MISADVENTURES

WITH A

DUKE

MISADVENTURES
WITH A
DUKE

BY
ANGEL PAYNE

WATERHOUSE PRESS

To you:
Every reader who loved Max and Allie's
story enough to ask for a sequel.
Every believer in the power of love that transcends boundaries.

CHAPTER ONE

BASTIEN

1789 — Orléans, France

Time is a ruthless wench of a bedmate. And no one knows it better than I.

A week ago, the witch taunted me with minutes that felt like days as I took steps that felt like miles through the Forêt de Marly. My boots were filled with mud, the days were drenched in rain, and the nights were consumed by the screams of traitors on their way to invade Versailles.

On their way to kill everyone inside Louis's grand palace—including the woman who possesses my whole heart.

If I had not joined my men in killing them then, she would not be here now, naked and wrapped in my arms. Those animals would not have cared that she was merely a chambermaid, barely paid decently to be in the building. They would have rounded her up along with the noblewomen she has loyally served and jailed or killed her in the same reckless manner.

A nightmare I cannot consider for another moment. Yet here it is anyway.

Bastien? Mon soleil? *Where have you gone?*

It is her voice, but I cannot find her anywhere in this

strange mist. No. *No!*

I push it out harder, begging to be set free from this dark chimera. From her woeful, agonized voice . . .

Bastien!

Until it is *her* face that I behold on one of the rebels I have killed.

"Nooo!"

Bastien. Bastien.

"Bastien! Please wake up, my beloved. Can you hear me? You are dreaming. Please wake up!"

My own woozy grunt pulls me out of my slumber. I blink hard before scrubbing a hand over my face. With my other arm, I pull my lover tighter against my chest. "Must have dozed," I mumble. "*Désolé*, little lily."

"Dreams are naught to be sorry for. Even the bad ones." With a fingertip, she traces a jagged line between the nicks that litter my chest. The feeling is heaven, especially when she marks the spot above my steady heartbeat. "Sometimes, talking about it helps."

"Not this time." I growl it strongly enough that she knows not to argue.

"Well, then . . . sometimes, you simply have to fuck it away."

Quickly enough, I switch to a throaty laugh. "Or pick up a sword and run a *bâtard* or two through."

She drops her hand. Jerks up an eyebrow. "*Tu préfère te battre que baiser?*"

"Hmmm. Tough choice." I rub my lips with a finger. "Fighting or fucking. Must I select this very moment?"

"If your *couilles* want to make it out of this room in the same sac, I would advise it."

My chortle bursts at full force now. "And now I know why all the ladies at court say you must be made of magic."

She twists her lips. "They do *not*!"

"All right, then. A simple sorceress?" I would not put it past those Versailles viragos to dampen her brilliance in such a way.

But I cannot let such ugliness cloud my thoughts when her husky laugh fills the air between us. When she punctuates it with a playful smack at my jaw and then a determined splay across my chest.

As soon as she plants her beautiful long fingers, I grin. I cannot be faulted, considering I can already predict her intent—and am damn pleased about it. Clearly, so is she. I feel it in the unique pebbles along her lightly freckled arms. In the desire that spreads across her face as she lifts up over me. In the decadent darkening of her gaze, shifting from springtime glades to shadowy forests, as she slides her soaked core over my hardening shaft.

Mon dieu.

I shall never take this feeling for granted. Her sweet little *livre* is quivering so hard. Waiting for me to flip her every sweet, hot page. To get lost in her secret sentences, paragraphs, and punctuation...

"Sorceress?" she giggles out. "Now I *know* you need to have the nonsense fucked out of you."

"*Mmmphhh.*" There is not much volume to it, and I am not sorry. She is already clenching around me, so warm and tight and perfect. "Why should it not be the truth? You *are* their little compendium of all the facts they refuse to keep straight, *oui*? And for that matter, their weather dial and their lice preventer and their—"

3

"Monsieur De Leon," she cuts in. "If you are happier discussing the behavioral patterns of lice right now, perhaps we should—*oh*!"

Her yelp is delicious as I buck my hips, stabbing my stalk deeper into her channel. "That is Monsieur le *Duke* De Leon, girl. And the only thing we should be doing is exactly this."

"Profuse apologies, your grace." Her last word quivers, already overtaken by the magical pout across her plush lips. I am captivated. Mesmerized. Especially as some of her paprika-colored curls tumble between the strawberry tips of her full breasts. "Oh, *mon dieu*, Bast. Are you truly a duke?"

I reach for my dusty satchel, still on the table next to the bed. I cast it down there last night in my haste to get the woman beneath me. Now, I reach for the inner pocket that possesses one of the most precious physical objects of my existence.

The scroll is printed on the finest paper and secured by a silk ribbon. With a deft tug, I loosen the bow. With an equally confident sweep, I extend the document to my beautiful Magique. With a chest that swells with pride on many levels, I watch her pick apart the words.

"Louis the Sixteenth, by the Grace of God and the Con—Consti—"

"Constitutions," I prompt, using the same gentle tone from when I first guided her into the world of letters, sounds, and all the magic they would open for her.

"Constitutions," she dutifully repeats. "And the Constitutions of the Republic, Emperor of the French, do hereby bestow upon my loyal subject, Bastien Eneas Jacques De Leon, the title of Bastien, Duc de Savennieres, to include all lands, properties, and dom—domin—"

"Dominion."

"Dominion thereof." With a gasp, she stops to look at me again. "Oh, Bast. It is like a dream."

I reach up a finger to lower the sheet of parchment behind which she has hidden her face. "Then why do you look ready to face a nightmare instead?"

Her face pinches. "Because now His Majesty will demand to know when you will be giving him new subjects with a proper duchess."

Her point is unsurprising. But so is my heart's answer to it. "If that is what he demands, then you should be fitted for a gown and a ring right away."

"I said a *proper* duchess, monsieur."

"As you shall be, Mademoiselle De Lys." For the first time, I push my brows into a scowl. "Hmm. 'Mademoiselle.' That does not sound right at all anymore, does it?"

Her fingers go limp. The parchment slips free, and I catch it with little effort, returning it quickly to the table. Only after I return my grip to her waist does she gain her voice again.

"*Bastien.* What are you saying?"

"Exactly what I mean." I curve a tender hand along the outside of her arm. "I love you, Magique De Lys. With all my heart."

"And I love you. But Bast—"

"But what?" I skim my fingertips over her collarbone, already imagining how beautiful the area will look when complemented by the neckline of a noble gown. "I love you. And, *dieu merci*, you love me too. And I already know my entire family will love you too. I cannot wait until you meet them all—especially Maximillian."

She laughs as if nervous. "And I think I would adore him too, based on everything you have said. But—"

5

"But what?"

I detest being so firm about it, especially this moment. Until today, I never thought there was room in my life, physically or financially, for properly keeping a bride. More rare were any dreams of offering the role to a woman I deeply cherish. Still, I am fairly certain that marriage proposals should be followed by things like happy tears and salty kisses. The weeping and affection that absolutely are not emanating right now.

"Bastien." Not a single sniff or dainty dab at her eyes either. "You are the Duke of Savennieres now. And I am a ladies' *maid*, nowhere near the station Louis would give you permission for."

"My love." I stroke my hand up to the side of her neck. My thumb traces her proud jawline. "The man adores you. Not too much, thankfully, or I would be obliged to call him to the Bois de Bologne to carve out his testicles—"

"Bastien!" she rebukes.

"Do you know that the king of Sweden married his own servant—twice? And the Archduke of Austria, with a common bourgeoisie? Genghis Khan did it numerous times."

"I assure you, Louis is *not* interested in Genghis Khan's nuptial habits."

I jerk my hips again, growing impatient—and amorous. I want to conquer this woman in so many ways, but most urgently from the inside out. With the tip of my cock down to the heavy sac at its base. And while I am doing so, to convince her that my way is the best way.

"Marry me, Magique," I demand huskily. "Marry me, and all this is yours for the rest of your days."

I emphasize it by thrusting up and then flipping her over.

The woman lets out a long and sexy yelp.

"All of . . . what, exactly?" Her grin is impish as she scores her fingernails over my shoulders. "I fathom not what you are speaking of, your grace. This ticklish delight is wonderful, but—oh *my!*"

The sounds from her throat are snagged and sensual as I push in deeper. I soak them all in, unable to speak myself. Utterly mute from the paradise of burying myself deeper. *Damn it, yesss.*

I drive in my length as far as her tight body can take it. A groan spills free once my balls hit her ass. *So good.*

"Still tickled, my sweet *magie?*"

She drops her head into the pillow. I suckle her throat, a column of inexplicably divine tension.

"Bastien. Ohhh . . . that is *so* nice."

"Damn right it is." I kiss away her giggle with a firm but adoring kiss. "And it could be the cock of your husband, giving this goodness to you every day for the rest of your life."

"Bastien!" She's shrill now, as I ensure she feels every thrust in the depths of her eye sockets. She gouges my shoulders harder. The pain only compels me to drive harder. Without stopping. Without mercy. "*Mon dieu!*"

I slide my forehead against hers. "Not the words I want to hear, little sorceress."

"*Fermé,*" she retorts. "Just shut up and fuck me."

"Hmm. Those are not the words either."

"Please!"

She rolls her hips, an unspoken plea for me to do the same. But I hold back, even if it is torment for us both, but I want something more than a burst from my cock right now. I need words from the sweet pillows of her lips. Specific words.

"Just say it, lily." I kiss her, using seductive pressure and tiny licks, utterly bold about my purpose. "'Yes, Bastien, I will marry you.' So simple, *oui*? And so perfect . . . just like you."

As the last of it soughs from me, I pull away by a few inches. I can already feel the concession in her limbs, softening to my demand, yet I crave the elation of seeing it in her huge green eyes too. But when I look, she has closed those divine worlds to me. Is that the sheen of tears across her lashes now? Why? Is she moved like this because of joy or sorrow?

I hate that I do not already know that answer. I hate the brutal catch of my heartbeat, confirming that truth.

But I would give up a thousand more breaths in place of what happens to my pulse next.

Its violent explosion as the door of my rented room is kicked in.

At once, the portal is filled by two glowering hulks. Protective fury drives me to haul the sheets over Magique's nudity. She is mine and no one else's. If I must prove it by running both of these miscreants through, so be it.

The thought is chased from my mind once the confusion crashes in.

I cannot kill either of these men. Nor do I want to.

One of them is Alonzo Mienne, who was more valuable than my sword arm during the recent skirmishes between here and Versailles. And the other . . .

"Marquette." I address Magique's brother aloud, though instinctively refrain from using the nickname he is called by friends. The name that he does not want from me right now. I know that much with awful surety. What is going on? Why is his mouth so twisted? Why are his eyes flashing like a beast with a knife in its gut?

"Well. Imagine that," the man sneers, tilting his head toward Lonzo. "It *is* exactly how you predicted, *mon ami*. Here he is with his cares in the wind and his cock in my sister."

"And not using a skin, I would also surmise," Lonzo adds. "Not more than five days ago, he told me he cared not whether he got her with child."

"Because my intention is to marry her!" I surge out of Magique and then off the bed, flinging a burning stare at both of them. "Or did you forget that I told you *that* as well, Lonzo?"

"Oh, I have forgotten nothing." He grunts before nodding at Louis's decree. "Including the fact that you made the assertion before becoming a duke."

"Which changes nothing."

"Which changes *everything*."

"Fuck you." I turn and grab my breeches from the floor. "Louis needs a strong hand to guide those lands back to prosperity. I am a fair leader, who has proven—"

"Proven?" Marquette's bitter bark is another harsh surprise. He bests it with an ugly chortle while watching me stab my legs into my pants. "Ahhh, Lonzo, you were also right about the *connard* being touched in the head by now. He truly thinks climbing to a dukedom on his friends' blood-soaked backs is leadership."

"Stop it!" Magique's outburst comes from the center of the mattress, where she stands with another sheet wrapped around her like a statue from the Versailles gardens. "Yes, Marquette Percival Dabriel De Lys, I mean *you*," she accuses. "How dare you, after everything Bastien has done for you? The favors he has extended for you. All the support he has lent, in word and in coin!"

"With plenty of return on his investment, I would say"

Alonzo verbalizes what Marquette states with one sweep of his eyes, up and down his sister's body with bald appraisal. I do not pause to consider which reaction enrages me more. I whirl to plow my shoulder into the chest of whoever has moved closest to me. Regrettably, it is Lonzo. He is taller and mightier than Marquette. The prick easily absorbs my impact before returning a brutal shove of his own.

Still, I grind my head into his collarbone with the intention of snapping it. The angle allows me to twist my face and fire a glare into Marquette De Lys.

"What the name of God has gotten into you? I am ready to make you my *brother*!"

The man huffs as if I have shit in his mouth instead. "Over my dead and rotted body."

Is he truly wishing for that? I almost spew the question aloud. Marquette must know that even a newly ennobled duke is shielded by all the protections of his title and that if word gets out that he and Lonzo have attacked me like this . . .

Unless . . .

All the whispers are true.

All the fears and predictions are coming to pass.

Reform. Revolt. Retribution.

Revolution.

But even if that is the case . . .

"You do not mean that." I give them a sign I can be trusted by displaying my own faith in them. Yet as soon as I slacken my hold on Lonzo, he flips the pressure and twists one of my elbows behind my back. "Damn it, Marq. Listen to your sister. Listen to your *soul*. You know that if I rise, you do as well. You *know* that I support strengthening the Third Estate. That I will be there when the Estates General is reconvened, to support—"

The two of them burst into laughs. My blood runs cold. Looking over to Magique is my strength but my curse. As always, her proud stance and lush face are what saves the center of my soul—until I take in the harsh quiver of her chin.

My lovely lily. Please do not cry. Your tears should be happy ones right now...

"Hmm. Perhaps you will be here indeed," Marquette murmurs. "Just not in the way you anticipate, sir."

My veins become sluices of ice. But that is not what I hate most about this moment. That comes when Magique jumps to the floor in front of her brother. Her eyes are vehement, her posture is shaking, and I already know what is about to happen next.

And dread it.

Smack.

Her palm connects with her brother's cheek in a louder blow than my imagination has ever created.

"*Branleur,*" she spits. "You ungrateful idiot! Whatever they have fed your mind about this folly—"

"No." Lonzo declares it with frightening zeal, intensified by the extra torque he delivers to my arm. "Not 'folly' any longer, my dear. We are a movement now. We have intent, we have motivation, and we have numbers." A new twist from him, and I can no longer subdue a pained grunt. "And now, it seems we have an appropriate symbol."

The color drains from Magique's face. "Wh-What do you mean?"

"What do you think?" My captor leans around, using his free hand to squeeze my chin. "Everyone will enjoy watching *this* head take a roll in the street, *oui*?"

And that does it.

The man has clearly forgotten that I still have a free arm too—now motivated by their disgusting barking. It is a simple matter to spear my elbow into his ribs. From there, even simpler to step free and reach for my woman's shoulder. Admittedly, at this point, the action is more for me than her. I need to know she is still here and whole. My lily. My strength.

"Get dressed, my love. Quickly. We shall ride within the hour. I can hasten the marriage banns in Loire easier than here."

"She will do nothing of the sort." Marquette slams a hand to the middle of my chest. "She will depart this building only with me. And *you* will be doing so in the back of a wagon."

"*No!*" she shrieks. "Marquette!"

"Marquette." I school my iteration to something calmer. "*S'il vous plait,* my friend. You want to reconsi—*unhhh!*"

The man curls his fingers until my chest hairs are also caught in his grip. "I am sick from my *considerations*, sir. We all are. And I am *not* your friend."

His emphasis comes with a virulent shove. I am sent stumbling back until caught by someone else. No. Not just a some*one*. Several men are at my back now. A flurry of rapid glances reveals them all to me. Chevis, Alain, and Gilles have all been such good friends that they tried matchmaking me with *their* sisters through the years. But clearly I am no longer their trusted *camarade*. I have become the convenient symbol for every crooked nobleman who cheated and mistreated them.

I am the reason they send up a rousing cheer as soon as Marquette snatches the long parchment from the table and then tosses it into the fire.

"No!" Magique screams. She runs to the hearth until

Marq grabs her by an elbow.

"Stand back, sister! I am ordering you!"

"Damn you." She scratches his face deep enough to leave nasty marks. "Damn you to h—"

"Shut up." He hurls her hard toward the bed. Too hard. Her skull collides with one of the posts, making her cry out in pain. There does not seem to be any blood, but I see red nonetheless.

And I am throwing off every man that holds me down. And heaving toward Marquette like a bull on the rampage. And stretching out my arms with one intent only. To strangle the man within half a breath of his life. Perhaps not even that.

His murderous look does not stop me. Nor am I deterred by the wicked dagger that he yanks from a hidden scabbard.

But the next moment, I do stop.

With a shallow choke. With my bare feet skidding beneath me. With my knees, now the texture of lagoon scum, collapsing in their wake.

I crumple completely as Magique falls into my arms.

As I again behold her brother's dagger—buried in the center of her chest.

"*Dieu. Dieu!*" But God is not listening. Not to my disbelieving rasps, nor the horrified rasps with which I underline them. Not as my volume increases when recognition flares in her glassy green gaze. "Magique. Hold on, my little bloom. This is not your time. Do you hear me? *This is not your time!*"

She rolls her head until it leans against my bicep. "Time." Her plush mouth twitches at one end. "Not enough. Not ever enough . . . with you . . ."

"But there will be," I press an urgent kiss into her

13

forehead, fighting to ignore my horror as a bright-red stain seeps across the sheet in which she's wrapped. "There *will* be, my beauty. But you must believe it. You must hold on!"

The words throb in my ears, drowning Marquette's sharp order for a physician. I do not concern myself with the bastard now. I cannot. Nothing matters but the precious lily in my arms. The woman who stepped into a dagger thrust for me.

"Hold," she mumbles. "I . . . hold you, Bastien. For better or for worse . . ."

I brush my lips across her temple once more. Her skin tastes like my tears. "No. Magique . . . please . . . no!"

"In sickness," she stammers on anyway, "and in health. Until death . . . but beyond."

"*No!*"

"Until the end of time, my love. Until . . ."

But no more words emerge. In their place, a long and shallow wheeze. A sparse echo of breath.

And then the new limpness of her limbs. The unblinking forests of her gaze.

Wildernesses to match the emptiness of my soul.

Until it is flooded by a tempest of fury. A storm so blinding, I really do see naught but crimson now. My senses are filled by no other sound than my primitive roar. In my tastebuds, there is only bile and blood.

But not enough blood.

Not until I can gouge open Marquette De Lys's chest. Until I am able to tear his heart apart, vein by worthless vein.

But when I emerge from my desperate red fog, only Magique and I are in the room. Shouts jostle each other on the streets below. The police are blowing horns and banging drums. They are answered by breaking glass and stampeding horses. Part of my mind orders me to move—I am covered in Magique's fluids, and it may not matter anymore that I am a duke—but I cannot let her go. I hold her tighter, promising everything I own if the Almighty will honor the force of my love and bring her back.

Praying for a miracle that never happens.

Instead, I blink in astonishment as this bizarre night takes another unreal turn. More accurately, gains another new cast member.

"Kavia?" I croak. "What...on..."

My throat cannot manage more than that. I doubt the woman has ventured farther than the outskirts of Loire her whole life, but the kitchen maid who has always been more like my second mother is here, at least a three day's ride from our family's Angers château. She looks the same yet is eerily different. She still wears her favorite kerchief, which holds her curly hair back from her strong features, but the rest of her clothes are different. Is she wearing... *trousers*?

That is not the observation that jars me the most. The urgency across her features brings my roughest jolt. Her gaze is so intense and unblinking.

"Bastien." She rushes over, tears coursing down her cheeks as if I have died along with Magique. No. As if I have died and come back to life. "Saints be praised! We found you in time!"

"In time? For what?"

"Carl! In here! I found him!"

I stare in confusion as her husband appears in the doorway. Carl is not the same as I remember him either. The last time I was home, so many months ago, there was only time for a brief visit with Father and Mother, so perhaps my

15

memory is playing games with me. But Carl seems bigger now, and not just in a physical sense. The man, usually the staid calm to Kavia's keen storm, paces into the room like a thunderhead in his own right.

"*Mon dieu.*" His triumphant growl is matched by his wide grin. "We did it. And just in time."

I shake my head, abandoning confusion for bewilderment. "Did what? In time for fucking *what*?"

"Yes," Kavia exclaims. "I told you we would!"

She drops down and yanks my head to her bosom.

I wrench away, which slams me closer to Magique. That aids with maintaining my sanity, but only a little.

"What the hell is happening?" I demand.

Nothing changes about Kavia's mien. Everything changes about Carl's.

"*Mon coeur,*" he mutters to his wife. "The boy . . . perhaps he has a good point. If he has to follow his heart out of this, but his heart is here, with her . . ."

"No," I retort, pulling my lost angel tighter as if to shield her from his bizarrely bleak words. The syllables that feel so small compared to the size of my love. And loss. "My heart is *not* here. Not any longer."

I struggle to imagine where she *has* gone, conjuring images from so many Sundays in church during my youth. But Maximillian was always more dutiful than I, listening carefully while I squirmed in the pew and fantasized about vanquishing Pierre Lacrosse at stick duels in the yard. The possibility of brimstone depths versus shiny clouds always felt far away and pointless.

Not anymore.

"We still have to try," Kavia insists. Her grip on my

shoulder is equally commanding. "We have to!"

"Agreed," Carl utters. "We have come too far. Risked too much."

I force my gaze away from my beloved's still face. "Damn it, what are you two talking about?" I mean every syllable. *Oui*, they are far from the château, but this is not the center of Paris. I am more concerned with his second sentence. "Risked too much how?"

"We can explain," Kavia says. "But not now. Not here."

As if her fervent tone needs more support, the chaos from the street gets louder.

"*Mierde*," Carl spews. "My boy...I am sorry. You must leave her here and come with us. Now!"

CHAPTER TWO

RAEGAN

Present day...

"Okay, woman. There's no time like now."

Before Allie's done with the command, she's acting on its implication—and earning herself my instant wrath.

"No!" I lunge off her big leather couch, flailing at a tattered sleeve of the *Moulin Rouge! The Musical* sweatshirt in her grip. But all I come back with are cotton pills in my palm and a cramp in my thigh. "Seriously?" I bark. "This is how you repay me for watching your place for a week while you and Le Prince Hottie screw your way across the Italian countryside?"

Allie balls up my beloved garment. "Not an accurate statement, missy, and you know it."

"*Désolé*, little Raegan," consoles the handsome guy who's appeared behind her. "But we both know *mon miracle* speaks the truth." As if he needs to kiss up to Allie any further, Maximilian De Leon scoots in and gives the side of her neck a string of sensual nuzzles. "The only prince in this apartment is the one in the *Purple Rain* film on the magic streaming device."

An affectionate giggle spills from Allie as her man seems to hit a sensitive spot. "I was referring more to the screwing-our-way-across-Italy part, Hot Stuff—and don't deny that I haven't been clear about it. *Work* trip, remember? Trend reports and fresh footage for the new season? Several hours of content we owe our generous network and their sponsors?" But she gasp-laughs again as he deliberately bites her earlobe. "Maximillian George Jean Valence De Leon! You promised you'd remember!"

The man steps back a little. "Hmm. But I also remembered the exact spot on your neck where you like me to—"

She stops him short with a sharp point toward their bedroom door. "Go. Finish your packing. That's a decree. Quinn will be here any second, and she said we couldn't dawdle. Traffic is a mess, so we have to get moving as soon as she gets here."

I sit up straighter, forgetting my beloved sweatshirt long enough to declare surrender on my hold. It's fine. Allie doesn't realize that a relaxed morning walk will get me to the theater district in no time, ensuring I'll have a fresh version of Satine and Christian across my chest before she and Maximillian go to sleep in Rome. But that's not my main thought right now.

"Hemline sent Quinn to drive you? On a Saturday?"

Allie waggles her brows. "Oh, yeah. In the *Escalade*."

"Ooh la. Someone is definitely a fashion channel's golden girl these days."

Her brows descend toward her rolling eyes. "Blink and you'll miss the moment, babe. Not about to give up my MetroCard yet." She adds a fast shrug. "I mean, the perks are nice but really just icing on the cake. You know that better than anyone, right?"

"Of course." I stamp my sincerity into both syllables. This isn't a new exchange for us: Allie, freaking out about letting her new fame and fortune going to her head, and then me, ensuring her it's not. But if it did, I'd tell her right away—ergo, her fresh push on the conversation's repeat button.

"Besides, it's not going to be forever. Very little in the fashion industry is, yeah?"

I swallow on a new weight in my throat. "You're talking to the girl who learned that one the hard way, remember?"

Allie's features widen. Her eyes are dilated in pure mortification. "Oh my God, Rae. Oh my God."

She plummets next to me on the couch, hauling me in for a fervent hug. It's weird. I'm usually the hugger, not the huggee. The moment affords me a second to study the framed photos across the apartment. Most of the images display Maximillian and her with hefty hitters in the fashion world's elite. Surprisingly, my ex-jerk isn't in a single one of them.

"I'm so sorry," Allie rasps with the subtlety of corn syrup. "I wasn't thinking. Not one damn bit. I'm so sorry."

I give her back a halfhearted pat. "It's all right, honey."

Except that it's not. But not for all the reasons that swim in her gaze when she pulls back to examine my face. "Mmmph," she grumbles. "What kind of guy in his right mind changes his name from Justin to Genesis, anyway?"

What she really means to ask is what kind of a guy, becoming such a formidable force in the fashion industry, would dump his adorable and outgoing girlfriend for a couple who call themselves Nefertiti and Akhenaten?

I force out a chuckle so Allie feels useful before having to leave. It beats me having to talk her out of canceling the trip altogether, which she was ready to do this time three weeks ago—nearly to the minute. I'd shown up in the lobby below as a blubbering mess after deciding to leave work early and surprise Just—errr, Genesis—with some Saturday sexy times. Instead, I'd found my boyfriend in our bedroom on his knees with his face between Nefertiti's thighs and his hand working Akhenaten's cock.

The second Allie buzzed me into the apartment, I'd raced to their guest bathroom and thrown up everything in my stomach. Now, even a prolonged glance at that door doesn't do a thing to my gut. Progress. *One step at a time...*

Despite how the entry buzzer makes me want to skitter all the way back to square one. The place where all the ugly questions wouldn't leave me alone...

Why didn't I know from the start?

Why didn't I see what he needed?

Why wasn't I enough?

Why am I never enough?

I shove it all aside as Allie pushes the button to enact the video connection with the building's lobby. Quinn looks like she always does, all polished business with her slicked-back blond pixie and tailored suit. Though she smiles—well, her version of a smile—she also lifts her wrists into the frame and impatiently taps her watch.

"No time for clicking more links, kids. You on your way down?"

Before Allie can answer, Max re-enters with a dance-shimmy step that he must've borrowed from one of the Central Park ducks. "Party over; oops out of time!" His attempt at singing is worse, earning Allie my gratitude as she cups a hand over his mouth.

"If you try 'Let's Go Crazy' in the elevator, I'll tell Quinn to push you out of the car at the bridge."

"Wrong album anyway." I hope the quip helps with

getting me out of the friend-who-turned-the-bathroom-to-puke-smell territory. I'm pretty sure neither of them notices, as Max dips in for another sloppy snuggle to Allie's neck. Too late. She's gasp-giggling again.

"Oh my God," I groan. "Would you two just get out of here?" *Before I really do vomit again—for very different reasons?*

Allie breaks from her lusty languor to quickly eyeball me. "Hey. Promise me you'll get out of here a few times. I swear, if we get home and the streaming queue is nothing but checkmarks..."

"And you think I'd be silly enough to use *your* account?"

"You have to get out and live a little, okay?" she urges. "There's a new waffle sandwich place up on 48th. And the sake bar just switched up its menu. They added udon!"

"Ugh! *Go!*" I laugh all of it out, but by the time they obey all the way, I'm sliding to the floor in a puddle of tears. The temptation worsens as soon as I hear them boarding the elevator with moaning kisses and nonstop gropes.

Envy, in its worst form, sweeps over my heart. Just like that, my self-loathing party is back in full swing.

Maybe *ugh* is right.

I love Alessandra Fine. I will love her until the day I die. So why do my cheeks burn with tears of resentment toward her? Why can't I separate my joy about her happiness from my misery about my heartbreak?

And why is it so hard for me to admit that Justin "Genesis" Jones was the worst choice to waste so much of my time and heart on?

Unless that's what I'm doing now.

Oh, yeah. That must be it.

I repeat it out loud while plodding into Allie's sleek

kitchen. After gathering everything for a big bowl of ice water and then dunking my face in it, I contemplate more constructive steps toward the goal.

It's still early, considering I'm in the heart of New York City on a Saturday night, but it's much too late to call Rue. The third member of our tight friendship trio has been on lighting and production design for a film crew in town, but the hours are long and brutal. Tonight is one of her few stretches to catch up on sleep. Couch-surfing and movie bingeing is also out. I'd likely gravitate toward one of my favorite angsty romances. Totally *not* what I need right now.

Guess I'm catching up on work tonight.

I'm pleasantly surprised when a smile crosses my lips. For the first time in a while, I'm zinged to be diving into a new project. Good thing, since *new* isn't just essential in the personal styling business. It's everything.

I go to the bedroom, open my suitcase, and pull out the wrapped item on top: a beautifully preserved corset from the late eighteenth century. Less than a week ago, the pretty pink undergarment was given to me during a consultation with actress Sylver Savoy, arguably my hugest client to date. She explained that it's a treasured family heirloom and *must* be a part of her red carpet look for Emmy Awards Night.

Good news? The Emmys aren't for six months, corsets are hotter than ever, and everything from the Enlightenment Era feels like perfect inspiration for me.

And the bad?

I've been in a massive creative slide ever since puking in my best friend's toilet.

No. That ends right now.

Allie and Rue have found their pieces of professional

happiness. It's damn time I grabbed that golden ring too.

"Focus, damn it," I order myself, accenting with a clucking tongue as I hold up the corset for a closer examination.

I cut myself off with another mutter.

"Wow."

The garment has solid construction. The stitching is intricate and precise. And the unique rose color ... *wow* yet again. This shade was probably achieved by using actual roses, mixed with things like cabbage and crushed cochineals for vibrancy, though God only knows what the original hue actually was. Time fades everything ...

Except my best friend's lover, the man who might have become king of France but left it all behind to get to my friend's side. Behind, as in two hundred years in the past.

So, yeah, they literally don't make men like that anymore.

And I'm surprised that Justin left me ... why?

"All right, you've got to let this go, girl." My grumble is as violent as the shake of my head, reflected at me from the mirrored front of Allie's wide closet. "Are you listening? You're not that Eeyore, Raegan Tavish."

The woman who actually occupies that role is across town, catching up from sleep deprivation. I love Rue, thundercloud and all, especially because that keeps me, the resident Tigger of our trio, from getting too hyped about everything from celebrity sightings in the Village to seasonal sticky buns at Amy's Bread.

Now I want my bounce back. Right the hell now. I long to look in the mirror and see a sparkle again. I want to smile back at myself and mean it. To even look at myself naked and appreciate what I see. To acknowledge everything about myself with something other than loathing and disgust.

Yes . . . even *that* part of me.

The spot I acknowledge with a fist to the center of my chest, pressing so hard my knuckles go white. Reminding me of *that* spot, between my breasts, that will never let go of my consciousness. The scar that never fails to remind me, at moments when I least need it, of the truth about the heart that beats beneath it. The facts it's learned the hard way.

Feelings aren't always my friends.

Friends aren't always that real.

Reality is rarely based on either.

But there's my silver lining. Because A, I'm always determined to find that elusive alloy in the clouds. And B, it means I can make reality whatever I damn well please.

Yesss.

I close my eyes. Lift my head. Haul in a long breath. But I'm taking in more than air. I absorb the energy from the whole city around me. All these people . . . I can't let them down. Not the millions who've survived heat waves, blizzards, subway derailments, terrorist attacks, and a global pandemic. What would anyone say if I admitted defeat to my own reflection?

You're better than this. Do it. Now.

With a determined huff, I jog up my chin.

"You're going to be okay," I command myself.

The words bring more than surface validation. They make me . . . confident. I start to actually . . . *like myself.*

Another sharp, long breath. Another effort to keep looking at myself—and affirming what I see.

"You're *really* going to be okay."

I smile as soon as my ears register the steadier tone. Its underlying—and enduring—strength.

"You're done with him, damn it. You're done being

ashamed because of him. *All* of you is done with it."

My chin wobbles, but my hands don't. I shake my head, letting more anger in. Why have I let a few inches in the middle of my body define how I feel about every other inch of it? Why have I let Justin, and others like him, keep telling me that's okay?

Because it's not.

And now it's time to prove it.

"Damn right it is."

I don't scream the words. But they're still a new manifesto, ready for me to put into action. I start that plan by leaning over and pulling my favorite pair of fuzzy socks off my feet. That's just the start. I don't plan on stopping until my leggings are off too. And everything after that.

Tonight, I'm going to love all of me—exactly the way I am.

CHAPTER THREE

BASTIEN

"Bastien! Are you listening? I said leave her, boy!"

Leave her.

Does Carl understand what he is demanding? Does he not see the grief that tears me apart like a morning star jammed down my throat? That walking away from Magique would be like ramming that spiked ball to the middle of my gut and then twirling it?

I tell him all of that and more with the violent lift of my head and the fierce grimace on my lips. He ignores it all and somehow hauls me to my feet. Kavia sweeps in too, speaking hideously soothing words while prying my fingers free from my beloved's lifeless form.

Magique slips to the floor with a sickening *thunk*. The sound is final and heavy, as if I have sobbed enough tears to soak her through. Perhaps I have. My sorrow eclipses my strength, rendering me useless against their pulls and prods. They guide me down the shadowed hall and the narrow back stairs. We cross the empty kitchen, not stopping until we reach the alley behind the inn.

The midnight air hits me in a chilled blast. It jolts me to a semblance of alertness, making me stare at the faded fichu in my closed fist. The scarf that once graced my lover's neck.

When I stare at the blood spatter on it, my other hand twists into a shaking fist. Chunks of my shattered heart pierce every inch of my heaving lungs. My steps are wooden as Carl and Kavia pull me farther down the alley.

Night creatures, still shivering in the shadows, scuttle into damp shadows at our rushed approach. Silently, I beg them to take me with them. The litany ends fast, as soon as we turn into the shallow inlet beside the inn's stable.

Unsurprisingly, the shallow bay is consumed by the girth of Carl's field wagon. I *am* stunned by what is occupying the majority of its broad bed.

"Why..." I blink, wondering if my addled mind has produced a skewed view. But no. Nothing has changed. "Carl? Kavia? What are you doing with the wardrobe from the *grande chambre*?"

Oui, this is indeed... *that.* The huge chest is not difficult to identify, despite having been laid down on its backside, so to speak. The pearl inlays along its doors reflect the few stars persisting overhead.

"Hush now," Kavia rebukes. "Please, boy!"

Her exigence is not in vain. Marq and Lonzo's compatriots are surging the main avenue like a rage-swollen river. For all I know, the pair of them are hiding in the depths of that flow: a couple of cowardly trout beneath the sharks who bellow and scream beneath their pennants and torches. That possibility actually brightens me. The mere idea of getting to sprint out there and tear the crowd apart to find them...

Kavia cuts the fantasy short with a jerk at my elbow. *Damn it.* The woman knows me too well.

"Come." She drags me to the cart bed. "Up here. Now."

I hesitate. "Because you actually mean to get through

that throng in this?"

"We will worry about that later."

I narrow an incredulous stare. "There is no *later.*"

She only harrumphs while hoisting herself onto the cart's bed alongside me.

"*Kavia.* Are you listening to me?"

"She hears you." Carl takes a position on the other side of the wardrobe. "But right now it is *your* turn to listen. Clearly and carefully."

The confused cotton in my mind thickens into down. "What are you talking ab—"

Kavia whomps a hand over my mouth. The top of her finger wall crowds the low end of my glare. "Hush," she grits out anyway. "But only if you value your neck half as much as we do."

I almost laugh. I *want* to, more than anything. To toss off her reproach with a smirk on my lips and a salamander in my pocket, as I did during simpler times. But there is no slimy little crawler to help me now. And the world is far from simple. I doubt it ever will be again.

"Get in," she dictates, preventing me from making the choice either way. She nods toward Carl, who swiftly swings open the wardrobe's doors. It's empty inside. I am not as bewildered about that than by the ongoing mystery of their ultimate plan.

"I still do not understand," I say, despite complying with her order. "If you want to smuggle me back home, there are easier means of—"

"You are not going home," Carl says.

"All right." I half expected that, considering every detail that has made it through the morass of my mind. The increased insurgent activity around Versailles. The murmurs of unrest in every tavern between here and there, likely spreading beyond that. The manifestation of it all in how Marq and Lonzo just burst into my room upstairs and—

Dieu.

How they did what they did.

And these rebels are calling *us* the monsters?

"All right." I use the words as a needed slap to my mind. "So you are wishing to continue to Versailles?" I do not fault their logic. If our family's château has already been comprised, seeking the king's protection would be a safe hedge. And the armoire ... "Ahhh, *oui.* I see now. Versailles it is. And *this* is your insurance through the gates."

The conclusion has me dipping a nod of fresh respect. The pair has done some thinking. We will not be the only party seeking refuge at Versailles' Court of Honor. The wardrobe stands out as a better gift for Louis than a mere vase or statuette.

"You are not going to the palais either."

Kavia's tone has me stopping. Never have I heard her sound so serious. Not even when I came home with salamanders in *both* pockets. "Then what is this all about? Kavia?"

"Just get in, Bastien." There is a wobble beneath her words now. Tears that refuse to stay at bay. "And obey every word I say."

"She knows what she is about, boy." Carl's assertion is easier to focus on, like a verbal light in the sudden darkness around me. Even the slim crack between the closed cabinet doors lends me illumination. My senses pick up on movement, but not the comforting sort. Not the rolls of the wagon or even a jingling of reins and harnesses, indicating we are about to get out of here. "Listen to her, Bastien!"

I grit my teeth to avoid snapping back at him. In the blackness of my strange new prison, I vacillate between desolation and frustration. Being addressed as if I'm twelve again is not a huge assuagement.

The moment I prepare to remind them that I am a man over twice that age, Kavia speaks again.

"Take a deep breath, Bastien. After that, take another."

Once more, her voice is something I have never heard before. Something that sneaks across all my pores and into the pulse of my blood. It happens between one blink and the next . . . one breath and the next. Though I've needed her first direction, it is impossible to pull in the second breath. For that matter, any air at all.

"Kavia?" I blurt. "Carl? What the absolute hell?"

"Ssshhh," Kavia charges. "You are going to be fine, Bastien. Just fine."

"This is not fine, damn it."

I raise both hands to shove the doors open again but encounter a small hitch. All right, not so small. My hands refuse to move. So do the lengths of both arms.

"Kavia! This is *not* fine at all!"

"Bastien!" Carl this time. "Calm yourself or this will not go well!"

"This . . . what?" I bellow, beyond caring if the horde on the avenue hears. It might be best if they do. These two people, the ones who sometimes saw me more in a day than Mother or Father, have now put me in the most horrific of cages. My legs have joined with my arms, shackled beneath invisible weights. *I cannot move!*

"Please, my sweet boy." Kavia nearly sings it despite her

fervent underline. Once more, it is nothing I have ever heard from her. What kind of creature has taken over the kitchen maid I love so much? "Please, Bastien. You must at least try for me."

"Do I have a fucking choice?" I still fight for strength, demanding my muscles hearken the screams from my mind. The effort is useless. Completely futile.

"Of course you do." Kavia's croon is still too gentle. And beyond strange. "You always have a choice, my little warrior."

"*Mierde.*" The woman has not forgotten any of her emotional weapons, including the use of the nickname I loved throughout boyhood. But it accomplishes her purpose. I surrender to utter stillness now. Resign myself to hearing her.

"Now close your eyes," she instructs as soon as I fill my lungs with my second breath. "And in your mind and your heart and your soul, envision her as completely as you can."

I huff. "Envision *who*?"

"You already know the answer to that, Bastien Eneas Jacques De Leon. The only one you can see, if you set your soul free and let your heart fly. Your true love, *mon petit guerrier.* The only one who is going to get you through this."

I shake my head—thankfully, I'm not numb from the neck up—with fresh ferocity. "Is this a joke? Why are you doing this to me?"

A low hum emerges from Kavia. I know it is her because there is still a tiny wobble in her eruption. But she does not stop. Now her drone nearly *is* a song—but not a tune I recognize. I would have remembered *this* melody. It's haunting but ethereal. Frightening but fascinating.

At least until she speaks again.

"Bastien. You are not reaching for the vision!"

I hiss with low vitriol. "Nor will I."

Because I want no part of remembering Magique as I last saw her. Because even with that resolve in my spirit, my conscience disagrees—disgustingly so. As soon as Kavia instructed it to activate my imagination, she is all I *can* see. Memories of all our laughter and lovemaking are mixed in with my last sight of her. The spreading blood on the floor. The loll of her head against the bedpost, and then in my arms. The pallor of her skin. The death in her eyes.

Fresh rage ignites in my spirit. The edges of my stare turn red again, even in this stifling gloom.

No.

That is not the case.

I am no longer encased in complete shadows.

Now, there are flames here too.

"What the *hell*?"

I wish I could be more facetious about it but am denied by raw facts. Actual flames invade the compartment now, clawing at my ankles, shins, knees, and higher. Instinct has me flinching again and again, and yet I do not *feel* a single thing. I am peering at pure fire, garish and bright and close to blinding, but every flame is like nothing but a blast of warm wind, buffeting my body and heating my face.

Curiosity takes over. Why not? The amber and orange layers bring more memories of my perfect *magie*, this time in those shades. The brilliant hue of her hair in the sun. The flecks of gold that spark in her eyes when she wants me inside her. The gleam of her tawny body beneath candlelight as I appease her need.

My mind's eye brings it all to me, and then some. The memories collide, heartbreaking and intense, until my mind nearly bursts from the glory—*and* the grief.

I can fully move my limbs again but no longer wish to. I pray to stay in my cage, seared forever by the memories of my precious girl. If the blaze consumes and kills me, so be it. I will be by her side that much sooner. Wrapped around her and inside her for all time.

Beyond the crackle of the invisible kindling at my feet, I hear myself growl in determination. The last answer I expect is Kavia's new exclamation, as impassioned as the conflagration itself.

"Yes! Oh yesss, Bastien!" Her voice comes from everywhere and nowhere at once, a mixture of fire and darkness. "You see her now. I know it. I can feel it. Perfect. That is perfect, my boy!"

"None too soon either," Carl joins in. "Woman, these shadows will only protect us for so long. *Depechez-vous.* Hurry!"

Hurry . . . how? About what? But the demands are naught but fearful grunts at my lips, hitting a solid wall of trepidation in my mind.

Carl and Kavia do not sound like they want to smuggle me out of here. That leaves me with some dismal options. They mean to kill me or trade me.

"*No*, Bastien." Kavia has never scolded me so brutally, even when I swore by three saints in a row after church one Sunday. "Do not let her go! Not for one second! She will guide you. Do. Not. Let. Her. Go!"

She pounds on both wardrobe doors. I lurch and battle an urge to punch back. My self-control is a dismal standby for what truly helps. The flood of Magique back to my mind's eye. Calm returns, along with my maid's praising croon.

"Ahhh. Perfect. That is it. Keep her there, Bastien. Right there, in the center of your spirit and soul. In the very beats of your heart, the deepest calls of your instinct. Reach for her. Stretch out to her with every depth of your dreams and desire until you find her!"

She drives on, raising her voice by impassioned octaves. And I hear every note. I listen to every syllable. I crave them now, whipping around me like sparks in the fiery wind. Obeying them like a wraith that already knows it's dead.

This time, the wraith is me.

Bizarrely, it is not such an awful acceptance. Nowhere near a chilling fear.

"I am looking, Kavia. I will not stop. I swear it."

The flames engulf me now, so I doubt she hears my vow. But then she answers, "Good. Very good, my boy! Now there is only one more thing to remember..."

The fervency of her words is consumed by the tumult of the fire. Then the smoke that thickens into soot. The dust that soon becomes dense darkness...

Then unbreachable night.

A blackness that brings me to...what? Takes me to... where?

If this is death, why do I still hear myself breathing? Why do I feel my muscles flexing, my nerves tingling, my heart thrumming?

If this is not death, what is going on? And why?

And how is there suddenly a sluice of brilliant light between the wardrobe's doors? Why does the alley's air suddenly smell like fresh linen and the queen's own amber? Where has the chaotic mob gone? Their shouts and anger already feel like distant memories, replaced by something so much better.

A soft peace.

A woman's humming.

But not just any woman.

"*Mon dieu*," I gasp out. Can it truly be? Do I dare believe?

Magique.

Have I really found you again?

RAEGAN

Wow. I'd forgotten how amazing it feels to walk around in nothing but my underwear. I confess as much to the pretty girl in the mirror, even winking as I say, "Damn, Tigger. Maybe you should be a topless hussy all weekend long."

But in less than an hour, my confidence wobbles. After several internet deep dives, I still can't find even one piece for Sylver Savoy to consider for the Emmys look. And *she* can't very well work the arrival carpet in nothing but her panties and high heels.

But the odd thought ignites a bizarre lightbulb in my brain. *At last.*

Maybe I actually do need to take a walk in the woman's shoes . . . figuratively speaking.

With perfect timing, I get a boost of encouragement courtesy of my showtunes playlist, pushing the sassy strains of *Moulin Rouge*'s opening number through the speakers mounted in all the bedroom's corners. Guess it's the theme for the night, despite my much-missed sweatshirt. But the sound quality of the speakers has me forgiving Allie a bit for the steal. *A bit.*

I swing off the bed, singing aloud with the naughty French earworm while grabbing Sylver's corset from the dresser.

Though it's impossible to lace myself fully into the thing, I'm able to twist my hands back and pull the stays tight enough to prevent it from becoming my hip girdle. Next, I step back into the stilettos I wore over here, a pair of hot-pink Jimmys enhanced with obnoxious bows, and re-approach myself in Allie's full-length mirror.

And instantly wonder why I don't own a corset of my own.

"*Dayyy-ummm*," I murmur. "Talk about hips and boobs you never had, darling."

I indulge myself in more of the self-love, dancing a little to the upbeat music, until I'm snagged into a fully shocked stop.

By a tidal wave of inspiration.

More accurately, by a why-didn't-I-think-of-this-sooner moment.

Belle Epoque inspiration ... given a structured update but an eye-popping satin train ...

"Okay, that could really work ..."

As I whoosh myself around, mentally playing with angles and movement, a small wince takes over my face. But not a full one. The dress would have to be a custom piece, since I don't remember seeing anything like it on any rack around town. I don't know how Sylver would enjoy the bump in price. But if we *could* pull it off ...

I'm too excited to sit still about it. Which leads to me yanking back the closet's mirrored door and reaching for one of Allie's satin bedsheets. I even sing with the guys' parts of the song while tucking the sheet under the corset's back edge and then flouncing it out like a train.

"Oh, *Allie*. You really *can* can-can, can't you?"

I finish it with a funny yelp, stumbling back as the bathroom's track lighting glints on the fabric. Another cry spills out as a second light flashes across the room. "Holy shit," I mutter. "The power of satin, indeed."

Fast revision. The power of *high-quality* satin. Maybe I should just ask Allie how much she wants for the sheet and then pitch the dark-crimson thing to Sylver as-is. Talk about an ensemble that would make headl—

"Ahhh!"

My shriek erupts in two stages. The first is pure instinct, a reaction to a *third* burst across the room. The second is a choke of pure fear. Because now I see where the flares are actually emanating from.

"Oh my God."

The inside of Allie and Max's armoire thingie has caught on fire. I'm surely going to vocabulary hell for calling it a *thingie*, since the baller-sized monstrosity used to be in a stadium-sized bedroom at the De Leon estate in France and dug deep into Allie's savings when she had it shipped over as Max's Christmas present. Weirdly, it's always looked at home in here too—except for now. In this moment, it's like someone's idea of a bad Mars rocket, with gold and purple light spilling from the seam between the doors.

And that's before it starts quivering.

"Nooo … freaking …"

I gulp and skitter backward.

And fixate on the rest of the story behind the huge museum piece.

The part about the cabinet actually being Maximillian's time travel machine.

Ohhh, yeah … *that part.*

The wardrobe into which he crawled, hiding from a mob circa 1789, only to emerge into the insanity of this day and age.

But that report has never been corroborated, since Allie and her secret prince decided to celebrate his arrival by banging each other until dawn.

They're probably doing exactly the same thing right now in one of the VIP lounges at JFK—a realization that isn't helping my scared confusion one bit.

"Oh my God." The moment merits the repetition. "*What is going on?*"

I try answering myself with logic. It must be a play of the room's lighting, or even some newly installed lighting inside the wardrobe itself, going haywire on dying batteries. Or maybe Allie and Max have stored something in there and it's in need of fresh batteries.

I let out a low growl. "Alessandra Fine, if I've almost peed myself in terror because one of your sex toys simply needs—oh, holy *shit!*"

The response to my growl . . .

Sounds more like another growl.

Only deeper. Harsher. And more real than I want it to be.

I kick off the Jimmys while cutting sharply left, toward the dresser. At once I grab my lipstick-case-that-isn't, twisting the tube to expose the blade concealed inside. It's not much, but I'll make it work. I *have* to make it work.

The resolve sets in as I whip back around—and confront a shirtless man who's pushing free from the wardrobe.

To rephrase, *a man.*

His hair's too long to be trendy. His muscles are too stunning to be gym-grown. He's new in town; that much is clear. The rugged edges haven't been primped out of him yet. But here he is, so enormous that he's ducking to step free from the cabinet.

But none of this can be right either. No way has he just materialized from the thin air inside that thing.

My brain must be more tired than I think. The logical explanation is right here in front of me, after all. Somehow, in some insane way, he's gotten in from the balcony and was hiding in the corner, just waiting—

To do what?

"Oh God," I rasp—already confronted by that answer from the gaze that locks on me. His irises are as rich as a Godiva sampler, except with twenty-four carat gold stirred in. But not the liquid dessert kind. The flecks that glint beneath his ungodly thick eyelashes...they've been extracted from the hardest stone. They're attentive and ruthless, not missing an inch of any move I make.

Of course they are. Because he's a criminal.

Which means I should be screaming. At the least, using my blade to back him off long enough to grab my phone and run for the bathroom. Behind that locked door, I'll at least be able to punch the emergency button and give someone enough information to—

But I'm not doing any of that. Because apparently, I'm an idiot.

I just continue to let this gorgeous Gigantor hold me in his stealthy thrall. I keep standing here, unmoving, as he shuffles another step closer. I quiver, which makes my blade noticeably wobble, encouraging him to scrape forward by another inch.

Wait. He's *shuffling*? And *scraping*?

Against all my better instincts, I glance down. Sure enough, the man isn't wearing shoes. On a *March* night. In *New York City*.

So maybe he didn't sneak in here to burglarize the

apartment. Maybe he's just after a little warmth and comfort.

And maybe you're a little insane.

The rebuke reverberates through my mind in Drue's voice. At once I spit back, "Just roll a giant one and take a drag, okay? Kindness is more on-trend than Docs, okay?"

Gigantor's mighty brow turns into a bunch of furrows. "You want me to drag rolls where? *Pourquoi*, my love?"

I join him in the realm of deep furrows. "Ermmm . . . I . . . uhhh . . ." Have no idea what to say to him now. My rudimentary French extends to a decent translation of his query, but all my brain can generate is a question for his question. *"My love?" Ohhh, no. Buddy . . . I think we need to talk . . .*

"If you need a physician, I can make haste to find one," he murmurs, coming closer. God help me, he's definitely no longer scuffling about it. He reaches over, grabbing both my wrists—startling me into dropping the weapon that never really was one. "What do you need, *ma magie*? Name it and it is yours."

If I had another switchblade—or, say, an AK47—the thing would be joining its predecessor on the floor. His words . . . *His words.* They're so forceful yet fervent . . .

They're so *French.*

The observation collides on top of others. Too many others.

Like the fact that he's shirtless and barefoot yet wearing pants crafted from a lush vintage silk in a decadent caramel shade.

Like the fact that those pants aren't pants at all—but breeches. Seriously authentic breeches.

Like the fact that I shoot my stare back up to the breathtaking grandeur of his face, finally plugging it in to the real reason why I haven't even tried to race across the room and summon NYPD's finest on his ass.

Like the fact that I'm not concentrating on his backside right now. Instead, I'm gawking at his face.

I'm *remembering* that face.

From a whole, crazy year ago.

From when it stared back at me from the wall of a private portrait gallery inside Château De Leon. It belonged to the subject of the painting mounted next to Maximillian's. I should know. I studied the thing for long minutes as Allie stood next to me, trying to accept the truth that the man who'd popped out of the wardrobe in her bedroom wasn't a lunatic stripper-actor but a nobleman named Maximillian De Leon. A hero who'd traversed time itself to get to her.

The realization does everything and nothing for me.

And neither do the words that it compels out of me, in pieces of stuttering shock. "Holy…shit. You… You're… *Bastien De Leon.*"

CHAPTER FOUR

BASTIEN

I laugh, but the eruption is forced. My scowl feels even more foreign, something that belongs nowhere near my face with her scent in my senses, her skin beneath my touch, her pulse beating so steadily with mine.

Her heart ... beating again.

Her *life*, so full and brilliant again.

For which I must be grateful, even if she still regards me as naught more than a stranger.

"Oui, *ma chérie*," I murmur. "It is me. You know that."

But does she?

The woman before me now is ... different. Not in the apparent ways, like her lush titian curls, lightly freckled nose, and elegant body. It is the way she presents all of that. She seems more fearless about the words from her lips and the wit of her mind instead of the allure of her beauty.

Why does it all baffle me so? This is everything I have been striving for with her! The self-confidence I have been fighting to instill in her for nearly a year. It is all as radiant on her as I anticipated, except that none of it feels exactly ... *right*. Not yet. That should come as no surprise either. The price we have paid for this to manifest ...

I scowl and heave those thoughts to the back of my mind.

She keeps gawking as if *I* am the one who has defeated death. No. Worse. She regards me like a complete stranger.

Mon dieu. Perhaps I am.

What if she journeyed beyond the veils, only to pay a price of her own for the return? The currency of her memories. But not all of them. She knows who I am but not *who I am.*

"Wh-Why are you here?"

Something inside me deflates. The bursting cloud of the hope that she was adopting a coy pretense about her bewilderment. But I see the truth now, etched across her whole face. She is not playing.

Which means I cannot do the same about winning back her recall. I have to combat her odd fugue with something more powerful. The potency of my truth. The power of my love.

"I think you already know that, little lily."

She looks ready to vomit and laugh within the same three seconds. "Just indulge me, Desperado."

Not an inaccuracy. I still am on the edge of desperation, though I sense that is not her meaning. I push aside the confusion to assert, "Search yourself deeply, *ma magie.* You know I am here . . . because of you."

A sizable swallow takes over the column of her neck. "Unreal," she mutters. "This isn't . . . it just can't be . . ."

"No!" I push past so many things that validate her assertion—the opulence of our new surroundings, the odd sounds from outside, her sudden preference for English instead of French—and grip her tighter. "It *can* be. You must believe that! *I* did, even when Kavia ordered me to do the same. You know that I was thinking she had jumped off into the loon lagoon, yes? But I *wanted* to believe her, *chérie.* I *wanted* to believe that somehow, she would lead me back to you..."

"Kavia?" She draws out the query, swinging her gaze back up to lock with mine.

At once, I clench my teeth to fight the sting behind my eyes. When I think of the last time she did this, forcing me to watch the light seep from her dark greens... *Never again.* I vow it from every parapet in my heart and soul.

"*Oui,* my sweetness. You... have heard me speak of her before. The woman who is like my second mother. The saint who helped raise Maximillian and—"

"*Maximillian?*"

I push out a long breath from my nostrils. "*Ma magie.* Please... you must try hard to remember. You *know* who Maximillian is too. And—"

She sweeps a hand through the air as if yearning to wipe my words free from it. Still, she blurts next, "So... Kavia... she's involved here somehow?"

I frown, now betraying my perplexity. "*Oui.*"

"Okay. And she ordered you... to do what?"

I lift one hand to the side of her face. To my delight, a small tremor moves through her. Whether her mind admits it or not, some parts of her still knows me. Still *needs* me.

"To do the easiest thing in the world," I whisper. "To envision my heart's utmost desire." I splay my fingertips along her hairline. Her curls... I swear by everything holy, they feel so much softer than before. I am beyond entranced. "That meant fastening my every thought on you, my Magique. Listening to Kavia, no matter how deep she seemed to be diving in the gammon. Hoping there was something to her plan. Praying that somehow, in some way, she would help me..." Before I can help it, a dazed chuckle spills forth. "And

45

now look. Here I am!"

Her reaction is not what I expect. At the very least, the pillows of her lips should be twitching in wonderment too. Curiosity should be brewing in her eyes, a faint smoke at the backs of those green fires.

But she is already darting that stare away. Averting it from me in full.

Why?

After a few seconds, she murmurs, "And where, exactly, do you think you are?"

I glance around. This room, appointed with flawless linens, decorated with intricate care, and smelling of such fine perfumes, presents luxury I have never seen before, even at Versailles.

"I do not know," I finally surmise, deciding not to share my initial assumptions. If I tell her it all feels like heaven, she truly will revert to gawking as if I should be thrown in an asylum. But one of the many reasons I love this woman is because she shares my skepticism about heaven, hell, and all the controlling trappings upon each by "spiritual leaders" who are naught but men in fancy clothes.

There must be another better explanation. We simply do not know it yet. Have not sought it out hard enough.

"Does it matter, ultimately?" I persist. "I am here, my arms filled with your glory again. And *you* are here, enjoying it." Unable to control myself any longer, I let my gaze dip—taking in the sight that compels me like dew to a morning flower. "Unless you are this . . . *enflamée* . . . for another reason?"

My description flares straight to her cheeks. Her gorgeous blush makes her freckles look like stars on satin.

"Okay, this *is* crazy," she mutters, curling fists against the upper swells of her breasts.

But she is too late. I have already seen what lies beneath. Peeked at the rosy puckers that are nearly spilling from that corset. Imagined the erect berries at their centers . . . and imagined all the reasons for it. That list is, thank God, very narrow.

She has to know that too but repeats nonetheless, "Very, *very* crazy. This has got to be—I mean—maybe it's just a dream. Oh, God. That's it, isn't it? I must've fallen asleep. I'm not even here. I'm probably drooling on my keyboard and—"

I drown the rest of her fuss beneath the crash of my kiss.

Crash.

It is the perfect word. I have fantasized about taking her like this, perhaps more times than I should, but never acted on the desire before this uncontrollable moment. Before I crossed the barrier between need and compulsion, desire and demand, choice and commandment. I have to conquer her like this. I *must* tame her, taste her, and take her to a wild mental island of my creation. A place where no other words exist on her feisty lips save one . . . *yes* . . .

When I finally release her, so many minutes later, her head stays tilted back. The copper tips of her lashes flutter up at me.

"Oh . . . *yes,*" she rasps. "Such a dream . . ."

A low growl vibrates up my throat. I am conflicted. Officially she has spoken the word, but it has come with friends. Unnecessary ones. I order them away with another smash of my lips against hers. Another plunge along her tongue. A tighter hold of her stunning curves, ending with my greedy hand against her firm little derriere.

She gasps against my lips. I answer with a scoundrel's smile.

"A dream, my luscious lily? If that is still so, then I pray we slumber a lifetime. Perhaps two or three."

Another taut breath escapes her. "You have no idea how right you might be, my lord De Le—*ahhh*!"

Her cry, a result of my gentle bite to her bottom lip, is nearly as perfect as her orgasm scream. *Nearly.* "Little girl, surely you have not forgotten so soon, hmm?"

And *there* are her eyes, in all their wide and wondering glory. "Forgotten?" she stammers. "Ahhh . . . what, exactly?"

I nibble her top lip this time. "That surely you meant Monsieur le Duke De Leon?"

"Duke?" Her greens pop even wider. *Mon dieu*, such emerald glory. "*Duke* De Leon? Okay, this plot *is* thickening."

Fate, in its divine humor, has that word corresponding to my next move before either of us can help it. As she spills the description, I am already swerving the spear at my center into the soft cleft of hers. We groan and laugh together. Suddenly, everything feels right again. Like *us* again. She admits it, as well. Not out loud, but in so many other ways. The weight that is gone from her mirth. The dimples that reappear in her cheeks. Most wonderfully, the acquiescence that eases into her body—and the soft awe that spreads across her face.

"Well, talk about awesome timing."

I push my forehead to hers and inhale deeply. "'Twould that we not talk at all, *ma magie*." Another long breath in, this time to appreciate the nuances of her new scent. There is no more trace of the blood and fear in which I had to leave her. In which I will *never* leave her again.

"Ohhh." She moans it out as my lips trail down the side of her face, tickling the curls at her hairline. "Okay, then . . ." The moan becomes a watery, sexy sigh as I continue my oral

ANGEL PAYNE

adventure, kissing my way to the delicate curve of her ear. "Should we forget about timing too?"

"Oui," I husk and recommence my nibbles along her sensitive shell. She trembles in my arms before wrapping her own around my neck.

"Maybe...we should just forget about the whole time thing, period."

I smile into her skin while pulling her deeper into my embrace. "I can think of nothing more perfect, my love."

RAEGAN

This is crazy.

No. What's the next stop past that? Then maybe a couple past *that*?

Because I shouldn't be here, melting like ice cream in this man's embrace. I shouldn't be letting my own arms turn to taffy, winding tighter until my hands are threading up through his damp, thick hair. I shouldn't be inhaling as if his whole chest has turned into the front door at MarieBelle and I want to consume every gorgeous ganache in the place.

MarieBelle would actually be a better place for me right now.

No. *Hell* would be.

Not that it isn't already swinging the gates wide, getting ready to send out the welcome wagon. How many commandments in the book am I breaking? Do I want to know? This man—*Maximillian De Leon's brother*—has somehow accomplished the same feat as his older sibling, despite the accounts of all the history books.

According to them, his body and head were officially

separated in early March 1789, right after a mob of revolutionaries killed his parents in similar fashion. So are the records wrong—or has he rewritten them? Did he elude the executioner by jumping into the family time machine as well? How did he even know to do it?

Max told us the only guiding light he had was his heart— that he had clung to a vision of Allie and then found himself in this century. It seems Bastien has followed the same premise, except his true love is someone named Magique.

Not me.

Really not me.

How do I tell him that?

Correction: how do I tell him that, when his mouth is like tendrils of fire along my neck, across my collarbone . . . down and over the peak of one breast? Oh, holy shit, and now the other?

And then . . . as he flicks his tongue into the space between the corset and my flesh . . . and snags my nipple with that hot, wet brand . . .

"*Unhhh!*"

Wow.

Wow.

Triple wow.

At this point, I'll even take help from the other side of the River Styx. I just need words. Lots of them.

"Ohhh, dear fuck!"

Better words than that.

"Well. You remember liking *that*, *oui*?" he drawls, gliding his licks across the valley toward my other aching peak.

Already my nipple pushes at the corset's confines, all but whimpering for his wanton attention. But I struggle to yank back. I can't keep doing this to him. Deceiving him.

No matter how much I like it.

"Wait," I insist, pulling at his hair until he raises his head. How have I already forgotten the mesmerizing alloy of his eyes? They're a darker gold than his brother's. Better. So much better. "Please. We need to . . . take a time out."

He hauls the rest of the air out of my throat with his slow, sideways smile. "What is this 'time' that you speak of, *ma chérie*?"

I huff. "You know what I mean."

"No." He's damn determined about it, turning him into the duke with the hands—and voice and smile and hip rolls—I can barely deny anymore. "I have absolutely no idea what you mean. We have left time behind, remember? Every day, every hour, every moment before this . . . it does not matter." He enforces that with a dip of his head, kissing me tenderly but deeply. "There is only this, my Magique. Only here and now. There is only me . . . marveling at the sheer perfection of you."

My Magique.

Shit, shit, shit.

The adoration in his whisper unravels me—in too many directions at too many speeds. I'm headed for disaster, a catastrophic collision, but I'm almost watching in glee as it happens. My mind doesn't feel attached to my body, which tremors in delight from his knowing, skating fingers. During every moment of the contact, I'm mewling like a dazed and stupid virgin. At the very least, like someone who wasn't quivering like this just a few weeks ago. All right, probably because I *wasn't*. Things with Justin . . . they were sideways before they went upside-down. So many signs were on the proverbial wall, especially when he begged out of Christmas with my family. I just kept refusing to look.

I never want to look away from this dazzling man. From every damn thing he's doing to fray me from the inside out.

He's already started anew, ignoring my sharp yelp as he expertly unties the corset. Next, before the thing even hits my feet, sliding his commanding fingers between the fabric of my panties and the swell of my ass. Last but absolutely not least, blending his growl to my hiss as the silk thong whispers through its own descent.

"Oh . . . *my.*"

"Oh . . . *oui.*" His hum, so satisfied and so male, dances through the inches between us. "My exquisite Magique."

My Magique.

Damn it, why won't he stop saying it?

Perhaps because that's who I'm supposed to be? The woman he clearly, adamantly craves—with intensity that has my whole body vibrating and my mind racing.

How would it feel . . . to really be her? To be drenched in the flood of his praise? To be basking in his worship and wonder? To be watching his gaze drop and center on *that* spot between my breasts, giving a look of nothing but awe in return?

To actually be his adored duchess?

"*Ohhh.*" I softly moan it as he presses several fingers at the center of my scar. "Keep that up and I'll be talking about dreams again, buddy."

"Dreams?" He leans in to replace his touch with his kiss. "Oh, no. This is surely naught but true magic."

Not *her* name again, but too damn close for my comfort— until he gets to work on my flesh with his beautiful mouth, spreading heat throughout my breasts that has the word tumbling from my own lips.

"Abra...cadabra," I blurt, twisting at his hair until I'm afraid of ripping his scalp off.

But the man must be a stud or a pain freak because his growl grows deeper as he suckles my left nipple with focused vigor.

"My God," I manage to croak as he trails toward my right peak. "My fucking God."

"Hmm. I do not think *he* is inclined to fuck right now, *ma magie*. But if you are open to a reasonable substitute..."

As he resumes his suction, my urgent scream spills out.

"Damn it! Keep that up, Duke Desperado, and the neighbors are going to call the boys in blue on us."

He lifts his head with a ferocious look. "*No* other boys on you. No boys, no men. Not in blue or any other color. Understood?"

He doesn't wait for me to answer. Only makes me moan once more with his awestriking animalism. His shoulders, tensing until they look and feel like the Adirondacks. His hands, digging into my waist to haul me close again. His bulge, pushing at my middle until my imagination conjures the NYPD again—at least in a few ways...

"I understand that you're packing one hell of a riot stick here, buddy."

He hums again, so knowing and sensual. "Only if you plan on rioting, mademoiselle."

I give up a light laugh. More and more, I'm forgetting what I'm not—and reveling in what I'm becoming. Discovering what he's seeing. Slowly but surprisingly, believing his words. Perhaps this really is just an intense dream, or a feat of incredible magic, but the man and his astounding body are obviously in for every second of the fantasy.

A bubble I could pop now, or later . . .

My inner Eeyore pushes for doing it now. My inner Tigger insists on taking over that narrative at once—especially when Bastien and I kiss again. This carnal, commanding man doesn't let up, dominating me with ruthless rushes of his tongue and grinding rolls of his magical hips. In return, I sigh and groan and suck on him with the same insane abandon. I breathe in, savoring his sweaty whiskey taste and his leathery, woodsy smell.

But this man isn't from some fictional forest with dancing tigers and pantsless bears. He's a warrior from a dark wilderness in another era, unafraid of kissing a woman with his whole being . . . and, God help me, all the mounting heat of his massive body.

My freaking hell . . .

No doubt about it; it's surely where I'm going now.

Because how is it going to be humanly possible to tell him at this point? Not now, after everything he's done to me. Every *magnificent* thing . . .

My whole body vibrates, blatantly confirming it. I'm naked but unashamed. Bared but emboldened. Perspiration glows along my limbs, reflected as decadent dew in the depths of Bastien De Leon's eyes.

Holy crap, how I want him. And how I know he wants me.

Then what on earth is he waiting for?

If he doesn't make a move in another ten seconds, I'll be more than happy to. Though I doubt he'll complain, it's still a weird concept. Yes, we may still be strangers—kind of, sort of—but he doesn't strike me as the kind of man to rest on his very fine haunches.

And oh God . . . he *doesn't*.

"Ahhh!" I'm not ready for the sudden splay of his palms on the spheres of my ass. The cry tumbles out a second time as he grips me harder, using the purchase to hoist me fully off my feet. Instinctively, I circle my legs around his waist. Inwardly, I throw a thousand celebrations about it.

Allie and Drue never stop teasing about my fixation with steamy moves like this, calling them my "in another reality with that romance cover model" dreams.

If they could see me now.

With a dark desperado who's better than a thousand steamy novel covers. Who's already ticked off a dozen of the sexiest moves from my fictional favorites—joined by yet another, as he spins around and launches us both onto the big, waiting bed.

CHAPTER FIVE

BASTIEN

I should have done this sooner.

But I hesitated, direly afraid to smash our dream by unleashing my full passion on her. I should have remembered that banked fires often burn the hottest. That restraining the hammer of my lust would only cure it into a mallet of unstoppable need. That it would be forged by my worship for this woman. The forever goddess in my soul.

The delusion I truly must be having . . .

Yet if this is delusion, let me never know sanity again.

Let me never remember how I had to leave her in a puddle of her own blood. How I never had time to put a diamond on her finger and call her mine before the world. How I watched every flicker of life disappear from her eyes . . .

Vitality that glows again at me, so perfect and whole. That flows through every naked inch of the writhing curves beneath me. Doing things to me.

By every saint I can no longer recall, the things she is *doing* to me . . .

"Oh!"

With every hot, hypnotizing repetition of that sole syllable . . .

"Oh *no* or oh *yes*, my sweet lily?"

My question elicits a response I have not predicted. Not in my dirtiest fantasies.

"How about you and this awesome cock trying for both?" she proposes, delving a hand beneath the flap of my britches.

While I flounder through my mind for an answering groan, she wraps her other palm around my backside, scratching my flesh with her urgent grip.

"Well," I finally choke back. "How about that being an excellent idea?"

She laughs, washing my jawline with her soft, sultry breath. "There are many more where that came from, your lordy dukeship of everyth—"

She slices in on herself with a tiny shriek that is, unbelievably, more arousing than her banter. It spills from her again as I slide inside her with a harder thrust. Our flesh slaps. My senses turn to star fire.

"My holy God," I grate. "Already so deep. Already so tight in your greedy glove."

More of that riveting fire in her eyes, the green depths like an otherworldly sky for my stars, before she rasps, "Greedy is right. I don't want to stop!"

"Then we most certainly will not."

I twist my hips and celebrate every note of her deeper moans. Then the tighter tugs of her sweet little *chatte*. Oh, especially those.

"But we have to. Oh, *damn it*, we have to. I was on the pill until three weeks ago but ditched them out of spite. Just let me up for a second. I'm sure I've got a few friendly Trojans stashed in my—"

"Trojans?" I halt my thrusts. Completely. Does she expect me to do anything else after mentioning a stash of men—however thousands of years defunct—that she wishes to retrieve? What kind of a freakish realm has the woman led me to? "And whom, I must request, does this regal cache include? The entire army, or just Hector, Alexander, and Cassandra?"

Her lips quirk.

I cherish every second of the look, preparing for the repartee to follow. The quick wit that entranced me long before the passions of her body.

No swift sarcasm erupts from her. Not even a well-paced barb. Instead, she is laughing. Not a few giggles. This is a laugh, full and rich, taking over her whole body until she is clenching me anew in all the right places. Yet in this moment, all the wrong ones. Not if she expects me to hold out...

"Magique."

Hold out? It is all I can to hold *on* now...

"Oh! *Desperado.*"

But not even now.

There is no more pausing for "time out." No more "letting up" to catch my breath. The enchantress, with her curls and curves and gasps and writhes, weaves a thickening spell around my senses... and the flesh still buried within her.

"*Magique.* I do not think I can—"

My choked groan cracks the air. My cock jerks of its own accord. It has become an organ under its own volition, ripped from the moors of my mind and speeding toward the siren call of her hot, undulating core. *Mon dieu,* no wonder she is evoking secret Trojans. Surely she was Helena in another life and it was *these* walls that distracted those poor idiots from the mission. Little shock they were slaughtered.

Shreds that pale in comparison to how she is ripping up my restraint.

"Oh...my word!"

"Mmm." I suckle the pillow of her bottom lip. "And what word would that be, my love?"

"*More.* Please! Just...right now...more of that. All of that, pl—"

A high cry from her, as soon as my shaft obeys her pretty plea. I swell and pulse, commanding every remaining corner of her sweet core.

"My sweet *lord,* Monsieur De Leon, who the hell taught you that nifty trick?"

"Hmm." I tighten my buttocks and swivel my hips, savoring the new shivers it all prompts from her. "Perhaps *I* have borrowed some sorcery somewhere, as well."

Her head arches back, putting an indent in the pillow. "Okay. Th-That works for me. *Oh.* Ohhh...*wait.*" Her breath hitches as I pull out and then slam back in, smacking her flesh with twice the force as before. "That works even better. Oh *shit,* mister!"

As soon as her deep greens flash up at me, I am ready with a darker stare...a tougher thrust. It is a marvelous thing to watch her jaw drop and her cheeks darken.

"Good?" I growl. "Talk to me, sweet lily."

"Can't...we just...discuss the *talking* thing later?" she stammers. "Because buddy, right now I just need—oh dear *God*!"

Her gasp comes courtesy of the new push I give with my pelvis. But only a push. Just a sample, reminding her drenched walls of exactly what made them that way.

"You need what, *ma magnifique*?" As a rasp invades my voice, her eyelashes flutter in surprise. She has the right to see her power over me, and I expose it to her in full. "Please, my beauty. Tell me all of it. Give me your filthy, fascinating words. The sorcery of your syllables . . ."

"Yes. Fine." She gasps. "But your cock first!"

I work a little more of myself into her. "You get it when I say you get it. *Your* words first."

"Damn it!" She locks her heels against my backside, attempting to force her agenda that way. "You don't understand!"

"Oh, but I do." I smirk without letting the mirth climb to my eyes. "What do you think obsesses me during those long nights on patrol for Louis? How do you think I get through the weeks of waiting, having to sneak peeks at you through the palais salon windows? Cherishing the days when the weather clears and you are asked to stroll with the ladies in the garden? Counting the hours, minutes, and seconds until time is on my side and gives you back to me?"

"Time." Her echo is more air than sound, once more spoken at some invisible entity in the room. "Not sure whether to thank or curse that bastard at the moment."

I smile. "More bees with honey, *ma chérie*."

"Not craving honey, Desperado."

"Then what *do* you desire, little lily?"

One edge of her mouth quirks up. "Why don't I just show you, duke of wonder?"

Before I can help it, my grin expands to a laugh. But also before I can help it, she again upends my expectations. I am shoved up enough to be free from her entrance, but not from her ministrations. A groan escapes as my cock is encased in new pressure. The long massages of her fingers . . . *Mon dieu.* Every inch of me stiffens beneath her intensely perfect strokes. Lust clouds my logic. The strength leaves my limbs.

She knows it at once. And, because of that, is able to topple me onto my back.

Where I receive every affirmation that I have followed her to heaven.

Nothing else makes sense once she switches the grip on my shaft. As she replaces her fingers with her mouth.

"*Magique*. This is such . . . it is so . . ."

But then my aroused haze spreads, taking over my mind. Words are impossible. I am choked and fevered. Caged but set free. Milked to the point of madness.

The best insanity I shall ever know.

Especially when she rolls her soft fingers across the sac at my base.

In an instant, I am broken down. And then broken out.

My liquid heat flows up. Explodes out. Drenches and fills the scorching cave of her mouth. But she does not let go, clamping my shuddering head with the back of her throat. I splay a hand against her head, keeping her in place. It's one of the happiest moments of my existence but one of the most despairing. Surely every drop of my seed must be leaving my body. All the De Leon heirs will have to come from my brother.

A price I shall joyously pay.

A joy that blossoms wider as soon as my woman raises up.

"You are still here," I say, treasuring it as fact. Only now do I recognize the trepidation at the back of my mind, nursing the fear that my physical finish would make this all vanish. But it is all the same. This warm cocoon of a room. This silken vision of a woman. Heaven after all.

One corner of her mouth hitches up. "And so are you."

"That perplexes you?" I grunt good-naturedly. "Ah, of course it does. An angelic life was hardly ever my ultimate goal."

"Worthy of celebration." Her tone does not commit that as complete humor, though certainly she is not serious. I transfer that curiosity to a slight scowl, which she addresses with haste. "Angels are only my thing if they bring their wings with extra garlic and a side of chipotle coleslaw."

A slight frown crawls across my brow. How long has she truly been in this realm? All these things I have never heard her say before . . . and meanings I can only guess at . . .

But even guesses elude my mind from the moment she reaches and palms my balls again.

I groan in stunned ecstasy, savoring how it sounds with Magique's sighs peppered in. Somehow, I raise my head enough to rake her anew with my gaze. The hoods that drop over her precious greens. The stiffness that claims her ruby nipples. The dewdrops that glisten between her gently parted legs.

Oh, *oui*. Most importantly, that.

A brief mewl spills from her once I rivet my stare down there. "More," I command, showing her my need by dragging my fist up my cock. "I need to see more. Spread yourself, little lily."

Incroyable, how she affects me. How much pleasure I have, returning so fast. I am even stiffer as she complies, revealing her wet, pink mysteries to me.

I lose my hand over the purple bulb of my crown. It is hot and hard, hating and adoring me at once. But I do not look away from her decadent cunt. The utter artwork of it.

"Holy hell. Look what you do to me, *ma magie.*"

Her hips jerk. More drops appear between her legs, collecting along her beckoning slit. "Look what you do to *me,* Bastien De Leon."

"Most assuredly," I rasp. "But now I want to *see*." I am prepared for the question in her eyes—and ready with an answer. "Spread *all* of your petals now. And then touch them. And fuck into them."

A nervous swipe of her tongue along her lips, which pumps even more blood up my cock.

"Was I unclear, woman?"

"No. *No*. I just—"

"What?"

"If I do it, I'll come."

"Well, then . . . you had best hasten about it."

RAEGAN

Orgasms and I have been good friends for a long time. Whether I should send a thank-you note to my free-spirited parents or the original *Gossip Girl* producers, I still have no idea. The conflict is especially acute as I frown at the clock on my drawing pad, indicating I'm wide awake at six on a Sunday morning because my bloodstream is still sizzling from the climax I rubbed out in front of Bastien De Leon. And then the next one, given with his own fingers, before he exploded for me again too.

It was the hottest no-fuck climax I've ever had.

No. It was the hottest climax I've ever had, period.

What would it be like to actually have the man ride me until he came? To ride *him* until I did the same?

Nate Archibald and Chuck Bass don't stand a chance against my new fantasies. *Sorry not sorry, boys*.

For the first time in my existence, I understand why some women emphasize the word *man*. Exactly what those underlines—and sayings like them—mean. Stuff like *wet till it hurts* and *weak in the knees*. So weak, I forgot I *had* knees.

Is this why so many people do the historical reenactment stuff? I mean, if everyone knew that the hottest sexual secrets of history have been stowed in the eighteenth century and then were given a way to start yanking the men out of there, what would that do to world history?

Though I'm pretty sure *my* eighteenth-century god doesn't know he's leapfrogged over the last two hundred and something years.

But how to tell him?

It's not like I can text Allie and ask her. After Max's jump, *he* was the one who had to convince *her* about the truth. Instinct tells me that won't be the case this time—which is why I'm here, counting last night's "sleep" as a total bust between web searches on my phone. Absconding from the bedroom either of my other devices wasn't an option, once I realized they were both stuck at the foot of the bed after Bastien and I made new dents in the mattress.

Oh my God. *Bastien De Leon.*

Just typing his name now is an invitation for every tingle in the building to visit the juncture of my thighs. I do it carefully, so as to avoid any conflicts with the search.

But I get no hits on the search. None that make sense, anyway.

Maximilian De Leon brother

Better hits but wrong results. Most of the listings are about Max's wild success on the Hemline channel, as a guest commentator on other shows as well as his hit partnership with

Allie. Turns out the modern world is in love with charming time travelers, even if they don't quite know it for themselves. None of the articles mention a brother.

De Leon family France + 18th century

Another list of clickables, though every link leads to the basics I already know. That the De Leons once owned massive lands in Loire, which were seized once the Jacobins and the Revolution inundated the countryside. That the family was given the land back once Napoleon took the throne, though a great deal of the family wasn't accounted for. Maximilian, Bastien, and their parents were seized early during the insurrections. The elder De Leons were executed at once. The next day, Bastien followed them to the executioner's block.

My chest hurts. My throat tightens. Still, I force my fingers to type in a new search string.

Bastien De Leon execution

I grimace but force myself to click the search bar.

The first results aren't enough to erase my tension. But I do indulge a long breath while scanning the page. Then another, as soon as I peruse the subject's second and third pages.

Once I hit the fourth, I allow myself to breathe easy again. For about ten seconds. "Doesn't mean a thing," I remind myself in a mumble. "Wasn't like Robespierre and his posse were logging every execution and then selling it for demographics."

So there's still a reasonable chance that Bastien's head rolled into a basket back then. But how does that explain the very beautiful head, attached to the equally stunning body, still snoring in the bedroom? And I mean *snoring*. The deep, lusty rumble actually makes me smile on the upbeats. The man can't even slumber without intensity.

On this day, in this time, Bastien De Leon is definitely not dead.

That opens up a few more possibilities. Crazy ones, but options I have to consider.

He's a substantial ghost. Or a soul reincarnated. Or a zombie. Okay that one's kind of cool, though he'd have to be categorized as a pretty zombie. Like that kid from *Warm Bodies* or the hottie king in *Army of the Dead*. But he'd likely rock the crap out of gory zombie too.

But that's probably not the case. Because I already hear what logic is screaming at me.

Like his brother before him, the man has been propelled through time. So that means he escaped or avoided prison. After that, he probably learned about the fastest way out of the country and vanished into Germany or Prussia. Maybe he even found a way to hop *la Manche* to England.

I'm so lost in a vision of him doing that, heart aching while I envision him trudging alone into strange countries, that his snoring dims from awareness. Once I realize he's stopped, the man is standing next to me.

Correction. Looming over me.

Holy shit.

His hands are fisted. His golden eyes are wide. He's really turned into my Desperado. He's frantic. Lost. Terrified. I can't say that I blame him.

"Oh, hey!" I surge to my feet. "Good morning." Within two seconds, I whip around to turn us into a pseudo see-saw, plunking him down to the cushion. "Okay, whoa. You're about to hyperventilate. *Whoa*. Bastien, you need to breathe deeper."

Thankfully, he listens. I still don't feel confident about letting go of his shoulders yet—having *nothing* to do with his huge delts beneath my sprawled hands—but it also feels good to have him near again. As if the world has been on a massive tilt and has leveled again.

"You." He lifts a hand that trembles harder than his voice. But when he presses his fingers to the scoop of my tank top, where my scar is peeking out, he touches down like my skin is chiffon. "You are still here."

"Yes." I run my own fingers along the back of his. "Exactly where I belong."

The pledge wasn't what my brain intended but what my heart means. It feels so right to say it. More than right to realize it. Almost as if I traversed centuries to get here too. As if *I* should be called *Desperado* as well.

"*Magique*."

Damn it. I liked Desperado Junior better. I even close my eyes and pray for it as he braces his other hand to my hip and tugs me down next to him. And then against him.

So close.

So warm.

So right.

"How is this possible?" He rumbles it with low ferocity, sending wonderful rumbles through his chest and along my cheek. "Last night, I nearly thought it but a vivid dream."

"I get it." I pull in a breath, sneaking an extra hit of his scent. There's a lot of my stuff, cherry body lotion and vanilla shampoo, mixed with the earthy notes along his skin. The effect is dizzying in all the right ways. "I almost threw down for the same theory a few times."

"Threw what down?" He busses the top of my head. "Perhaps your precious garlic wings and the cold slaw with chips a-laying?"

My giggle nearly becomes a spit take. It's tempered by a glaring realization. Even animated corpses know the almighty goodness of garlic wings.

So, I really have to accept the base truth now. And the conclusion to where it leads.

I have to convince Bastien of what's happened too. And, very possibly, why.

And something—a pounding, dreading something—tells me he's not going to hop on the time travel parade float as easily as his brother.

CHAPTER SIX

BASTIEN

"Alll riiighty then."

Magique's evasive expression is not just words from her lips. She looks away quickly, as if having a debate with herself before deliberately raising those pretty greens back to me.

Eyes that have become too bright. Above a smile that is too forced.

"You know, now that we've danced toward the subject, you hungry at all? I haven't had a chance to check kitchen inventory yet, but if Allie's only got old stale saltines and diet soda, we can order in . . ."

Words that are too hurried. And truly make no sense at all now.

I clasp both of her hands. It is the only way to halt her progress from nervous to petrified. If I know nothing else about her, it is assuredly this. "Magique." I squeeze to emphasize the mandate. "To me, you are already my duchess. If you desire some food, I can send a servant to—"

"Oh, holy shit." She chuckles despite my puzzled gape. "Sorry. I didn't mean it like— I mean, it's just that servants aren't going to be—" She stops again, though with significant purpose. "Maybe we'd just better sit for a second."

I *knew* I was premature, thinking her tension was gone.

Still, I give an inviting tug to her stiffened fingers. "Why sit when we can lie?"

She adamantly ignores my suggestive glance back toward the bedroom. It gives me no choice about looking elsewhere too. And wondering, yet again . . .

Where am I? What is this place, with its grand architecture, gleaming surfaces, and bustling sounds?

If I were here alone, the chaos would indeed be daunting. But as always, Magique De Lys is the sight hole of my armor. The only light upon which I need to, and must, focus. My touchstone and sanity, despite the alluring words that fall from her next.

"I'm not likely to trust myself with you on your back, Desperado." Her gilt-tinged eyelashes catch the morning light, ensuring my morning oak now matches the thick armrests of this overstuffed furniture. Not an inch of the development escapes her notice. "On that prominent note," she pointedly says, "Do you mind fastening up all the way? *Save me from me.* Catch my drift?"

Unbelievably, I am able to nod and mean it—though surely it is *me* from who she will need ultimate rescue. If her smile inches any higher or her curls turn into a full halo of sunlight, the bedsheets may have some company this morn, after all. But I will let her speak her peace first. Landing an arrow is as much about awaiting the wind as releasing the bow.

"You know I adore every one of your *drifts*, my little lily."

She laughs, but it does not result in her wider smile. All too swiftly, the expression twists into a grimace. A look that hooks into my gut like her death stare did.

Like a goodbye.

No.

I twist my grip tighter around her. She does not fight me, which sharpens every barb in my stomach. The brightest light is comprised of constant motion. Every decent soldier knows that. A man who loves a woman like this is well-served to remember it. But her movements are sparse and reserved, even when she lifts her head and once more fixes the twin forests of her gaze on me.

"Okay...that's kind of the thing here," she says. "I'm...not exactly your 'little lily.' Or your *chérie*, or your *magie*..."

As soon as she trails off with a strange shrug, I stiffen. "I do not understand."

"I know you don't. What I mean is that I *look* like this Magique person of yours—I mean, I think I do—but that I'm not her."

She adjusts our handclasp, flattening my palms together with the determined presses of her beautiful hands.

Her... *hands.*

Why have I not noticed them before this moment? How did I not marvel about how the strained work lines have disappeared? The dry spots from washing other women's underthings in boiling water? The callouses from hauling that water through the back halls of Versailles? And after that, a myriad of other physically brutal tasks? A life I am determined to take her away from.

But what about now?

"I still do not understand." My cold tone comes from instinct. I wish that it were not so, especially as she straightens her own posture. "This 'person' of mine? What are you about? You...you *are*..." I stop as soon as I push a hand up, landing it to the center of her chest. The chemise she wears is pliant, allowing me to trace the line of her valiant scar. "Do you not remember *this*? How you earned it?"

Her next laugh is as disconcerting as its predecessor. "*Earned* it? Well, I like that take on things better than most."

I press harder with my strongest two fingers. Demand of her, my voice still tinged with frost, "Meaning what?"

"That of course I remember how it got there. Mack Deluise wasn't easy to forget, even before he planted his switchblade in my chest."

I let up on the pressure. I have no choice. My fingertips are suddenly icebergs. Even Magique reacts with a significant shiver.

Magique?

Dear God.

Can I be truly sure it *is* her?

Does all this feel so different because *she* is?

I close my eyes after a few seconds of the supposition. It is my only fight against the agony. A battlefield strategy to get through this mental mire. *One piece of information at a time.*

"Mack. Deluise." I purposely give the words their own boxes. "Perhaps you mean *Marq De Lys* instead?"

I pray that my intonation will jar her memories loose. She left mortality so swiftly, without warning. Perhaps that garbled things for her. Because of that, I deliberately leave out the part about her own brother putting her in this state.

But all too quickly, she shakes her head. "I'm sorry. I don't know anyone named Marq De Lys. I *do* know Mack Deluise, the schoolyard tyrant who accidentally stabbed me instead of Harker Bowe over half a bag of Funions during morning break. And no, I *won't* forget it just because it happened when I was thirteen. Bullies grow up." She is not so still anymore, twisting her lips and darting her gaze. "And that's when people need to stand up to them even more."

Her confession is not one I expect, or even want to, hear. But I comprehend so much of it now, even the parts she does not express in words. I am speared by the horror that takes over her face but am also moved by the aspect of her that overrides it all. The compassion of her spirit. The humanity of her heart.

The things that are so special about her . . .

That are so much like Magique.

My Magique.

I do not know how I get from beholding her to kissing her. But here I am, where I need to be. Where I *should* be. Taking her mouth with soft persistence. Tasting her tongue with warm languor. Not pushing or insisting. Waiting, with held breath, for *her* to do it. To give me all her signs.

And she does.

And I am rejoicing as she lets me inside a little more. Offers me her sighs and moans. Circles an arm under and around to score the narrow valley along my spine with long, lusty scratches.

And that easily, we are together again. Wound and wrenched and knotted around each other with heat . . . with *heart*. All the way *inside* our hearts. I cannot deny it. I *will not* deny it. And neither can she.

"Oh *God!*"

But she does. So fiercely and urgently.

I catch a glimpse of the sheen in her eyes as she pushes back and shoves to her feet. It develops into salty rivers, flowing down and seeping beneath her fingers as she smashes them against her lips. As if she's trying to push her frantic breaths all the way back to her lungs.

"OhGodOhGodOhGod." The words pour out in a matching torrent, almost indecipherable. Thankfully, she lets them fall before demanding, "What was that? What the *fuck* is going on?"

Surprising her, and likely myself, a smirk takes over my lips. "You said the same thing when I kissed you the first time."

She frowns. It is more adorable than her profanity. "Last night?"

"Last *year.*"

Her expression changes. Still beautiful but not so adorable. I loathe making her look so sad. "No, Bast. No, I didn't."

Bast.

My casual name...on her trembling lips. It sounds stilted and unsure, as if it is the first time she has uttered it in that way. So softly. So intimately. But I know it is not...

It cannot be.

She presses a hand to my jaw, scraping at the scruff that lines it. "Damn it, how I want to tell you differently. How I long for all of that to be true. How I want this piece of my heart with your name already on it to be okay about pretending for you. But you deserve better. And...so does Magique."

As she rasps those last words, she shifts back by small, unsteady steps. From the darker expression on her face, I expect her to cross herself any moment. Or vomit. Or both.

I do not wait for either. There is too much at stake now. Too much about her rasps that nonetheless feel like screams. Worse, like the truth.

"What the hell are you saying?" I do not rein back my seethe. "The *complete* truth of it, woman."

Her chest, beneath that painstakingly flimsy chemise,

billows in and out. "You kissed Magique last year... but that was her, not me. I don't remember a thing about it because I wasn't there."

My head rolls in something like a denying shake. "Is that the part I am supposed to understand now?"

She readjusts until securing my forearms beneath her grip. "I wasn't there last year because for me, last year was twenty—"

She completes the assertion, but my mind does not register her last numbers. They are inconsequential beyond her century marker.

Her century marker.

My head rolls around again. For a moment, I wonder if it will just easily snap off. It will be easier to realign all the contents. Clearly, something has gone wrong. Very wrong. She has not just told me... if so, she cannot be serious...

"Bastien? Hey, are you ok—" Her harsh huff penetrates my mental vortex more than her babbling. Which is only that, *oui*? Her own way of explaining all of this. Her personal denial of being murdered by her own brother. "All right, you *aren't* okay. Come here. Maybe you'd better sit down again."

I jerk away. I must. Sanity will not come when being so close to her.

"Leave me be." I march across the room while stabbing hands through my hair. "Just... leave me be. Please."

At once, I want to retract the nicety. It is not *nice* at all, gashing the air like an angry expletive. In my periphery, her fast flinch confirms it.

"I know it's a lot. And... I'm so sorry about that. But that wardrobe in the bedroom... it's some kind of time transportation thing. You've used it to get here, to New York

City. It's in the United States of America, and—"

"America?" My jolting head leads the way for my whole body to spin back. "The backwoods where Lafayette went?"

Her spine stiffens. "Backwoods, hmm?" she murmurs, nodding toward the window. The muted dawn beyond the big glass panes is at least bright enough to illuminate the vista beyond.

An entirely new world.

"*Mon dieu.*"

There is a vast river, though not the Thames or Loire. It cannot be. The landscape . . . There are so many lanterns, all illuminated at once. They are in so many *colors*, as if we are inside a brilliant seashell. Noises echo back at us the same way, cacophonous and loud . . . and once more, so *many*.

"What . . . is . . . this place? How can those ships move without sails? How are those carriages pulled without horses? And why are they so far aw—"

My stunned grunt is my own interruption.

"*Putain de merde.*" I save myself from spraying it across the window by scrambling back as frantically as I can. "The carriages are that small and far because we are . . . this high and far?"

"Okay, breathe," she urges. "You're perfectly safe. I promise."

Her statement does not confirm my theory. But does not deny it either. After learning I am not so dizzy when looking to the horizon instead of the park directly below the windows, I can construct clear thoughts again. "Exactly . . . how high . . ."

All right, *reasonably* clear thoughts.

"Twenty stories," she supplies, as breezy as before. "I'm not sure what that adds up to in exact feet, but—"

"Not necessary." I underline it with a sharp wave of one arm. The other, I use to steady my descent onto the nearest safe surface: one of the couch's sturdy arms. "I already want to forget the approximation."

A long pause, filled by her full but unsteady inhalation. "You *are* perfectly safe, Bastien."

"As you have insisted before," I growl.

"This building has been standing solid since the eighties. Everything is up to code. And it's not even the tallest one in the ci—"

She clamps her lips with an audible sound as I grunt and grip the couch tighter. While my head swims, my torso gives in to a watery kind of weave. I fight the urge to fall all the way over, back to the cushions next to her. If that happens, I will long to touch her again. And if *that* happens, we will never get to the actual reasons behind the bizarreness of last night. What was real. What was not. What parts were dreams and what parts were, pray God, just deranged nightmares.

Or . . . a mystifying mix of both?

An explanation that becomes the safest buckle in my brain, as I home in on a new object of fascination.

Of terrible recognition . . .

Step after dreading step, I close in on the weird little box. I stop but do not want to. If I freeze, so do the images inside the box.

Images? Am I certain about that? *I have to be.* If this is not an elaborate trick of mirrors or play on paint, what in the actual hell is this thing? Is this cube a creation of angels or demons? White magic or dark sorcery?

Cease your ramblings. You do not believe in sorcerers. You make your own destiny, damn it.

The last of it tumbles out aloud—and I am unsure whether to thank or curse myself when the picture in the box seems to respond. I startle and step back. The image reacts again, this time becoming a whole new scene with whole new movements.

"*Mierde!*" I abandon all my caution, which feels foolish now. I lunge over and grab up the box. "Maximillian?" I demand to it. "Brother? Can you hear me?"

The couch's leather creaks. There is a defined shift on the air. But the female behind me does not move beyond that spot. Her effort is pointless. The distance she keeps does not prevent me from feeling her longing. From comprehending her need to rush to my side.

How?

How is it possible for me to sense her like this, to know her heart so clearly, if her claim is true? If she is not my Magique, after all?

One of us is subscribing to the wrong truth.

I hate the increasing surety that it is me.

I fight the sensation by picking up the rectangular box and shaking it. I turn it end over end, struggling to comprehend what I am looking at. It must be a trick of light and mirrors, but there are no hidden latches or doors to lead me to those intrinsic secrets.

"Max," I demand past locked teeth. "Damn it! Talk to me! How do I get you out of there?"

That has to be the substance of it. No matter the diabolical methods they have utilized, mysterious wretches have taken my brave brother captive. Perhaps not so mysterious. Are Marquette and Alonzo behind this? Have they found more ways to betray our family? Or is this the work of someone else in the insurgents' ranks, who has unearthed the deep secret—and likely truth—about Maximillian's heritage? That he has the king's own blood in his veins?

That would make him quite a prize to keep under glass. 'Twould also explain why his hair has been markedly shorn. Why he is not wearing so much as a scarf around his open neck, let alone a cravat. Why his shirt, striped with a bizarre red and blue pattern, is so plainly tailored. Most notably, why it is tucked into a pair of full-length pantaloons, with a thin black belt around his waist. But there is no constraint attached to *that*. Perhaps that means he has somehow escaped his jailors. Perhaps that is why he waves at me again. I have no reasoning for his wide smile—which might not be that at all. He is so small. How can I truly tell?

"I need more information, brother. I know not what you need me to do! Maximillian?"

My absorption with the box is so consuming, I have not heard the approaching footsteps at my back. When Magique—or whoever the hell this is—appears at my side, it is too late to render any reaction.

"He can't hear you," she says with entirely too much patience. "It's a video box."

"*Pardon moi*?" I roll my head in more random patterns. "But it is not *vide*, my sweet. Not empty." I wave the box before her. "You see this? What is inside this? *Who* is inside this?"

Her tranquility does not garner the same from me. How can she be so calm about this? There is a man—*my brother*—trapped inside this deranged detention! "Let me play with it for a sec?" she asks. "I think I can make him talk. Or at least light him better, so you can see—"

"The hell you will."

I draw on well-practiced instincts to put a lot of the room between us in a few seconds. My speed is spurred by a gut-wrenching conclusion.

Perhaps she has been right all along.

Maybe she is not my Magique but a shell only appearing as such. Another part of the elaborate illusion that has put Maximillian in a box that fits beneath my arm. In a place that makes it possible for her to reference his torture as if she merely plans on changing the straw in his cell. *I can make him talk. Light him better.*

I cannot bear to envision what she actually has in mind.

So why does her new approach not chill my blood and raise my defenses? Why, even now, does my breath quicken and my groin harden? Why does my gaze latch on every expressive angle of her face and my imagination liken her light freckles to wildflowers in a fairy glen?

Magical. She is still so magical.

But she is *not* my Magique. She was the first to tell me so. And now I must force myself to believe it . . .

But I cannot. I refuse. If Magique is gone, what else is there? What do I have left to believe in?

Not the rest of what she has told me too.

There has to be another way. Another explanation. Another reality.

But not here. Not in the same space in which I can see her, smell her, *feel* so much of her.

"No. Not here."

It is a croak on my lips but a roar in my spirit. A rally cry in my senses, waking up the rest of me. I have to get out of here. But where *is* here? And does it matter? The chamber possesses a door. Whatever lies on the other side cannot be as complicated, conflicting, and chaotic as this. The first step has to be getting away from her.

As far and as quickly as possible.

CHAPTER SEVEN

RAEGAN

"Bastien! *Wait!*"

An extra *whomp* of adrenalin provides extra power for my shriek, not that the apartment's new fugitive is paying attention.

Damn it.

Of all the reaction scenarios I played out for Bastien in my head, this wasn't one of them—but it should've been. To a guy like Bastien De Leon, who's clearly more into the rough-and-tumble side of court life than his brother, *magic* doesn't mean frogs, princesses, and disappearing warts. For him, it's curses, snakes, and certain damnation—like the kind he's clearly convinced he's facing now that he believes I'm not his real Magique.

In his mind, I'm now the fraud who ripped him away from her. Who tore him from his world. Who even "imprisoned" his brother in a "box." Insult atop all that injury, I got him naked and nasty before confessing to any of it.

"Naked!"

I gasp it out while sliding on the polished foyer tiles. I look down, blatantly reminded that my attire is nothing but a pink tank top and Fruity Pebble boy shorts.

"Oh, God. *Nasty.*"

Though technically, I'm still dressed in more than he is.

"Shit, Shit, shit," I spew during my limp-sprint back into the bedroom. It feels like an hour instead of a minute before I find yoga pants and a basic hoodie to throw on. I indulge an extra ten seconds to shove into my Crocs too. Usually, the plastic clogs never see the light of day beyond quick tromps to the park or pool, but every rule has an exception.

It bears repeating, albeit in my reluctant mutter, as I scoop my phone off the top of the dresser. "And it's six thirty on a Sunday," I add. "Nobody's even out walking their dogs right now."

Clearly, I've never been a dog owner.

I'm forced to admit it in full as soon as I finish the elevator ride and burst out onto the street in front of Allie's building. It's not a complete dog parade but way more leashes, poop bags, and eyes on my smudged plastic shoes than I expected. Under other circumstances I'd be in heaven, grabbing as many snuggles with the furballs as possible. But there's no time for that fun because I can't see Bastien anywhere.

Not a single glance of his fine ass in those luscious breeches or the torso rising from that waistband in its musketeer-worthy glory. I even still myself and listen for extra sounds on the air. Anything abnormal from the cars, motorcycles, bicycles, boats, and airplanes that form their usual twenty-four-hour symphony. Something like a surprised outcry from anyone along the boulevard. Better yet, a spike of Bastien's discernible growl.

Everything stays too predictably normal.

Meaning my pulse rate edges toward cardiac arrest range.

Still, I ignore the Pomeranian taking a Labrador-sized

dump in front of me and frantically look right and then left. Though the first option beckons with the sparkling stretch of the river, getting there from here equates to crossing the FDR, which would intimidate the staunchest d'Artagnan.

My instincts tell me that Desperado has ducked left, toward the blocks where trees with new spring leaves arch toward each other over the avenues. But also toward the heart of Midtown East—and beyond that, more of Manhattan's confusing tangle. Oh yes, mulls the girl who grew up in this city.

The girl who, seven blocks later, has run herself out of breath—with no scowling and shirtless hunk to show for her efforts.

A man who's never experienced anything like sidewalks, crosswalks, and skyscrapers before.

A man she's officially lost in a city of millions.

I moan in frustration while smacking a palm to my forehead. They've predicted a heat spigot for today, which explains the slide of my phone in the sweat of my other hand.

At once, I break into another anguished sound. I forgot to slip my spare key card to Allie's apartment back into my storage sleeve.

It's time to call in reinforcements. Probably in more ways than one.

"Mmmph. Huhhhlo?" comes a sleepy mumble after I've hit one of my top redials.

"Hey. I know you're in recovering-from-the-set mode," I blurt, "but this is kind of life-or-death."

"What?" In nanoseconds, Drue pops from half-comatose to fully juiced. No sorting hat needed to know she belongs in the fifth house: Hyperthorpe. "What is it? Are Fashion Wench and Prince Hottie okay?"

"Yeah. Of course," I assure, wishing I could chuckle at the nicknames she uses for Allie and Max only when they're not around. "She texted me earlier from FCO. They're safe and should be having hot Roma sex by now."

"They'd better be." Her grumble is rough and low. An equally scratchy sound has me picturing the frustrated hand she's running through her bright turquoise waves. "So why the panic dial? Is the apartment okay?"

"Yeah. I mean, I hope so."

Another grunt. "Which means what?"

"I sort of locked myself out."

"Oh. Is that all?"

"Not . . . exactly."

"Shit."

"You're going to need more bad words than that."

A lot more.

★ ★ ★

Thirty minutes later, Drue is actually proving me wrong. She stands here in Allie's bedroom, her spare keycard in her hand—and zero words on her lips.

She's so silent and still, I reach up to deliver a small nudge.

"Hey. You believe me, right?"

The question drips with desperation. What am I going to do if she doesn't?

"*Drue?*"

"Yeah. Sorry," she finally says. "Of course I believe you." But she still stares into the wardrobe as if she wants to retract it right away. I'm not encouraged by her scrutiny of the bed, where the rumples confirm my tale in ambiguous ways at best. "It's not like I can call you insane, right?"

"Wouldn't be the first time."

"I don't think this compares to taking that commune vacation with your parents."

I surrender to a small chuff. "And here I was, thinking you'd drag out the second date with the professional hot dog eater."

She turns green. Nearly literally. "You mean after the *first* date that should never have been?"

"Similarly, none of *this* should have been." My own words have my chest clenching and my arms spreading. "Maybe . . . it wasn't. I mean, what if it really wasn't? Maybe I really did just dream it. *Shit.* One glass of wine has never done shit like that to my dreams before . . ."

"*Raegan.*"

"What?"

"Why are you doing this?"

"I don't unders—"

"Of course you do." She tosses turquoise bangs out of her eyes while hooking thumbs into her trendy jeans belt loops. "You know exactly what I'm talking about, but you're trying to explain it all away. And *you* were the one refusing to let Allie get away with that shit last year."

I snort. "Allie had the truth walking around in front of her."

"And you've got it in the form of some impressive beard burn along your neck, as well as an armoire that still smells like a campfire and a story that does you no good to fabricate."

I clutch at my nape. "Yeah. You're right. I just wish you weren't."

"Then I'm not going to make you feel any better now," she rejoins. "Because if you're really after the truth, let's remember everything we learned of it during the trip to Château De Leon last year."

I push out a hard breath. "What makes you think I haven't already?"

She jogs up her chin. "Okay. So have you checked every fact?"

"Twelve times each since this morning." I hope she sees, as I wave my phone, that the statement's literal. Even on the toilet, with eyes still bleary, I'd started the fact-checking marathon. "But there's hardly any mention of Bastien, except as footnotes to Maximillian's story. But even those are unchanged. They all allege that he was put to death shortly after his parents. So unless someone lied to the historians or went to the block in his place—"

"Oh, fuck me to Christmas."

Guess I wrote off the profanity too early.

I'd even be laughing about the thought—and damn it, really want to—except that D's eruption comes with a lot of emphasis. As in, almost too much.

"Does Christmas get a say in that?" I volley, despite detecting that she's not going to play in the banter. The intensity across her face is still focused on her own device. "D? What is it?"

She doesn't look up. "Did you search for images in your little web jaunt this morning?"

"Why would I?" The question is valid. "If there were barely any website hits for Bastien, what makes you think an image search would spit back anything different?"

"You mean something like this?"

As she turns her phone around, I lean forward.

Just before I grab the device and drop back, thankful the bed is here to catch my descent.

Correction. My stunned-as-shit fall—courtesy of the label on the painting that she's found for me. My eyes grow dry because I gawk at the image for so long, wondering if I want it to be real or not. Not getting any clearer answer as I tap on the link and read off the piece's supposed title.

"*The Execution of Bastien De Leon.*"

Drue folds her arms and rocks back on her heels. "Except that's not the Bastien De Leon I remember from the private portrait gallery at the château."

I nod. "It's definitely another guy."

"Says the girl who really knows by now."

I tolerate her waggling brows, if only because my shock is still playing boss babe with my senses. But I give back as good as I get with a wide and amazed look. "It has to be a crazy coincidence. Another nobleman with the same name—"

"Who was painted like this, the exact same year that your Bastien went to the block?"

I glower. "He's not *my* Bastien."

"Right. Uh-huh."

"Knock it off." My narrowed stare gets nothing but her rolling eyes. "You were listening during the part where I said he's a gallon of whipped cream over someone else, right? And the only reason he cruised erotic city with me last night was because I look like her?"

"Right." She folds her arms. "And all of that was simply by coincidence, then? Enough to trip a destiny-driven time machine by *accident*?"

I punch back to my feet. Shove her phone back to her.

With matching purpose, I slam the wardrobe's doors shut. "We don't know that for certain. I mean, yes, it's a time travel mechanism. And yes, it's obvious that another De Leon used it. But because of *destiny*? You remember the part about him being obsessed with another mate, right? And that he's lost somewhere in this city because he thinks I'm a witch who took over that woman's body before shrinking and imprisoning his brother?"

"So . . . what?" She leans against the dresser. "You going to give up right away just because he's pining for a woman who's only bones in the ground by now?"

I drag in a sharp breath through my nose. "You're implying there's something to give up *on*. And before you invoke everything Max and Allie, consider that Max arrived from his jump with an open mind and heart. He was *ready* to believe in the impossible."

"Ahhh. Yeah. You're right." The words are there but her tone isn't buying them. "So having to fight a little harder for your own prince's heart isn't worth it. I mean, I get that too."

"Duke," I snap. "He's a duke, okay? And I never said anything about him not being worth it."

"Not in so many words."

"Not in *any* words." Right away, I recognize the priority of more calming breaths. Fortunately, they help with restacking my thoughts in some semblance of order. "Because there's no *heart* to be won here, okay? I just want to be sure he stays physically safe until he can wrap his brain around everything. In the process, maybe we'll learn what really caused him to transport here. But first things first. We've got to track him down. I'm damn sure nothing from the eighteenth century, even Paris, France, has prepared him for Times Square in a pre-matinee crush."

It's a weird relief to watch Drue's gaze go wide. "You think that's where he went?"

"I don't know," I confess. "It's just what my gut says. If I were a stranger here and having to pick a direction out the building's front door, I'd head toward the shady sidewalks and full trees."

"Beyond which is the craziest place in the city."

"Where Bastien De Leon will either go equally crazy or drown in five dollar bills from everyone wanting to pose with him."

I grimace to show how little I enjoy saying that part. At the same time, something urgent, anxious, and protective rises in me.

The man can handle himself physically, that much is obvious. It's his mental exposure that I can't stop stressing about. His total rejection of the truth, despite how gently I tried to break it to him. Right after that, his fast flare of aggression—understandable to me but not a great tactic to turn on some tourist who thinks Bastien's just a cosplayer waiting for his next acting audition. He's barely wearing more than the Naked Cowboy!

Drue seems to reach the same tension level at the same moment, thanks to the fact that it took me one sentence to sum up the man's time travel attire when she asked.

"We need to roll," she states while jabbing at her phone again. "I'll cover the ride. Pre-tipping to let this guy know we need warp speed."

This guy turns out to be a gorgeous non-binary human named Dash in a lime-green hybrid, with driving skills to match the rock star exterior. We're at 42nd and Bryant before

I can finish checking my emails. I'm still tapping out a reply to Sylver Savoy, who's psyched about the updated Belle Epoque stuff, when we make it onto the main flow at 7th.

The stretch of concrete that even now, before noon, feels like the center of the world.

That, for the first time in my life, has me cringing on the verge of panic.

Never has Times Square done this to me. When I was a girl, I thrived on dragging Mom and Dad here once a year, on my birthday. We'd go shopping in one of my favorite toy stores and then out for an equally overpriced lunch. From the age of thirteen on, I was allowed to pick a Broadway show instead. During one of those shows, I certainly fell in love for the first time. I'm not sure if it was with a French Revolution idealist, a masked phantom, a cocky rogue from Oz, or one of the many heroes after that. I only knew they wore shiny clothes and sang with perfect pitch.

Right now, I'd trade all of them just to find one runaway duke.

Drue and I navigate the sea of humanity for six blocks, up to the Red Steps and back again. Nowhere between the tourists, theatergoers, musicians, desnudas, and restaurant flyer guys do we catch even a hopeful glance of a shirtless god with a stunned gawk.

We seem to be the only goggle-eyed ones on every block, peering so hard into the throngs that I'm shocked we haven't been arrested.

Sure enough, D slumps against one of the barriers between the concourse and the avenue and mutters, "Okay, we've got to chill before Officer Stink-Eye over there gets any closer. Either that or line up why we're casing this crowd like

Dickens pickpockets."

My shoulders slump as I settle next to her. Out of habit I open my phone, as if expecting there'll be some kind of text update from Bastien. Or at least *about* him.

"How come nobody told me the hot duke was going to need a tracking tile?"

"Because...hot freaking duke?" Drue whips back. "We're all human, girl. No shame in basking at the De Leon oasis after being parched in the Desert of Justin for so long."

Well, that takes my mind way the hell away from Officer Stink-Eye paranoia. "Hold up. You think I went for it with Bastien as just a rebound from Justin?"

"Didn't you?" She's wise about averting her stare, choosing to look up at the ribbonlike marquee of the nearby media studios. "Because no way is it anything more, yeah? Because he's a wolf who's bonded with another mate. Whose dick didn't want anything to do with you, after his head branded you as a nasty seductress. I'm getting all *that* right, aren't I?"

Her smartass tone gives her real message away. She glances over, watching the deeper tone of my blush as she gets around to paying homage to Bastien's crotch. I don't know whether to hug her or hit her for it. I don't want to remember the man's resplendent ridge, but its glory consumes my mind all the same. I recall how it looked as he approached me with that accusing glare. *After* he'd concluded that I was a bad, bad witch. Stalking like he yearned to turn me into his bad, bad girl.

And holy shit, I would've let him. So damn readily.

I've never had angry sex before. Two seconds more and I would've been begging him for it...

But no way am I going to admit that part.

"Are you *getting* the rest of the story here?" I retort instead. "About how traumatized he looked when bounding out of that armoire in the first place? About how furious he got when I tried telling him the truth?" I lock my hands to the top of the concrete rampart, purposely scraping my fingers to keep them in place. "And about the fact that he might be here . . . by mistake?"

After a couple of seconds, Drue spills an uncomfortable girl growl. "*Pleh.* Are we seriously back to that?"

"And are you seriously saying that you've ruled it all the way out?" I volley. "Up until last night, every historic record told the world something completely different about Monsieur le Duke De Leon. Who, don't you think, would be mentioned *somewhere* if he actually did become a duke of the regime? So what if there's been a malfunction? What if he's really not supposed to be here? Maybe the reason we can't find him is because he's already been zapped back to the seventeen hundreds, and—"

"Oh, *no.*"

D looks up like someone's injected her brilliant blues with liquid silver. It's one of her prettiest looks but also one of her most unreadable. Has she gotten real now, or am I still being played for fun?

"Oh my God," I utter, banking on the latter. "Are you even listen—"

She slams a hand over mine. I'm about to swear with some vigor now, but she's already groaning, "Ohhh, no-no-no."

"*Hunnnh?*"

It slurs out with strange emphasis because my chin is a victim of her other hand. Damn it, the woman's grabbing me like needle-nose pliers.

"*Dudette.* He hasn't been zapped back."

I get it then, that she's ordering me to focus on something besides the nervous jiggle of my left leg. Up, up, up and to the right, to be exact—at the updated news feed that ripples along the front of the media building, via that artistic electronic strip.

At first I only scowl, thinking she's merely strapped on her rough and relentless side because of the marketing blurb on a massive billboard above the electric display.

KNOWLEDGE

IS NEVER

A MISTAKE

"Okay, okay. I got it, all right? Shit, D. What on earth are you getting—"

Only now, when the huge video screen is switched from an eyeshadow ad to a breaking-news feature, do I understand that she wants me to be reading the headline ticker that's thrown in between stock market and weather updates. The words that justify why we're looking at choppy footage from someone's cell phone instead of professional camerawork. The sound bite that's really not. The click bait that's even worse. The only intention of this line is to stop people in their tracks. Literally.

And one for all? Half-naked lunatic breaks into NYC French Consulate with a broadsword . . .

"Holy *crap.*"

I rasp it while watching my worst nightmare take life on a digital plateau over my head. Not a bulb of the supersign shows me mercy, in much the same way a pair of guards treats Bastien on the marble floor of the consulate's rotunda. I cover my mouth, ordering myself not to get sick while viewing his sweat and blood slicked across the ornate surface.

"Oh my God." I gasp it into my palm as the video feed is split in half.

The right side still displays the live events, with at least three people keeping Bastien pinned to the floor. On the left, they're replaying a clip that's timestamped from ten minutes ago. It looks like the videographer, likely a consulate employee, turned on their camera after Bastien burst in past the building's 5th Avenue entrance.

Bastien's tumbling hair and Conan-like shoulders are exaggerated by the light pouring in from behind him, even with the mansion's awning in place. But not in the shot? The broadsword that's so giddily noted in the ticker description. More cheap click bait, at the expense of a human I already care intensely about.

I'm well into an incensed growl about the injustice, only to choke on it after Bastien seems to exchange shouts with an aggressive security guard. As soon as the officer charges forward, Bastien swings to the right and yanks the weapon from a mannequin in a display beyond a velvet rope. Without a doubt he does the sword more justice than the statue, not that I have time to overly appreciate how spectacularly he gets his Conan on.

I can only groan harder, awash in new dread, as he swings out the blade with expert precision. But he's so good that he only shaves the top of the guy's hair—not that the guard notices that his life's been deliberately spared. He keeps charging forward, invigorated when a couple of buddies back him up.

Another gasp clouds the air. I can't deny it's mine, since Drue is already in Eeyore mode down to the last sardonic speck. "Please tell me that's not really him," she mutters from beneath her rain cloud.

I don't bother offering a virtual umbrella. We're not going to be standing still that long.

"No time to lie about that right now." I don't wait for her comeback. I'm already turning and heading down 44th, barely refraining from breaking into a full run. "I've got to help him."

"You mean *we've* got to."

Eeyore vibes or not, the woman keeps perfect pace enough to give me a shoulder bump of encouragement.

While returning the gesture, I add, "You're getting a full hug for this when I don't have to dread telling Max that his brother's been thrown into Manhattan Detention."

"Not going to happen," she volleys.

"The hug or the Max convo?"

"Both." She barely pauses as we hook a left onto 6th. "Good call, taking it this way. Cutting through the park won't be pretty today."

I give only a fast nod. Depending on the day, Central Park can be either a sanity restorer or stripper. On a sunny Sunday like this, it's likely to be the latter—and I'm currently needing every shred of lucidity I have left. Yes, even the parts of it that make me face valid fears.

Even if we sprint, the consulate is over a mile away. Waiting on a train, or even calling for a ride, will equate to the same amount of travel time.

What if we get there and they've already taken Bastien

away?

And what if they get him to prison and ask him about his identity? His birthdate? His next of kin?

What if he decides that his jailors in this century are no better than those of his last?

If he's even come to accept that he's not in that time anymore...

The what-ifs don't stop there. Not by a single, awful bit. I'm getting so dizzy at processing them all, on top of fighting to keep up with Drue's half jog, that I'm only focusing on our surroundings with half a brain.

The half that doesn't recognize the lime-green hybrid that's slowed to a crawl next to us.

"You guys look like you're escaping fate or chasing demons," says the driver past their half-dropped passenger window.

"And you look like you hung out over at Bryant, hoping we'd resurface," Drue answers Dash, who has instantly become our new best friend of the day.

"Did it to yourself, fancy tipper," the driver rejoins with a fast wink.

"Which I'll double if you get us to the Consulate of France like green lightning."

At once, Dash pops the locks. "I'm your fast finisher, baby."

"You really want me to riff on that one?" Drue quips as we climb in.

"I don't upcharge for banter. But seriously, which is it? Fate or demons?"

I sigh heavily. "All of the above."

And damn it, how I wish that it's really only banter.

CHAPTER EIGHT

BASTIEN

"Do you know who I am?"

Why do I expect this iteration of the demand to earn me a different response than before? That these idiots in officers' wear will opt to do anything but chuckle, grunt, and ruffle my hair like I am a stray dog they are preparing to torture and throw in the river? A fate I nearly yearn for, since decorum and civility seem to be missing factors in the twenty-first century.

The twenty-first century.

My senses have not yet recovered from their shocked raze, though how can I blame them? Two hundred years has changed the world. It is a place full of so many more colors, textures, *people.* Languages, lights, *people.* Vehicles, voices... *people.* Human beings that I understand but do not.

Like everyone else here, I have been in a hurry too. Deciding that if I just go faster, I will find the ultimate destination I seek. The place in all this insanity that shall extinguish the frantic fires in my mind, all burning with the same crucial question.

Why am I here?

I thought this building would have that answer. As soon as I saw the plaque that declares it as my homeland's consulate, with the flag containing France's traditional triad of colors, hope soared in my soul. Surely we are still friends with America, since they borrowed the colors for *their* standard. At once, I felt secure enough to rush in here. To do so with eager joy, expecting I would be met with courtesy, honor, and refuge.

Courtesy.

Honor.

Refuge.

Words that will never mean what they once did. I know that as a surety while straightening my stance despite how it strains my shoulders. The three guards responsible for my capture are not impressed. They keep up their chuckling and preening, until fresh footfalls resound across the atrium.

At once, the soldiers are sober. Their spines straighten. They dip their heads with deference at a tall fellow who enters, the clove shade of his skin lending to his kingly air. As he reciprocates their nods, I notice that his thick black curls are coifed similarly to Maximillian's new fashion. He is bizarrely unaffected by the clamoring horde that has gathered beyond the building's awning.

He is different than anyone out there. From anyone in *here.*

The observation dims behind my fascination with the sleek tablet he pulls from an inside pocket of his jacket. He holds it like Moses with one of the sacred slabs from Sinai: an ideal comparison since the entire front of the thing lights up when he touches it with a long black rod.

But my gawk does not deter him. Yet neither does he regard me like my mind is made of pudding. He seems to see me as one of Carl's staff would. There is honest respect in his gaze, despite his open curiosity.

"Good afternoon," he intones, his accent as pedestrian

as my attackers. But his words are similar to Magique's—well, the modern version of her—in that it has subtle music because of its underlying consideration. "Monsieur . . . De Leon?"

"Oui," I say, remaining cautious. He nods, seemingly understanding of that. As if he knows what I have just been through. As if he was watching from beyond the bright, flashing lights as the trio of churls took me down and bound me like a common dissident.

"Detective Liam Logan," he states. "But you can call me Logan if that floats your boat better."

My fascination with his light board makes it impossible to answer right away. But when he dips his head again, becoming the first in here to pay me some basic deference, I return the courtesy as best as I can with my hands bound at my back. Tucking a shoulder and extending a leg, I bow a little lower than I thought possible.

Before I am finished, Logan frowns. His perplexity does not wane, even as he speaks again. "Well, okay then." He clears his throat. "So now we're clear on *me* but not you. Catching my drift?"

His drift is not as enjoyable to contemplate as the goddess who warmed the sheets with me last night. "*Désolé,*" I mutter. "I am afraid not."

"You know my name now, but I'm still not officially aware of yours." He focuses back to the glow of his tablet. "Bastien Eneas Jacques De Leon? That's all of it?"

"*Oui.* Just as I informed your colleagues."

His confusion, even after my statement, prompts more of my bewilderment. That and my abysmal choice of words. *Colleagues?* Surely something more accurate could have come to my mind, such as *underlings* or *thugs.* The same jackasses who congregate nearby, reminding me of gossiping whores with their open disdain of Logan and his fitted attire, compared to their ordinary livery. 'Twould seem *some* things about the world have *not* changed over the centuries.

If Logan notices their pettiness, he does not indicate so. "Well, we're having trouble matching you up to the databases, man. I mean, *any* of them. That's part of why they called me in to help out. You hear me on that? *Helping out.* So twist your heat to low because I can't legally arrest you for now. Technically, you're still on French soil."

"I … am?" I glance out the window. Nothing at all has changed, meaning I have to advance his narrative for myself. "I mean *I am*, of course." This consulate must be similar to the ceremonial tents that foreign dignitaries insist on erecting at Versailles that are symbolically treated as an extension of their own country. Confidential—and untouchable.

"But only for *now*," the man reiterates, as if I have reasoned all of that out loud. "If we can't clear up your citizenship, I'll have to remit you back over to these NYPD boys. No more having your back."

I snort. "Because of what? Walking in the door?"

"Not my job to make sense of another country's laws. Or, for that matter, my own." He rolls his gaze back toward the mob outside the windows. "But right now, just give me something to cover a few of the databases, okay? Then I can let you blow this popsicle stand."

"Blow on it? Why? And where?" I emulate his modest rear back, though am prepared to go on. "As far as bases, if you enlighten me about these *day-dahs*, and what materials with which you would like to cover them, I am certain I can help. But if it must be today, I suggest wood instead of bricks. The skies have grown foreboding, and rain might be—"

"No," he interjects, but not soon enough to suppress the snickering gossip gaggle. He quells them with a sharp glance before addressing me again. "What I mean is that we can't find you, buddy. Like, anywhere. You don't have a viable home or work address, here or in France. We can't find a single background document to link to you. You don't have a social or NIR number. No driving license in either country. Certainly no birth certificate."

I stiffen my jaw. "Oh, I was born."

"Of which I'm well aware." His mild sarcasm goes well with mine, though he does not indulge it for long. "But how and where and when?" he persists. "Come on, De Leon. Don't make me try to rhyme anything past that. Just press me with some numbers that prove you didn't show up out of nowhere, so we can cross-check things and avoid you getting snack-receipted out of here."

"Getting *what*ted?"

"Stuffed somewhere dark and tiny then eventually forgotten."

I snort, newly enlightened—yet pained. The expression sounds like something my modern *magie* would say. But just as my silent pining grows into inescapable ache, the woman is back with the best surprise of all.

"Nobody's forgetting anyone."

Herself.

Logan and I nearly collide skulls as we swing around, reacting to her determined decree from the gilded hallway leading to the back of the building. Even so, I am inundated by the waves of his new puzzlement. Thankfully, my senses fight back with waves of warmth and solace. It is a selfish but necessary choice, soaking in the strength of the voice that she has stolen as much as Magique's face and body, and I promise to plead forgiveness from her ghost later. But right now, I am unable to swipe away my triumphant smirk as she approaches. Triumphant—and transfixed.

With everything about her.

Those fierce and determined steps. Those flashing, glittering eyes. Her attire, with the tight breeches similar to other women I have observed in this era, that now seems so new . . . so damned alluring.

That brings on more guilt and bafflement.

Why all this attachment and attraction to a woman I know barely better than a street doxy? A stranger dressed in such garish trousers and a formless jerkin?

The answer defies all logic. But last night, I also would have scoffed at the "logic" of being pitched forward in time by hundreds of years.

"Who are you?" Logan demands before she gets too close. "And how the hell did you get past the security perimeter?"

"Can we just cut the niceties?"

This time, the retort is not from my pseudo-Magique. I know this because I have not broken my stare upon her, even as she seems to physically split before my eyes. Quickly, I realize the impression is because of her companion's smaller stature.

The friend, who brings a smirk to match her open audacity with Logan, wears a crimson knitted cap atop black hair that resembles a monk's blunt tonsure. Perhaps it is, considering the strictness of her overall stature. Despite the coiffure—or perhaps, in some strange ways, because of it—she reminds me somewhat of that little fellow Napoleon, without his nervous twitches. Her attire is similar, with a dark-blue jacket buttoned down to her knees and shiny black boots covering the rest.

"Senior Special Agent Lautrec, FBI," she states, flipping open a small leather case to show a shield-shaped medallion for all of two seconds. "And this is my partner, Agent Degas."

Logan snorts as the women resettle their postures. "Lautrec and Degas?" He escalates to a chuckle. "Is this a joke?"

Female Napoleon tilts her head. The cap stays perfectly in place. "Do I look like I'm joking?"

"And you're FBI?" Skepticism glinting even brighter in the detective's eyes. "No disrespect intended. I'm simply confused. You don't look—"

"Right. Because we're supposed to pass for ad execs even when undercover. Dude, if we put a buck in a jar every time we got that..."

"My bad," Logan mutters. "But begging your pardon again, and all things media mob being considered, why are you here? We've yet to determine if this altercation is a two-country concern or a misunderstanding on both sides."

"Misunderstanding? You've got that much right." Again, the cap is uncannily secure as she swings her head the other way. "And moreover, should be damn glad you all aren't facing group and individual charges right now."

"Damn. Cool the rocket fuel." He darts a nervous glance my way. The stress doubles before he turns back to Lautrec and Degas. Though he is far from trusting them, I am of a different mind.

Those are solid names. They connotate nobility. But even before Kavia and her sorcery propelled me into this insanity, *nobility* was becoming a tarnished word. An honor no more substantive than dried ink on parchment. Paper that could easily be burned...

Logan grunts with enough frustration for us both. "Once again, with all due respect, why wasn't anyone on my team informed about this? I would usually be called at once if the FBI had been—"

"Well, of course you would've been," my gorgeous not-Magique cuts in. "If we were following *normal* procedure."

Logan finally gets his full grimace. "And this time you're not?"

She scrunches up her nose, which causes adorable distortions to her freckles, until she looks more awkward than the Queen Consort at the Grand Couvert dinner. But something tells me this gaffe will not simply add up to the king's displeasure.

"Ermmm...no. I mean, we're not. We're definitely not." Once more, her intrepid friend is the situational savior. "I mean, isn't that obvious?"

"Obvious?" Logan double-takes. "Ohhh, shit. Is this a covert op?"

"Errr...yes. Exactly. *Very* covert." Little Napoleon almost overcompensates by wrapping a possessive hand around the back of my bicep. "I mean, that's why we were stunned too. We thought you at least knew who *this* was."

"Holy shit," Logan growls. "So *that's* the scutts on the informational duck-and-dodge?"

"Shit. Sorry. We really thought you knew, man."

Logan snaps around, stabbing me with a glare. "Damn it, De Leon—or whoever you are. You couldn't have pulled out the special handshake for the dog in the trenches here? Some subtle heads-up at all?"

Two seconds of a glance from the green eyes that have hardly veered from me, and my instincts take over. The same instinct that tells me where to look for foxes in trees and spies at court has leapt to high alert, ordering me to go along with this ruse despite only comprehending every third or fourth word of it.

"*Mon ami* ... secret handshakes are only possible if one has hands to use, *oui*?"

"Crap." Logan motions at the guard standing closest to us, already motioning toward my back with a firm sweep of his closed journal. "Sorry about the crossed wires, man," he offers while the officer frees me. "But tell the gang at Federal Plaza to shoot the prairie dog a little higher with the next op at this level. Then nobody ends up looking like an idiot."

The redhead between us smiles with entrancing serenity. The expression scatters her freckles into new patterns and turns her mouth into the definition of elegance. "But sometimes it's called infiltration for a reason, Detective."

"Well-played, Agent Degas." Logan shakes his head while returning his tablet to its interior pocket. "So how can I help you further? Do you need to give a debrief to anyone here? We ordered the Consul General and his staff to lock their doors and stay put, but I can have reception call them now if—"

"Thank you, but not necessary. As you can surmise, it's probably best that we salvage and sanitize whatever we can. That's best done elsewhere."

"Of course." He pivots around, indicating to the uniforms that they can return to their posts, which they answer with scuffing reluctance.

I glower, barely refraining from adding on more. No men

on any of my patrols, at Versailles or elsewhere, would be so insouciant. Logan nods at my two gorgeous rescuers.

"Can I get your numbers and emails," he asks, "in case I need any other details for my report?"

I hope I am the only one who notices how pale both the females turn. If Logan does too, I am certain no one will know it. The gentleman is fluent in the language of self-composure. The next moment, I am certain Little Napoleon attended the same subterfuge school.

"Sure. You can have mine." She reaches for a device that Logan produces from an outside pocket this time. The thin rectangle is similar to his magical tablet but a quarter of the size. I attempt not to gawk as the woman taps rapidly at it with her thumbs. My fight is for naught once the front of it changes, as if responding to her actions. "Give a shout day or night," she offers. "Sorry if you have to leave a message. Believe it or not, the service at HQ can be shit sometimes. I'll call back, though."

Before Logan finishes tucking the device away, I have been guided down the regal hallway, through a sumptuous room denoted as the bookstore—how are there *so many* books in here?—and then through a small door that should be illegal in its deception.

Dainty doors do not belong on kitchens like this.

I sweep around with an awe-stricken stare, but my new awe is overtaken by a larger perplexity. Why is no one in this mansion not *using* a single one of these modern culinary wonders? How is that possible? Unless this is their second kitchen… But how is *that* possible? I cannot imagine a cookery grander than this.

Ponderings I must, and do, set aside.

The most important matter is that we are finally away

from prying gazes. I celebrate that by finally exhaling in full. But neither of my rescuers does the same. I should be more concerned but do not wish to be. It feels too wonderful to be fully on my feet, free of shackles on my wrists and trepidation in my senses. The immaculate floors in this place are much better appreciated without my face mashed against them. The stunning redhead at my side is no awful hindrance to the cause either, despite the scowl that crunches her sleek features.

"'Give a shout, day or night?' Are you kidding me?"

Her spew is so ferocious, I instantly assume they are sisters. But aside from their high cheekbones and full lips, there are not enough other similarities to support my supposition. The woman next to me is tall and curvaceous, with fire in her strides to match her distinctive curls. That is above and beyond the verdant spells in her eyes and all those gorgeous freckles. Her friend, now leaning against a big silver machine that hums in daunting ways, is shorter but formidable. I have no doubt that if the guards changed their mind and rushed back in here, she could knock them out of their boots and then force-feed the footwear back to them.

"What?" she retorts, folding her arms. "Should I have gone with something else?" And then bats her arresting blue eyes, obviously mocking. "Gosh, Detective. I'd totally give you my number, except I just lied about my name, occupation, and imperviousness to your hotness. But let's go get some drinks and tapas sometime, okay?"

"So . . . you gave him a bogus number?"

The woman pushes fully back to her feet and yanks at the beret, which is indeed attached to her short dark hair—which proves to be naught but a wig. Beneath that, her hair is still contained, held in place by a matching black net of some sort.

"Let's just say the guy will be in luck if he wants a to-go order from La Barca."

The woman at my side spurts out a giggle. "Ohhh, excellent pick—kind of what you need for that wig too, sweetie."

"Are you kidding?" She rocks her head back, regarding the frayed black mess. "It's been in the bottom of my satchel for a week and got there by being crusted with too much stage blood. I'm just glad the beret was down there too. Hopefully it helps Dick Gorgeous to remember me fondly."

"Excuse me?" exclaims my redhead. "Dick *what*?"

"Oh, come *on*. That fine, fine male . . . He was better than a large malt in a heat wave." She adds a fanning motion with her hand. "Sweet frosting on my cookie, Tigger. I must really love you."

"Oh, you *do*." They hug with palpable affection, which has me forgetting the new emptiness in my hand. "And I'm so grateful, honey. Honestly and truly."

"Yeah, yeah. You can repay me with Crémant and croissants some other time."

A hungry groan leaves my lips before I can help it. "I like her," I say in time to their laughter. As she yanks off the black head net, revealing her actual hair in its cobalt and turquoise splendor, I emphasize, "Especially now."

She chuckles again, the droll sound a perfect complement for her dazzling locks. "Well, props back to you too, Pompeii."

"Huh?" The woman between us blurts. "And what part of your backside did *that* come from, Drusilla Daphne Kidman?"

"The obvious part." She drags a hand through her long, bright plumage. "If you IMDB *Pompeii—*"

My magnifique rolls up a hand with a new laugh. "Why don't I take your word for it?"

"On that note, why don't you two find some shadows to hang in while I get moving? Because no way are we going to be to transport *him* anywhere with *these* still on display."

I cannot control the smirk that teases my lips as D illustrates her words with fast pokes at my chest and arms. I nearly let my lips take on a chuckle of their own as my woman— at least for now—responds with a defined verbal simmer.

"Settle down, Raegan," her friend admonishes. "We don't have time for a bestie showdown."

"All right," my redhead grumbles. "So what *is* your plan?"

"That cute consignment place is still open around the corner. Matter of fact, it's where I got these." She raises a foot, showing off one of her impressive boots. "Let me duck in there real fast and grab something that won't scream 'hunky but horribly doomed' so loudly."

At once, the female at my side is giving up a new smirk. While any expression is alluring on her, this is my preference to her open stress.

"Lovely little Lautrec, I officially love you."

"Of course you do, Diva Degas."

Before any more witticisms can be traded, D and her cobalt locks have vanished out the door, leaving me alone in here with a woman too close to ignore anymore—and too mesmerizing not to resist. Not anymore.

As if I have finished a confrontation of mortal consequences and finally arrived at safe shelter, all the resilience leaves my limbs—yet never have I felt so strong, so vital, so alive.

So aroused.

I cannot hide it from her anymore. Nor do I wish to.

I pull at her elbow to draw her closer to my frame. My

effort is so adamant, the momentum has me stepping back until my spine is flush with the big noisy machine. The big *quivering* machine...

And sometimes, one finds surprises in the oddest places. Like a different century.

I am tempted to ask *Diva Degas* exactly what this modern wonder is, but why waste our precious, private minutes on trivialities? Or so they seem now, when compared to how her body feels as soon as I reposition her. Spreading her legs from the back, ensuring the warm triangle at her center settles upon the surging length of mine. Squandering not another second to work her up and down my bulge, making it necessary for us to bury our moans in each other's necks.

"Oh *my*," she rasps. "Oh, Desperado..."

At once, I spread a smile along her silken skin. And then breathe out with one word.

"Raegan."

"Ummm?" Her sultry moan vibrates along the length of my collar bone. "Yesss?"

"Raegan," I echo in a seductive murmur. "That is... your real name."

This time, her lips tilt up in equal measure. "Wow. How have we not gotten to that part yet?"

"Because, during many of those parts, I was behaving like an ass?"

"Ah. Yeah. All *those* parts." Her soft laugh is a gentle bounce of sound around the sterile room—but most beautifully along the lips I dip closer to hers once more. By the Almighty, *her lips*. The mere sight of them stirs me to fresh madness. A spell that combines with her flowery scent and supple body to enrapture me in such new and stunning ways.

She is not Magique.

I do not require my mind's reverberation to be certain of it now. I still know the fact without a single doubt. But this change across her countenance, from the inside out... This is a new creature, separate and fascinating. I am dazzled, wondering what new, wonderous thing I will discover next about her.

Such as how she likes to be kissed when danger is a thing to be *enjoyed.*

As soon as the decision stamps my mind, it coils through my actions. Flexes down my arm and into my hand, twisting through the ends of her thick curls. Invades my libido like wildfire, until I am pulling her head back. Rumbles up my throat as I kiss my way along hers, up then down and back again.

So delicious...

It commands my other hand to roam lower, not stopping until I am squeezing her flesh with brutal demand.

So succulent...

Until I am working her harder against me, grinding her trembling crotch along my urgent ridge. Until I am ready to yank down my breeches *and* hers and then impale myself in her soaking wet channel. And *oui,* she *will* be wet. She already is. I hear it in every note of her husky gasps. I feel it in her tightening hold around my neck.

And at last, I receive it in all the passion of her kiss.

So. Perfect.

Our mouths meet and mate. Despite the brief pain because of the cut I endured in my lower lip, I welcome her inside. So fully. So openly. We spread each other wider, wrestling for access to the intimate pocket of where our voices live. Using this fusion to speak instead, with stabbing tongues and swirling wetness. Learning each other... despite all the ways in which we already know each other.

My heart forgets a beat. Another.

I know her. *I know her.*

Despite all the *here and now*, there *is* so much of the *then and before*. The woman that was there too. Not just the scar I peek down at now, still there at the center of her chest. It is because of other things. Little but not-so-little things. The tiny pink spot at her nape, slightly bruised because she grabs it when she's nervous. The way she clutches *me*, curling fingers into my hair until I feel the sweet sting in my scalp. The way she does it again and again, knowing how much I like it.

And, more than all of that, the way she pulls back to gaze at me now.

And how her endless greens sting me all over again.

As the rest of her face contorts with so many questions...

As if she senses it too. As if she feels it all, along with me.

Everything that is not the *here and now*...

"Bastien." Her sough is fortified by a sharp breath. "Bastien?" But again, naught but sparse air for that incredulous query. Perhaps one of the most beautiful sounds I have ever heard. "Wh-What's going on? Why do I feel so ... *Monsieur le Duke? Qu'est-ce qui se passe?*"

All her frantic blinks are good for countering my wide stare. I want to smile and kiss her doubly as hard as before, but the horror that conquers her face has me scrambling to simply keep her in my arms.

"*Mon amour—*"

"No." She shakes her head as if a thousand bees are swarming around it. "Don't!"

"All right. *All right.* Be calm now. I am here and you are safe, *ma chérie.* Just—"

"No." She shoves away and stumbles back. I have not stopped to notice her small-heeled shoes, but they make significant clatters across the pristine floor. "No! Stop it! I'm not your *amour* or your *chérie.* I just . . . can't be, okay? I'm *me.* I'm Raegan Karlinne Tavish, and this is *not* seventeen eight-nine. But I still have no idea what's happening. What the freaking *hell* is happening to me?"

CHAPTER NINE

RAEGAN

I should've eaten breakfast.

I should've listened to all the preachings of every lifestyle blog I know and had a proper combination of fruit, starches, and protein. *Lots* of protein.

I seriously wish I was kidding about it. Because right now, in this dizzily insane moment, it's the only explanation I can find in my mind's panicked whirl. The only viable reason to connect to the French I've never heard in my life, let alone spouted as if it were my second language. No. My *only* language. I can't even think of an instance, during the time I was there for Allie's birthday last year, that it got in subliminally.

"Raegan. My sweet little lily. Can you pause and take a breath for me? I cannot help you if I do not know—"

"Don't touch me! Oh God, I'm sorry." The first part accompanies my flinch; the second brings my new grimace. "Bast. *Bastien.* Just give me a second, okay? Maybe more than one."

I can't verbalize more than that any more than I can welcome his touch back to my body. Not because I can't bear it. Because I can't bear the thought of being *without* it. This feeling, so overwhelming, that collided with the moment our bodies did. The flood of longing and lust, as massive and beautiful as a seventy-foot evening gown train, that took away my air with matching majesty. That made me crave his skin all over mine, his flesh *inside* of mine. That had me wondering if I could reach down and free us both that way, without anyone knowing...

Until the second I remembered actually *doing* it.

But not here. Not in this way too public kitchen or anywhere in this city.

Not in this time.

In the vision, we were at someone's wedding. Someone of stature, I think, because the garden was abundantly decorated with flowers and ribbons. I don't remember a lot of everything else, except that he was the picture of fuckable in his velvet finery. The Prussian blue fabric made the gold in his buttons, and his intense eyes, stand out like fine jewelry.

Oh, yes. Fuckable.

And I did just that.

In another kitchen—if it could be called that. An old-fashioned place of stone and damp, though we could still hear the bride and groom laughing outside. We listened to the musicians striking up for a *contredanse,* just before he swiveled his hips enough to drive me to the edge of ecstasy. As I decided the edge wasn't enough, so I reached for the buttons at his crotch...

"Oh my God," I choke out, fighting for why that doesn't feel like a fantasy at all. Instead, why it feels like ... a *memory.* "Oh my God!"

"Raegan. *S't plait, Laissez-moi vous aider.* Let me help you. What do you need?"

I duck my head and quip beneath my breath, "Nothing more than what I needed at that wedding."

Suddenly, he stumbles backward too. His breath audibly snags. "*What* did you say?"

I straighten with as much urgency. "Nothing. Forget it." Because that's what it is. Absolutely nothing. "I just need to eat. What time is it? Ohhh yeah, definitely time to eat. No wonder I'm dancing with all the boo-boo bears."

"There are bears nearby? How do all the horseless wagons not hit them?"

Thankfully, I don't get a chance to decide on a reaction to that. Someone's swinging open the kitchen's back door with comforting intensity. Never have I been more grateful to see Drue, but never has she seemed more wigged about seeing me.

"Whoa. What's happened? You're whiter than bleached cotton but more worn than this T-shirt."

"Thanks," I deadpan as she produces a massively sized souvenir shirt from *Spiderman: Turn off the Dark*. The garment is way more faded than it should be. "Okay, wow. That's worth either ten thousand bucks or ten cents." Inwardly, I'm leaning toward the latter. "I still can't believe what you always find at that place. You probably forked up a twenty and walked out with change."

She bites her bottom lip. "Hrmmm, not this time."

"Wait. What?" My gaze bugs. "You paid more than twenty for this? On consignment?"

"No. I paid more than twenty for *this*."

Her emphasis overlaps with my louder-than-acceptable gasp. Can't be helped it. "*Drue*. Are you serious?"

She smirks. "Would you speak to me again if I left this behind?"

As I take the denim jacket from her, with its rear panel covered by a hand-painted Moulin Rouge windmill and the words *Come What May* in elegant lettering, I almost tear up. "Now I *really* officially love you."

"I know." She preens. "Especially because *this* should complete things perfectly."

After she unpins the beret from her wig and hands it over, I tackle-hug her until we're exchanging loony giggles. "Thank you, woman," I say with soft sincerity. "This is going to help in more ways than one. I'm starving, so that means we've got to grab something on the way back to Allie's place."

It takes her less than three seconds to fully stiffen away from me. "Ah, no," she says at once, earning my answering glower. "The more I think about it, definitely no. Logan has no way of quickly tracking Agents Lautrec and Degas, but how long before he wonders if *this* De Leon is related to the guy on the main marquee of the Hemline Studios building?"

"Shit," I mutter. "I didn't consider that."

Bastien's reaction is blessedly more reserved. "Maximillian," he murmurs, seeming to connect more facts for himself. "So . . . he is here too? In this time period? Is he thriving?"

I reach for his hand, reacting to the stress it clearly took to get both questions out. "Yes to both. He's happy and in love with our friend Alessandra."

"The woman in the other images with him," he supplies. "The ones that moved in that box."

My double-take is instant—as is my new awareness of his fast-thinking mind on my too-damn-aware libido. "Yes," I finally say. "The mini video keeper. Errr . . ." A new mini whiplash, though not with such pleasant effects on my crotch. "Wait. Holy shit. Bastien? What did you do with that? The video box? The one that you had when you first left the apartment?"

His brows push toward each other. "I...dropped it." But he really gets me with his sharp blush. "And after that, it was crushed. My sincerest apologies, Raegan. I was guarding it like a treasure, but I heard a crowd yelling from below my feet and a massive crash. By the time I went down the steps to investigate, I was pushed forward and into another moving box. A much larger one. I was jostled, and the one in my hands fell somewhere into the tunnel..."

Forces stronger than stress are clearly taking over him now. I squeeze his fingers harder, hoping my reassurance helps. When he only swallows like there's a grapefruit in his throat, I speak up.

"Bastien. *Hey.* Take it easy. The box is replaceable. You're not."

"Replaceable?"

I hear every drop of his continuing torment but can't take the time for a full explanation.

Not when my epiphany of shock gains a mirror across D's features. "Yo, Pompeii. Back up that lava spill. The loud sound you heard...was it more like grinding and screeching? Something like panicked reindeer in a raging snow storm?"

"Oui!" He regards her with half a smile and a lot more wonderment. "Those are quite accurate descriptors." He regards her with new interest. "You would make an exceptional court spy, Mademoiselle Drusilla."

"Now *there's* a moonlighting goal," D quips, though she's not done riding her intel-gathering train. "So the big steel box probably had a number on its side. Something inside a colored circle. Do you remember what that was?"

"Indeed," he states. "A six, emblazoned on a green circle. It was dazzling. I was puzzled about how the artist achieved perfect paint color for all of them and then applied it so smoothly."

I give myself permission for a soft giggle, already seeing how D is using her sarcasm to battle her shock. Effective tactic, especially in light of what she says next.

"And when the train—errr, the big steel box—stopped again, why didn't you get out of it along with the other people?"

Now he's cocking a stare like *she* doesn't comprehend the full scoop. "More people remained inside than out. And I was . . . curious."

"About what?"

"All of it. The variety. The colors. The *speed.* All of it . . . all of *them* . . . going by so fast." By now he's returning my rough grip with climbing energy. But while his hold is still harsh, his words are uneven.

"It's okay," I murmur, wrapping my other hand around our clasp. "You made it. Congratulations. You're no longer a virgin to the New York train system."

"Hmph." His fast glance is a screen capture of beautiful irritation. "Giving up my real virginity was less frightening."

"Let's hope so," Drue drawls before popping her attention to me. "You know the really scary thing? They caught this big boy on camera *after* all that. He was full-on Pompeii all the way from Allie's neighborhood to Grand Central and then hopped on the Lexington line for three stops. If he'd been a real barbarian out for blood, there'd be a mighty miserable blood trail up the middle of Manhattan's belly."

Bastien tenses. "If a blood bath *was* my intent, there would be no evidence after the fact." He scrutinizes Drue again. "Barbarians leave messes. Trained warriors do not."

"*Touché*," Drue replies. "Oh, my, my. You're more in touch

with your snarly side than your brother."

Unsurprisingly, that rips the wind out of Bastien's gruff sails. Also not a shock: the way he quietly turns back to me, his noble features possessed by stark emotion.

"How long ago?" he pleads. "*Maximillian*. How long has he been here? In this . . . world?"

He stumbles on that last noun, but not before I sense where he was really headed with it.

In this time.

He's starting to believe it, though he doesn't want to say it. And that has to be okay too.

"About a year," I offer. "But obviously, strict linear logistics don't rule the magical mystery era-jumping armoire. If they did, then none of this—your own trip—would've been possible."

He frowns. "How so?"

I sigh. My God, even his confusion is beautiful. "Well, because you'd be—"

"And that feels perfect for this episode's cliffhanger." While D saves me from myself without a second to spare, she claps her hands just once. But with that kind of authority, once is enough. "Especially because you're good to go now, Pompeii. Uh, wow . . . in all the best ways."

There's not a sliver of room to argue as she gestures to Bastien with a one-armed sweep. Though he's squelched the Pompeii factor by slipping into the T-shirt and a pair of scuffed loafers that D miraculously managed to find in his size, he's still a beautifully scruffy hottie. The shirt's hem hides the outdated crotch of his pants, making it look like he simply splurged for a pair of khakis on his way up 5th Avenue. Even the loafers look like they were styled on purpose to "relaxed" mode.

"Web of wonders," I utter.

"Looks *so* much better than a spider can," D adds.

"Very nice work, Miss Kidman." I'm the one cracking my hands together now, leaving them in prayer position while amending, "And you know there'd be heaps more mush where that came from, if only—"

But the prayer hands aren't any help, illustrated by the new swing of the kitchen's door. This time, it's not the good one that leads directly outside. It's the portal that connects back to the consulate's bookstore and then the rest of the building. Oh yes, including the atrium where we left Detective Logan and Bastien's original aggressors.

Who are now *here*.

Mercifully—*thank you, prayer hands, for working* this *time*—not all of them. One of the guards has stayed behind, but Dick Gorgeous has clearly vowed to make up for it with the force of his glare. The livid look is copied by the pair of security goons behind him.

Shit, shit, shit.

They've definitely taken off their diplomatic gloves. But hell if that's made them forget they have fists. At least the two officers. Logan's too busy recovering his balance after his stunned skid. Clearly, he didn't plan on finding us so soon.

As the guards collide into him at top speed, creating a Larry-Moe-Curly moment that I long to enjoy for longer than a second, I seize Bastien's hand. In turn, Drue seizes my elbow as if hellbent on dislocating it. Thankfully, that doesn't happen.

And that's where our luck runs out.

After twisting from my grip, Bastien refuses to move. The hothead stubbornly stands his ground, barking at our intruders in rapid-fire French that I don't understand—and probably don't want to.

"No," I sputter. "*No*, Bastien! *Please.* There's no way you'll win this!"

He arches one sharp brow my way. "Then you do not know me very well."

He's wrong. I don't know him at all, no matter what I'm told by the most bizarre visions I've ever had in my life. The *only* visions I've ever had. "I know *them*, okay? The jig is up now—for all of us!"

"Well, would you listen to that, boys?" Logan's free from the human pile-up and stomping at us again. "Something from *Agent Degas* other than a lie."

"Crap," I choke out, though barely—because now Bastien is hauling me out the door with more impatience than Drue.

Wait. No. Not Drue. Not anymore.

Where the hell did she go?

I want to echo it in a full shriek but don't dare. If Logan's already doubled back with the FBI and dissolved our masquerade, the wait time on our real identities likely won't be long either. No need to give him any more help. More exigently, I've got to focus on keeping up with Bastien as we run toward the end of the narrow alley behind the consulate.

Wasted urgency.

We see that before we even get there. Together, we stop and gape at the very tall and very locked gate in our way.

That's before fate screws us again.

When two cops appear on the other side of the black iron barrier and make short work of unlocking it.

"Damn it," I spit out.

These boys look more fomented than their air-conditioned buddies on the inside. They're sweaty and harried, probably pulled from media mob duty out front on orders to hold us off at the urban pass if need be. As soon as they see us, they rig up for the challenge. As if pre-choreographed, they unsnap their holsters and whip out their batons. One of them brandishes his to our left. His buddy does the same, only down and to the right.

"Holy shitballs," I say, louder this time. "They're serious this time."

"Good." Bastien twists his grip around my fingers until it hurts. But not half as much as my intimidated heartbeat. "So am I."

"Oh, God. Why don't I like the sound of that? *Bastien?*"

He pivots until he's fully facing the stern-faced pair. But he doesn't let me go, instead curling his arm so I'm flush against his honed slab of a back. But all these muscle striations, along with the sinfully soft breeches beneath, aren't the leading reason why I choose to stand by him.

Bastien De Leon... Once more, he just feels more right than anything else. So bold and mighty. So arrogant and confident. So inexplicably wonderful.

Yes. This is exactly where I need to be. Even if that means going to jail with him.

"Okay, everyone take it easy now." From behind us, Logan assumes high command. "De Leon, I'm talking to you too. To both of you."

Remarkably, the decree brings me an easier breath. I'm still just a *you* in the detective's syntax, meaning he's not yet determined who I *am*. I can enjoy the anonymity for at least thirty more seconds, until one of the officers closes in enough to grab my crossbody—damn it, I probably won't get the gorgeous new Fendi back either—and hunt down my ID.

After ten seconds, because I may or may not be counting down on my freedom, a crow lands somewhere in the alley. I don't know why I notice or care, but it's an obnoxious thing with its repetitive caw. I tilt my head to try rattling him back. This ambush is already tense and terrible without a cocky corvid frying everyone's nerves.

But there's no shoo'ing this pest.

Because this bird isn't a bird. Well, not literally.

The painful *scrawk*s are coming from a human.

One of *my* humans.

Right now, all I can see of Drue is her head and neck as she pokes out from behind a door marked *Gallery Personnel Only*. She keeps up the merciless bird calls, but never have I been happier to have my eardrums continuously assaulted.

I don't waste time expounding on the fact—nor to think anything else but twisting hard on Bastien so that he's alerted about our new plan of action.

A here-goes-nothing sprint toward the door that my friend still cracks open.

Another urgent race through rooms I don't recognize, dodging canvases and shipping crates and worktables piled with assorted tools and large wire spools.

At last, a burst into the main gallery itself. We rush with care since they're installing a new show, and I already hate the mere idea of accidentally ruining a canvas. Between my frantic apologies, I want to shudder from the thought. At once I'm flashing back to the night I watched a glass of red wine get splashed across the A-list party looks I styled for Jaden *and* Willow. Why does heartbreak strike at the worst times?

But right now won't be one of them.

I vow it as Bastien and I get to the sidewalk on 75th. Drue cuts a quick turn to the left, already starting to weave between parked cars. By the time Logan and his posse regroup enough to shout up the street behind us, she's dashed between a couple of luxury sedans and guided us beneath a low awning emblazoned with one word.

Fourteen.

The face of the liveried doorman beneath it seems to say *If you have to ask, you can't come in.*

We don't ask.

The stodgy gatekeeper isn't happy.

"Pardon. Me!"

Drue pivots like an elegant pop star, one eyebrow arched with disdain. "All right, if you insist. You're excused."

Super Stodge isn't amused. "Sunday clients are by appointment only." He rakes us all with a judging sweep, appearing nauseated once he reaches Bastien's shirt. Clearly his Broadway Hits mix tape doesn't contain anything without an overture. "Do you have an appointment?"

Drue's other brow jogs up. She weaves her head, winding up to tear this guy apart. But no way can we afford that mess right now. I have to think *fast.*

"How do you do?" I reach for the man's hand. "My name is Raegan. What's yours?"

"Errr . . . Arthur."

"Beautiful name. So Arthur—can I just call you Art?—the thing is, we had to keep our appointment off the books. Way, *way* off." I lean in, wrapping him tighter around my theoretical hook. "Just wouldn't be good to have the fans swooping in on the duke while he's trying to get inspiration for the gala."

The man's eyes grow as big as Caesar salad plates at

Carmine's. "*The* gala? As in ..."

"What other gala is there?"

Plenty, if he really thinks before answering that—there are three giant society things happening between now and the extravaganza at the Metropolitan Museum of Art—but I'm not ripping any seams out of an opportunity that's going so well. Arthur's now fawning, fussing, and welcoming us all the way inside the shop—and just in time. A handful of seconds after the etched glass door closes behind us, Logan leads the charge up the sidewalk outside, toward Madison—and hopefully beyond.

"Madame is upstairs taking some tea and her medications," Arthur explains as we step into the shop's main room. "I'll just dash and wake—errr, *inform* her—that you're here."

After his careful emphasis of the words, my mind fills in the blanks about the not-so-veiled code. I take it as a formidable slice of great karma. If the proprietor is getting as relaxed as Arthur implies, she won't be so incensed when the duke and his team decide on a fast retreat from her showroom. But on our way through, I grab a business card from the counter and make a mental point to throw a few clients her way in gratitude for the temporary shelter. There are some cool pieces on these racks.

We slip outside on the Madison side of the shop, which stresses me about what to do next. Logan isn't clueless. All too quickly, he'll claw at the wool we just threw over his pretty brown eyes and double back. But which way will he look? Or will he split the manpower and go a multitude of directions?

I don't have to voice any of those thoughts aloud. One look at Drue, and I already know we're sharing brain cells about it. But she's quicker about taking action on hers, thank God, already snagging Bastien and me by an elbow apiece. She keeps up the momentum, rushing us across the street and into the small crowd that's bustling onto the M1 bus.

"My madness comes with a method," she insists, even as Bastien looks wary about entering the thing. I have to admit, her voice strikes *me* as too eager and cheery. "Get off at 109th and then cut toward the park. Go past the Duke Ellington statue—say hi for me—on your way to the North Greene."

"The north *huh*?" I retort. "What are you talking about? I don't do woodsy and buggy unless there's good hooch involved. You know this already."

She also knows she's telling us to ride all the way to Central Park's northern border—and that means sections like the Loch, the Ravine, and the North Woods. In short, the woodsy and buggy parts.

"Not the north *green*," she stresses. "The North *G-R-E-E-N-E*. It's a hotel. Okay, technically a guest house."

"Which you know about *how* and *why*?"

"Because of the picture I've been working on. We're shooting a lot of complicated scenes out in that part of the park." She smirks. "Turns out you're not the only one allergic to nature, and our generators can't spare enough juice for all the main cast trailers."

"Seriously?" I counter. "Who all is in this movie?"

She shakes her head like a weary toddler mom. "Bigger discussion than we have minutes for. Anyhow, the studio's bought out all six rooms of the Greene for at least the next ten days, but nobody's in it right now because of the production halt due to the coming storm. The big names have escaped for downtown hotels if they don't already have a place in the city.

The rest of us have gone home."

"Except for you." I pull her close for a heartfelt hug. "*You're* out here running around with your friend, under skies that are about to dump angel tears. And that friend is so damn grateful."

"Ohhh, no. Not yet." She steps away. "Be grateful once you get to the Greene. A night or two of lying low there, and then Dick Gorgeous will be yanked away to more interesting leads. Actual break-ins. Grand theft. Dead bodies." After fishing a pen out of her purse, she turns my hand over and scribbles on it. "Here's the addy. Just walk in there, put on your Anna Wintour face, and tell them you're with the crew for *Apples and Oranges.*"

I flinch. "Please tell me that's the movie's dummy title."

"Hell *yes* it is." She copies my cringe but for different motivation. The woman has always been freakishly good about delineating sounds of the city, a talent that serves us well as she pushes Bastien and me into the bus. Her urgency coincides with a new rise of shouts from up the street. Up *which* street, I can't tell. It now seems like Logan is leading cops to us from every direction. Thank God we're already rolling.

Bastien sticks close as I pay the fare and find us a pair of seats. We fall onto our butts with heavy sighs. Before I inhale again, the man is squeezing my hand with agonizing intensity. I don't complain. In a lot of ways, in the insanity of this moment, I welcome every painful degree of the pressure.

"Bastien." I actually deliver a vise grip of my own. He's zoning out but not in a leave-me-alone way. I see it in his glassy eyes and feel it in the continued sprint of his pulse. "Hey. *Desperado.*"

He finally snaps his head up. I smile, hoping he knows that

it's not just because of his response to my special nickname. At least not all of it.

"You're okay," I murmur. "Look around. Come on, do it for me. Do it *with* me."

I tug at him harder, not relenting until both of my hands are encasing his fist at the center of my sternum. I press his knuckles there, compelling him to feel what his nearness does to my heartbeat. How, despite all the crazy events of the last few hours, there's no place I'd rather be than on the M1 line with his hand wrapped in mine. With his big body pressed close. With his breaths easing as he leans in and utters curious questions in my ear. As I answer every one of them in a matching murmur. Words meant for him alone . . .

They aren't afraid of the city burning down because there aren't any candles in the lights. When the ones over the street turn green, the bus driver knows he can go.

The bus runs on the same kind of power as the lights. A lot of the cars now too.

Yeah, we pay money for raw food. A lot of money, actually.

I don't know why more people aren't talking to each other. Everyone's in a rush, I guess.

And it hits me then that this is the first day, in so many, that I *haven't* been in such a rush. When was the last time I sat on a bus—or a train or plane—and simply watched the world go by? No checking texts or working on sketches. No opening my ereader to get lost in another world. Not that other worlds aren't awesome, but just *look* at the one right outside my window.

Our window.

The pane that feels reserved for just Bastien and me. Dedicated to our special cubicle of the bus. Our unique moment in time.

A moment that feels over two hundred years old.

I tense up but disguise it as a position shift. Thankfully, Bastien's too absorbed with his own relaxation game to notice. He does take advantage of my new proximity to snuggle and kiss along my neck.

Now I *really* don't miss my texts, messages, and responsibilities.

Well, not in any real sense of the word—except that they'll help my senses stay rooted in *this* century.

I mean, this is getting weird.

These temporal disconnects...they're intense. And terrifying. I wish I could talk to someone about them. But there wasn't any down time with D at all, and I'm afraid that asking Bastien will have him dragging me to the nearest psychic, demanding Magique to push me aside for *her* twenty-first century entrance. Now, I'm always up for copious drinks and a trip to Shakti's Studio for some tarot deck fun, but this is different. This stuff is weirder than the darkening sky outside.

As if high-fiving—or maybe middle-fingering—my musing, Mother Nature lights up the city with a lightning show. A few seconds later, thunder goes bowling up and down the avenues. Umbrellas pop open along the sidewalks, and none too soon. Seconds later, the skies rip open with a true deluge.

I look out into the storm, blasting the heavens and blurring the windows, and silently thank Mother Nature for the dramatic fit. The spring storm comes nowhere close to the thoughts I've just been trying to untwist.

And I had to go and get that Zen about shit.

Because as the bus stops at 106th, I already know I'll be pressing pause on the atmospheric ASMR tracks.

The weather forces a lot of people to get on the bus. A couple of them are elderly women. I know this because we're close enough to the front of the bus that Bastien rises at once to help them climb the entrance stairs. The first woman receives his personal escort to the seat he's just vacated, next to me. As I make sure the sweet apple face with purple-dyed hair and matching flowered scarf is comfortable, he's already carrying a grocery bag for the second woman. But the seat is occupied by someone else. A budding musician, surmising from the drumsticks he's beating on his knees and the earphones hugging the shaggy sides of his head.

Meaning he sees Bastien but doesn't hear the distinct De Leon rumble that conveys a glaringly clear message.

Meaning that he also doesn't understand why he jogs his head up with a yo-bro smirk and receives a daunting glower as reply.

Meaning that when the guy adds a friendly wave of a drumstick and watches Bastien snap it like a twig, he doesn't hesitate to leap to his feet.

Just like I do.

Because even as Bastien helps the woman to sit, smiling as if everything's right with the world, I already know it isn't.

I don't know what to be more freaked about now: the fury on Drummer Boy's face or the fascination on everyone else's as they whip out their phones and start recording the rumble.

CHAPTER TEN

BASTIEN

"Hold. *Still.*"

Though this is Raegan's third time around with the words, their vehemence does not wane. But none of her communication has been jovial since the commotion I caused on the bus, causing the driver to swerve, stop, and order us both off the conveyance.

It mattered not that *I* was the one with blood joining the rain down my face. The woman had jabbed hands into her jacket pockets and turned as if I had insulted her in eight different ways. Without waiting to see if I followed, she tromped across the street. Her pace did not falter even as I completed my crossing too late, earning me obscene screeches and blares courtesy of the people inside several of the car machines.

One of those *enculés* wanted to waltz into my memory a little more, cutting sharply at the corner to lob an empty glass bottle my way. I picked it up, perplexed why someone would be so wasteful with glass, especially etched with such a dazzling message. *Share a Classic with a Friend.*

Raegan Karlinne Tavish does not look like she wants to be my friend anymore.

Now, as she pushes a washcloth against my left cheek, I

wonder if she has any *considerations* left for *me* anymore—as friends or beyond.

I should not be weathering that as if *she* was the one who punched me on the bus. *Oui*, the first *and* second time. I should not be feeling as if she is the one who grabbed one of the broken sticks from me and then lunged it toward my right eye socket. Thankfully, the bus's driver swerved his wheel at just the right moment.

"Hold still," she intones. "This is going to sting a little."

The second she presses the cloth to my cheek, I jerk back with a howl. "*Mierde!* What the hell—"

She rolls her eyes. "I said—"

"A *little*," I bite back. "*That* is what you said. Not that you had squeezed peppers onto a cloth and thought it would be a good laugh to use the foulness on me."

She slams the cloth down. "Do I look like I'm laughing?" Her shoulders fall and her eyes darken, but she makes no further move to approach me. "It's old-school antiseptic. It's all the innkeepers had at the desk. You want an infection from those welts, that's on you."

I hold back from flinging words or a tone that I'll regret. Moments like this are sometimes better than arguments. *Sometimes.* The conclusion aside, I seize a chance to study her in full. My poor little rescuer is seething, soaked, and spent—and still beyond beautiful. It still does not feel wrong to admit that, despite knowing her real identity.

It is a force beyond the obvious impetus: her tiny slip of fluent French, so much like Magique, that stopped me as hard as it did her. Nor was it her mumbled comment afterward, when she thought I was not listening anymore. A memory from sheer vapers for her but from last month for me.

But neither of those factors are the grips at my sanity now.

It is her. So many things about *this* woman, of *this* moment. The female who should have given up when I fled from her this morning. Who broke the legalities of this time to come and find me instead. Who has turned her life inside out to continue being here at my side, despite how she looks ready to fall asleep on her feet for it.

She inspires me as much as Magique ever did.

And somehow, I sense Magique smiling about that. Approving.

Telling me to care for Raegan Tavish in all the ways I took care of her.

Even if that means pulling in a long breath to strengthen my lungs for the next words on my lips.

"But that is . . . not the only thing that would be 'on me' today, would it?"

Raegan's chin hikes up. Her gaze goes to green velvet, soft but still so dark. "No," she murmurs. "It certainly wouldn't be."

"Then I am sorry." I withdraw the cloth from her hold and cup her hands in mine. "You did not ask for any of this. For your existence to be upended like this. I truly regret that."

"Like you regret bolting from me before we could talk about it and I could've helped you in a way other than impersonating a fed?"

I comprehend enough of the words that a sheepish reply is warranted. "*Oui.* All of that."

"And you also regret getting into that guy's grill and then snapping his stick?"

I understand all of that, as well. But the part about giving her my true contrition? I refuse to insult her by bearing that falsehood.

"He had another one."

She yanks her hands away. "They had *drums* in your time, right? Ones that needed to be played with *two* sticks?"

I unleash an open seethe. Hers clearly wants company. "And we also had human beings who reached the achievement of their elder years and were shown respect for that. Respect that never had to be enforced with nudges, glares, or fisticuffs."

A sigh tumbles from her pursed lips. "Fine. You're not completely wrong. But you're not totally right either." She slides her eyes closed. When she reopens them, she sends a visual plea to the plain pendant light overhead. "Holy crap. I just hope nobody got viable footage for any decent posting. If they did and there's a connection between the stuff that got streamed from the consulate, we might be dealing with more than just one peeved percussionist…"

Her trail-off is perfectly timed. Another few seconds would not have been enough to quash my enraged spike. "Peeved?" I spew. "*Why?* He was being a complete toad. That woman was carrying food and supplies! He was toting *sticks.*"

"Okay, whoa there, Trigger." She lowers her sights back to my face and slides her touch along my shoulders. "Was he a total asshole amphibian? Yes. And were you right about reminding him of it? Technically and morally, super yes. But in the eyes of our law, that's a hard no." She throws one hand back up, halting my objection in my throat. "Hold up there too, buddy. Everyone in our day and age isn't a boorish cretin. The nice guys are still here, but the battlefield has gotten a lot flatter. As you can probably surmise, that's a good *and* bad thing."

I push to my feet. This conversation is heading into different nuances, though I do not fully hate the recognition.

I *can* surmise that, *merci beaucoup,* and it feels good to have someone simply recognize the fact. As thoroughly as I worship my big brother, it has been maddening to be brushed off as the denser brother simply because of our birth order. Why? Doesn't second in line merely mean I've just germinated a little later?

But vocalizing all that will not change it. I embrace her bigger point instead. Her better point. "Equality for all means even the toads, *oui*?"

"Exactly." Her whoosh of the word coincides with her backwards flop onto the room's large bed. "Regrettably and unfortunately," she adds, "but . . . exactly."

That repetition falls out of her with more heavy breath—a sound I also recognize well. The rush of an exhausted whisper is likely known to every warrior throughout history. I am reassured by that, at least, just as I smile while predicting what will spill from her next. The full breaths that predict she is approaching deep sleep.

Quietly, I close the two steps to the bed. Assuredly, the woman's eyes are solidly shut. Her lashes are thick umber sweeps against the cream and ginger dapples of her cheeks. I'm halfway toward touching her there, so tempted to trace those dots like she's my human constellation . . .

But all too quickly remember what happened the last time I reached for heaven.

With the drive of a dagger, it was ripped from me. She was gone.

She is still *gone.*

It is my self-imposed dictate, over and over in my mind, while I lift the bed's top cover and gently wrap it around the woman who *is* here with me.

Raegan Tavish, who chose to run for me after I ran *from* her.

Raegan Tavish, who has literally worn herself out to keep me safe in this danger-strewn new world.

Raegan Tavish, who now shivers before jerking the blanket away from me. Who proves that her keen intelligence is working even in its subconscious state.

Oui, little one. Stay away. I am clearly not the Duke De Leon. I am the Lord of Chaos.

But I promise you—I promise—once I know you are safe with your friends again, you will never have to deal with my insanity again.

I do not leave her side until watching her breathing even out. Once I am certain she is warm and comfortable, I step over to the radiator device that she hurriedly activated once we arrived in the room.

"*Incroyable,*" I rasp, fanning my hands in front of the steel grill that gives off the heat of a small campfire.

Once the chill has seeped from my own limbs, I strip off my shirt and drape it across the back of a nearby chair to dry out a little more. For a long moment, I gape at the garment—before deciding that who or whatever Spiderman is, the eighteenth century will surely seem like an emptier place without him.

But I will learn to live in a world without the web tosser just as I will abide in a world without Magique.

And . . . without Raegan.

The woman who entrances me all over again, even from the couch onto which I flop across the small room. Who already has me wishing to turn into a pillow as she rolls over and wraps her arms around one. Who has me timing my breaths to the gentle air flowing in and out of her soft form until I am ruthlessly engulfed by slumber, as well.

Then just as savagely ripped from it.

A shriek explodes across the room. As I jolt into consciousness, it peters into an agonized wince. I gain my feet as another scream tears the air.

"Mag—*Raegan.*"

I sit on the bed next to her, already observing how deeply her nightmare has ensnared her. A mere shake of her shoulder will be useless against her subconscious wraiths. As she cries out again, I sprawl all the way next to her.

"Raegan. Wake up, *chérie.* 'Tis but an awful dream."

I have to repeat it several times, tucking her face close to my chest, before the rumbles of my voice penetrate her in that other world. Before fully crossing the bridge back, she flails at me. "Nooo!"

"*Oof.*" It takes the place of my favorite profanity, even as she lands a whack to the middle of my injured cheek. Swearing about the sensitivity of this wound, despite the noble intentions that led to it, does not feel like the correct call right now.

But nor does letting her go.

Even as she sighs into the middle of my chest and softens against the middle of my body. The part of me that changes as well—toward the opposite end of that tactile spectrum.

Mon dieu. This woman's breathtaking body . . .

"Huh? Oh, no. Oh my God. Bastien?"

And her voice, so effervescent even when half-awake . . .

"I'm so sorry. Did I hurt you?"

And her benevolence, even when there is no reason for her to bestow it . . .

I chuckle. And before I can control myself, I am turning my face and kissing her sweet fingertips. "Nothing I have not deserved, *n'est-ce pas?*"

Her lips twist. Her gaze is dark sage, like a forest just minutes before dawn. The thought makes me wonder about the actual current time in our day. Deep shadows shroud our little room. I can only see her because of the small light from the adjoining kitchenette.

"Deserved or not, that's going to be a hell of a shiner, buddy."

I arch a brow, indicating toward the rain-spattered window. A low thunder roll portends of more to come. "I doubt that *shining* will be a viable task anytime soon, *ma magnifique.*"

Her lips perk but her eyes remain solemn. "And now you're being too nice. Magnificent isn't the word I'd go for in the Raegan media kit right now."

"Bah." I grunt softly. "I have never been much for mead. Should we just assume you are a sweet wine instead?"

And *this* is the comment that banishes her doldrums. I struggle not to let my confusion take over my scowl as her bursting giggle lights up the room much better than any daylight. "As you wish, Monsieur le Duke. But if I had my real preference, we'd be doing whiskey flights and stuffed potatoes somewhere in the Village."

Every word of her pronouncement makes sense on its own. Together, they baffle me all over again. Still, I reply, "I will never walk away from good whiskey."

"Then it's settled. When we can roam freely again, I'm parking your fine ass at the Flatiron Room and treating you to—" She stops in the middle of enthusiastically patting my chest. "Oh, my. Speaking of your oh-so-fine bod, my lord . . ."

"Here at your service, my lady."

I grin in time to her cute smirk. Excellent move, in time

to veil my bittersweet tinge. I never had the chance to address Magique with those words. Though I am still really not, it feels close enough to feel her smile in my soul, inspiring the words that continue on my lips.

"That applies to *all* of my body parts, Raegan. Including everything up here."

Her mouth purses with mirth as she watches me tug at an ear. "And exactly why do you suggest that, mister?"

I do not mirror the blitheness. "Do you want to talk about it?" I move my fingers from my ear to her forehead. "The nightmare?"

She closes her eyes and keeps them shut for a long moment and then pushes her face back into my chest. "Damn. How come you still smell so good?"

I steel my composure, fighting the effects of her moving lips and silken breaths on my skin. Directly beneath her mouth, my heartbeat surges anew . . . and pumps fresh blood to other body parts. Anatomy I should not be acknowledging at the moment . . .

"You are evading the subject." I direct the growl at my cock as equally as her. My body ignores me. Thankfully, she does not.

"Because there *is* no subject." Though she mumbles it, there is purpose to her volume. "Mack Deluise doesn't get that honor anymore."

"Deluise," I echo but swiftly stamp it with a snarl. "The one who tried to stab you in the heart."

"It was an accident," she counters. "We were kids." She pulls back but not completely. I am glad, despite the continuing torment she issues in the form of a light fingertip on my breastbone. Up, up, up she traces with that caress, until pausing at the hollow of my neck. "I just wish my subconscious would get that message."

I swallow hard, knowing she can feel it. "I understand that more than you probably suspect."

She hitches her face up. As soon as her wide stare thoroughly rakes my face, she murmurs, "You're right. I don't get it."

I finger one of her curls. Our longer-than-expected tromp in the rain had a wonderful effect on them. They are softer. Curlier. I cannot resist. "Usually, it is—*was*—Magique shaking *me* awake from the nightmares." Already knowing that will intensify her frown, I steel myself to give her the rest of the explanation. "Taking a man's life . . . it is not as romantic as the traveling actors and court minstrels paint it to be. Even after one crosses that breach once . . . the decision you have, about knowing you are strong enough to snuff a life and then actually doing it . . . there is no traversing back to the other side. Not until you are faced with that decision again. And then you *are* on the other side, with your sword at someone's throat . . . and you are God again." I drag in desperately needed air. "And it is the most sickening feeling in the world."

There is gentle pressure against the side of my face. It is from Raegan's newly raised fingertips. "The kind of sick you can only feel in nightmares," she finally whispers. Before I look back up, I already know . . . that *she* knows. She simply . . . does. "How many times?" she asks then. "That you've had to scale the breach, Bastien?"

I gulp. "Many." My voice is strangled. My eye sockets are hot. "Too many."

She slides her hand in, palming my whole jaw now. Those seeking digits of hers are now strands of warmth against my damp ones. "But why?"

"I am the second-born. You know Maximillian as more than a passing acquaintance, so you must know that. While I was always sure that my parents would not let me go destitute, I cannot expect them to carve my entire path for me. After all, they have Max to worry about."

"You mean they *had* Max to worry about."

"*Oui.* Of course." I am perturbed about the forced correction, but not because her allegation is so obvious. Because her *sadness* is. There is a discernible, nearly touchable, certainty beneath her words...

She knows something. A something she does not feel ready to share right now. After my humbling lesson from the bus about being an overbearing oaf, I force the curiosity to the back of my mind. It will keep for another time—when her poor mind has not been battling a monster named Mack Deluise.

"Go on," she prompts after a short lull. "So what did you do about carving the path?"

I am grateful for the subject change and tell her so with a small smirk. "Well, I was a devious child. Nobody was surprised when I grew up to be a man who could discern the same trait in others. It served me well when I was a guest at Versailles and thwarted an assassination attempt on Louis."

Raegan's eyes flare. "Shut the front door!"

I glance the general direction of the guest house's entrance. "I believe the innkeeper already did..."

"Now *you're* evading." She pushes up, resting her weight on an elbow. "Knock it off and tell me what happened."

I shrug. "Several of the men in the *Grand Veneur* slayed a huge stag for dinner. When they were about to wheel in the carcass for the king's inspection and praise, I saw it move."

"Ahhh!" she yelps, pressing her free hand to her mouth. "So wild!"

"Not what it was supposed to be at that point, but I think I grasp the point. Since my mind jumped instantly to foul play—"

"Or that maybe it was a zombie stag?"

I meet her light laugh with a wondering snort before continuing. "Louis was impressed with my observation. I have served the crown faithfully ever since."

"Which is why he gave you a dukedom."

"Ah." Though I am done chuckling, I hold on to a lingering smile. "So my big brother *has* been bragging about me."

Her sunny mien gets tucked behind a strange, subdued cloud. "Ermmm . . . not exactly," she murmurs, earning herself a visit from my own inner storm front. I can only push back my overbearing thunderheads so many times.

"Meaning *what*?"

She averts her gaze. I do not have a chance to properly growl about that because she twists and settles to the bed again, all the way on her back. The plain white ceiling suddenly occupies her whole attention.

I silently seethe. Is the query *that* arduous to answer?

"Raegan?"

"*Bastien.*" She whips a hand back up, sprawling it across my lips. "Please . . . Just for now, can't we just say that it's awesome you survived getting here at all? And that *we've* done well at surviving the insanity since?"

Beneath her fingers, I compress my lips. I haul in air through my nose, determined to regain the upper hand of the exchange but am struck by a fresh wallop of her fresh floral scent. That sweet tinge along her skin, overlaid with the smoky damp of the rain . . . In seconds, I am almost undone yet again. But that's when the storm intensifies, a perfect companion for the tempest that still spikes my temperament.

"Insanity," I husk, battling the din from the new sheets of water plummeting outside. "So that is what I have caused for your life?"

"Oh, lordie." She sighs while dealing a chastising push at my mouth. "I'm going to start calling you Eeyore 2.0, mister."

I snort and pull away. "I know not of this pointy ore—or, for that matter, what you continue to speak of besides answers to my honest questions."

She pulls her hand back. Splays her fingers along her furrowing forehead. "You know what? You do make me insane. But not in all the worst ways. *Hey.* That was a *joke.*"

I relent my glowering mope, though not swiftly. "Understood. But perhaps 'tis best that one of us keeps to the *not worst* side of sanity."

She bats at my chest. "Oh, that doesn't sound like any fun."

"*Désolé,*" I mumble, already reveling in the way she leaves her hand there, working her sorceress's magic through every available pore in my body. "Fun has been a rarity in my schedule as of late. Situations with His Majesty have become more and more . . . complicated."

A sound spills from her, humor wrapped in odd nettles that I cannot interpret. "Gee, you think?" As soon as my frown deepens, she burrows her hand farther up on my scalp. "Okay, I'm *désolée* too. That's a subject for a much different midnight. Or whatever time it is."

"You cannot check on your small tablet? The one that lights up?"

She copies my arched brow. "That would be my phone, remember?"

"Ah. Yes. *Phone.*" It would be easier to recall the word, so closely tied to its Greek origin, if she actually used the device for speaking. But that feels like another subject for a different midnight, as well.

"But your point is valid," she inserts. "Though I'm not in a hurry to get across the room. The less I wake that thing up, the better. If Dick Gorgeous has figured out I'm really not Degas's long-lost-great-great-grand-something-or-other and is already tracking my apps for location alerts . . ."

I am proud of following the majority of her comment now. I am *not* comfortable with the meaning it infers. "*Tracking.* Logan can do that to you without actual tracks? Through the phone device?"

"If he tries hard enough, yes."

"But he has to thread a few fine needles."

"Or get permission from the proper authorities. Which, I imagine, is a little of the same thing."

I suck in a sizable breath. "What about other things to distract him, as you and Drue discussed?"

"That's a possibility too," she offers. "And obviously the scenario we want. But traipsing out of here now, assuming that's how all the morsels have melted, would be a big mistake. They gave me a dining guide when I ventured over to the front desk to ask for a phone charger. I think we can find some decent take-out, once we're hungry."

"Take what? Out of where?"

She snickers softly. "It's one of the better things about living in New York. I guarantee you'll approve."

I huff. "That is welcome news, since my list of the good

things about this place is sparse."

Her focus spikes up by an obvious notch. "What's on the list so far?"

"You."

She laughs again. "Excellent start. What else?"

"That is all."

"Then that's a shitty list, buster."

My own chuckle comes quickly, due mostly to the enchanting flush that flows over her cheeks. At once, I want more of it. The demand does not even scream solely from my cock anymore. The pulses between my legs have expanded to unmistakable intensity in my mind and a primal pull from the center of my chest.

Primal . . . and undefeatable.

And intimidating.

Because, for the first time in my existence, I cannot explain away any part of it.

This attraction is unlike any other, including my passion for Magique, because there is no logical reason for it. Every woman in my life, most especially in my bed, has always been there with valid justification. The way that female has excited me with a flirting stare or engaged me with a silken jest. And, *oui*, loath as I am to admit it, the advantage of gaining some new court gossip.

Raegan Tavish is none of these things and yet all of them. And beyond. So far beyond. She is open flirtation and racing excitement. She is a gateway to a thousand unexpected jests and has even given me her own version of court gossip: the intriguing tales about the celebrities of this time, their personages often occupying entire windows in the Madison Avenue boutiques. She was in the middle of such a story when

I ruined the day for her, adding another canto to the chaos I have wreaked upon her life.

And yet here I am, ready to do it again. So weak about fighting the spell of it...the enchantment of *her*. The unabashed intensity of her eyes. The small squirms of her whole form. I cannot resist.

I cannot resist.

That makes me one hell of a pathetic man.

And yet, as I hover my mouth above hers, I have never felt like more of one.

"The list is fine the way it is, *ma chérie*," I murmur, letting the syllable puff across her slightly parted lips. "It simply lacks certain elements."

"El...ements? Like...ermmm...what?"

She is suddenly not so glib, and I savor every pretty drop of her agitation. Every adorable inch of her uncertain thoughts...while her body responds in very definite ways to mine.

"Like subheadings." I dip in a little more, teasing every syllable along the plush cushions of her mouth. There are fresh skitterings up and down her form, new beacons of her inexplicable hold over me. "Perhaps you can help me fill a few in."

CHAPTER ELEVEN

RAEGAN

He's looking at me like *that* again.

The way he didn't rip his gaze from me back at Allie and Max's. Those incredible minutes right after he emerged from the wardrobe. The hour of carnality that turned into one of the best and worst things that's ever happened to me.

Except this time, it's different. There's something missing.

But that's not necessarily a bad thing.

The moment Bastien presses in, transparent about his intention to kiss me, the recognition gongs through my mind.

This time, there's no sadness in his attention. Not a shred of desperation in his tender passion. He doesn't kiss me like I'll disappear when our lips graze and tingle. He doesn't pull away to impale me with raw stress from his worried goldens. His attention is still reverent but not in that memorial service kind of way. He's taking his time with all his caresses because he *wants* to this time, not because he's afraid he'll shatter me.

This time, he's looking at me because I'm *me* ... not Magique.

Which should have me rejoicing, right? It's good to be the real person in his head. The correct person receiving his soft caresses.

But for some reason, I'm trembling. And this time, it's not a great development.

I'm scared. In the big league fire-and-brimstone way.

Which is so freaking ridiculous. Because that first encounter over in Midtown . . . it was my own game of show-don't-tell too. A medley of all my defensive mantras. Show skin, not what's within. Give him the screaming O but not the lonely tears. And I'd done just that—which meant the discovery about Magique was a not-so-small blessing in disguise. The pressure was off, and I was damn grateful. I still am. I mean, I think.

Aren't I?

I don't really have to be the Allie to his Max. Because clearly, I've got some work to do in the *knowing a guy's needs* department. Having to figure that out with a twenty-eight-day limit due to an old gypsy curse that will end his life without the magic of true love's kiss is pressure I don't need right now. It's been shitty enough to figure out what Sylver Savoy is going to wear to the Emmys.

This way, everything is blessedly simpler. We just have to get Bastien back to the time travel machine for his journey back to Magique's arms. No mess. No confusion. And thank *God*, no awful aches in my heart.

Or so I thought.

Until right now.

This time, there's way more meaning in this man's exquisite kiss. More intent in the longer mashes of his lips, the heated sweeps of his tongue. The kind of more that makes me moan, beyond conflicted, as he opens me wider and delves to my tonsils with his ardent assault. And as he groans in return, pushing his beastly roughness through my system, it's the kind of more that has me not even caring.

I whimper again. Louder. Longer. I bury my hands in his gloriously thick hair, twisting at the thick beauty of it. He keeps up our primitive conversation, growling in return. Not making it possible to breathe for fear of missing a moment of his bold carnality. His magnificent force. The addicting heaven of his passion.

As more thunder rolls through the clouds above the city, a similar sound rolls from the mighty depths of his beautiful chest. "Ahhh, *ma chérie*. How I savor this sweet, succulent mouth... Now *here* is a fine subheading item for my list."

"Ummm." My senses soar. My heartbeat takes wing, attempting to chase them. For once in my life, there's absolutely no clever quip in my brain or at my lips. The only thing I have left for him is just that pitiful mumble...

Until the man next drops his head to the valley of my breasts.

"Holy crap!" I gasp harshly from the moment his scruff abrades my cleavage. My nipples stiffen, already fighting the pads of my no-frills bra, donned so long ago when I was rushing to follow him halfway across New York.

We ended up going so much more than halfway—an idiom, I now realize, that's applying to more than just subway and bus stops. There's a familiarity along with our connectivity, like the warm glow of a lamp after the electrical spark that turned it on. A sensation that glides through me, making it easy to unzip my jacket and then unhook my bra, obeying the unspoken plea from his hungry eyes. That molten gaze that wants to see all of me...

The part of me that yearns to give him that and so much more.

This is beyond simply exposing my breasts and nipples. It's about the spot between them too. The line of puckered flesh I'll never fully escape that always feels like my huge risk. An exposure that always leads lovers to ask so many questions. And after that, all my answers—leading my lovers to decide things about me.

In this moment, I always become one of three things for those men. A Madonna, a badass, or a charity case. While any one of those can lead to some role-playing fun, none of them are real. None of them are *me*. When I thought I found a guy who finally seemed to get that, it turned out that *me* wasn't enough either.

So when is Bastien De Leon going to spring the same news on me?

And why, as he licks my scar between worshipping my nipples, do I not bother to care?

Because, apparently, I'm the shallow missy with the breasts that haven't felt this good in a damned long time. Perhaps in *ever*.

"Ohhh! *Bastien*. Are you . . . oh, damn, are you *biting* it?"

Okay, definitely not in ever.

Because this is definitely not anything I've ever experienced.

"You are enjoying, *ma magnifique*?" But he concludes that with a chuckle, since my high-pitched gasp has already filled out his figurative memo. "*Mon dieu*," he murmurs, teething his way up the swell of my other breast. "How has a delicacy like you never been enjoyed like this?"

"Because nobody else knew what they were doing?"

It feels good to reclaim my sarcasm even as he steals another chunk of my sanity by closing his teeth over my other erect tip. The pain is intense, forbidden...exquisite. I'm writhing now, growing more aware of every place my body rubs against his, a pleasure that's doubled once he releases my throbbing peak. At once, fire tumbles through the rest of my form—especially toward the pulsing button between my thighs.

Ohhh...yesss.

The words are a sharp keen on my lips as my hands spread along his scalp. My moves are desperate and raw, as if I think it's possible to absorb his thoughts that way. The boldness of his mind and spirit. The riveting, carnal confidence that he bends and rasps into my ear...

"Oh, these fancy cakes are getting their own subheading too, *mon petite rayonnement.*"

And right away, I'm at a loss for returning anything resembling bright wit. For that matter, forget anything that sounds like normal breathing.

Rayonnement.

I have no idea what it means, but I'm good with it. So much more than good.

Because it's mine.

I'm no longer *little lily, sweet fleur,* or even *ma magie,* though that last one can stay if he wants to switch it up sometimes. But right now, I only smile and whisper my way through the one that matters most.

"*Rayonnement. Rayonnement...*"

And I'm already forgetting how to push air past my vocal cords as he continues downward, kissing fresh awareness into my skin before stopping at my belly button.

"It is very fitting for you," he says, licking around the shallow dimple above the waistband of my yoga pants, "Such effulgence and light. Such fervor and ferocity. A luster of life force, even in the darkest part of this endless midnight."

I should thank him for that. Like, in a million words just as beautiful and sigh-worthy. But the man is holding my oxygen hostage, and I'm helpless to bargain for that freedom. All I do is burn for him. Moan for him.

Shine for him.

And I'm there, from the moment he fully flicks his tongue into the sensitive skin inside my navel. From the second he tantalizes me in all the best ways, ending up with my arching torso against his whole face. So many sweet shivers. So many pulses through all my muscles . . . especially down there. That place that strains and tightens for him. Needing a bigger piece of his attention than this.

"Bastien!" Thank *God* my voice finally breaks free from the shackles. "Oh *please.*"

He hears me. And he gets it too. I know that as soon as he lifts his head, the depths of his stare fiery and alive, like the focus of a wildcat in the dimness of a forest. A shiver takes over me at once, but I don't feel like his prey. I'm ready to be his she-cat, giving back as good as I get.

"Do it." I speak to the one aspect of his gaze that doesn't match the rest. The tiny hitches of hesitation, lingering at the corners between his eyebrows and eyelashes. I run a soft finger across one of them. With my other hand, I push the waistband of my yoga pants into the area between his parted lips.

Do it.

Holy shit . . . please!

But he twists up and away, pulling the rest of his body a similar direction. When our gazes meet again, it's only from inches apart. He's lying beside me again, his weight back on an elbow, one hand sliding over my ribcage. The light from the kitchenette limns the stunning landscape of his shoulders. But I hold back from exploring those muscled hills. My need to fulfill other cravings is much stronger.

So. Much. Stronger...

"Wrong direction, Monsieur le Duke." I grab his wrist and push his hand back toward my throbbing groin. "Here," I plead, raspier now. Harsher.

"*Mierde.*" Bastien gulps with similar brutality. Drags in air past his locked teeth. "Raegan—"

"No. *Here.* Help me. You know how."

God, do you know how. I tell him that part with a grateful sigh as he slips his big hand down, cupping me from the outside. But after a few seconds, it feels like trying to tango to a waltz. Doable but wrong. Incomplete.

"Please," I husk—and slide his hand beneath my pants. Yet this time, there's not even partial satisfaction. He's at a full stop as soon as his fingertips graze my trimmed mons. "*Please.* Like this."

"Raegan." His voice rides the same sandpaper tone as mine. "If I touch you... flesh to flesh... I do not know if I can stop."

I palm the side of his face, hoping my expression conveys gratitude for his sweet concern. Yeah, the stuff that pours out of him even as his erection announces itself along the top of my thigh. Oh, my *word.* What did they feed those eighteenth-century secret service guys? Whole sides of beef?

"Then we'll have to get creative. We did before, right?"

He closes his eyes as if the waltz has hit a record scratch. Mutters something beneath his breath in French. For all I know it's a nursery rhyme, but every membrane in my pussy reacts with filthy connotations instead. That's an extremely good thing, since the man clearly comes to a decision—*thank you Jesus,* the *right* one—and pushes his hand a few inches lower, sliding easily into my freshly soaked core.

"Oh, Bastien!" I buck up by a similar number of inches, reveling in the double hit of contact that brings. More of my leg against his hard-on, straining between the annoying barriers of our clothes. More of my intimate tunnel around the length of his firm, long finger. "That's . . . nice," I croak out somehow. "Oh, yeah. Really . . . nice."

The last part is my stammering effort to encourage more of his verbal finesse. Along with those hefty eighteenth-century dinners, someone must've been making those soldiers read up on silky love song lyrics.

"Get these pantaloons gone with glorious haste, woman. I must behold the nirvana of your nude flesh."

Especially a little ditty like that.

As soon as I hurl aside my yoga bottoms, my moan is punctuated by lightning glare from the window. During the thunder roll that quickly follows, Bastien is quiet. Too quiet for a man who's kept his fingers buried in my sex this whole time. Who's kneading me there with matching intensity despite his new attention to the mute button.

It's bizarre but kind of hot.

Not as hot as the moment he hooks a leg around mine. His hold turns into purchase for his increasingly urgent pushes along my thigh. I turn my hand over on that side, hoping to help him out. Since there's already a damp splotch in the fabric there, I get immediate friction.

He groans hard. Harder still as he rolls his hips to work more of his magnificent dick into my grip. But he's already so massive. Too much to wrap fully with my fingers due to the thickness of his breeches.

He doesn't seem to care. He's as frantic as me now, chasing his pleasure with urgent pumps into my hand—but still with no words at his lips. Nothing beyond that single moan. Is he even still with me? Or has he finally flown off, nearly two hundred and fifty years into the past, to instead be with Magique? Should I ask him? Or say anything? And what if that answer is yes? Does it change my mind about wanting to surrender to him like this? About wanting to watch *him* giving in to *me*? About gazing at the open desire across his face and knowing I was the one who brought him here so far?

About being the one who gets to hold him, even as things go even further.

He's grinded hard enough now to unseat a button on his breeches. And from the moment I feel even the firm, wet tip of his perfect penis, I long for more. Especially because it's so easy to get it now.

Two twists of my wrist have him falling into my palm, swollen and hard and huge.

And then his snarl is in my ear, lusty and heavy and bursting.

"Raegan. Oh *Raegan*."

Ohhh, yes. Definitely *my* name.

And ohhh, yes. Now I'm inspired.

I stroke him harder. Longer. Treasuring all the new ways he comes alive beneath my touch. The subtle jerks of arousal. The extra fluid that spurts from his slit and then spreads between my fingers. The clamoring coals in the sac at his base, so entrancing to rub and explore . . .

"Stop."

Until he spits that out.

"Wh-What's wrong? Bast—"

He grabs my hand, pulling me up and away from his cock. He leans deeper over me, sliding the center of his body impossibly closer to the place where he doesn't want to be.

The place in which he'd fit so perfectly . . .

"*Mierde*," he utters, dropping his head as he pushes up with both arms. "We have to stop."

Stop, stop, stop.

Don't, don't, don't!

I blink fast as the battle takes new form in my head, with the jukebox taking the cue and switching up—*Don't Stop Me Now*—except it's the London Cast version from the West End show, not the original track with Freddie and his guys. That doesn't ease the agony of this conflict at all, especially as Bastien battles to do just that. He's practically in a high plank over me. His shoulders are coiled, his abs are a solid ladder of flexes, and his thighs are shaking. He's giving me all the time and opportunity to roll away, but I don't move.

I can't.

My body is drawn to his like a supersonic magnet—if that's not really a thing, it should be—needing to be fused to him. Drawn to him by a force beyond understanding. A power, I'm now sure, that permeates more than my body. It lights up every corner of my spirit and soul . . . perhaps even my heart.

I slide my hands together over the matching part of him. Press them close, right over the center of his chest. My palms are filled with the urgent thrum of the vital organ inside, as if it's calling to me. Talking to me. Determining the cadence of my own pulse so it can adjust to match.

I'm silent, letting him listen and feel. Searching me out . . .

And finding me.

I want to find him too. So desperately.

"Bastien." I roam my hands outward until my fingers are splayed on more of his flesh. This time I grip the expanses of his biceps. "I don't want to stop."

His whole body slackens. But not for long. He shifts to one side, pressing his weight onto one bent knee and one braced elbow, while muttering loud enough for me to hear now.

"*Dieu aide moi.* Neither do I."

His words are like the release code for more power to the magnets. We're nuclear, replacing all our reactor cooling rods with the fierce stabs of our tongues into each other's mouths. It already feels like they're glowing, so hot and beyond combustible. My defenses are liquified, my logic blasted into ash. No more lingering doubts about where Bastien is either. One steady look into his eyes brings the indelible certainty. He's right here, ready to breach the dangerous core.

Mine.

And dear God, I want to let him. Yes, right now, just like this, knowing that a huge part of his heart remains with a woman from his own era. Knowing that after he returns to her, I might learn that there's a special gift he left behind and that I'll be raising that child by myself.

But being Allie's sounding board about her family planning with Max has made me think about—and yearn a little—for my own. I'll be twenty-seven in a few months, and while the big biological clock isn't deafening yet, I know I want a child sooner than later. Why not a little boy or girl to carry on this man's beautiful DNA? And why not set myself free to consider it now?

I don't think about the subject any longer. Not when I can

do something better—like act on it.

"*Bastien.*" It's barely more than a breath as I wrap my legs around his lean waist. "Do it. Please. I can't wait any long—*oh!*"

I shriek it with all the best versions of shock, coinciding with the moment he lunges long and deep into me. I'm fully ready for the union, my core slick with desire and soft with welcome. He moans his appreciation for that with some more erotic things in French. I'm unable to translate, since thinking of words in my *own* language is impossible right now.

I'm wrapped in a new cloud of lust, body trembling and mind flying. Everything around me is heated passion. Everything inside me is aching pressure. I'm filled to the brim, and yet I ache for more. Bastien's cock, deeper inside my core. His massive thighs, ramming harder between mine. But most of all, his white-hot desire—calling mine to our ultimate fusion. The place where the magnets totally melt together.

The place called here.

The time called now.

No. Not even that.

Because time has ceased to exist.

The only moments that own us are these. The only people we know anymore are each other. The only existence we have is the center of our climaxes, pure molten sensation and endless vibrations. Explosions that spread through my lust cloud like electricity, fissuring but strengthening it at once. I carry new bolts of lightning and pounds of thunder. His beautiful currents buffet me. His wild winds carve my psyche into so many new shapes.

I hate knowing that with such certainty. And admitting how much that terrifies me.

Worse that, even an hour later, well after we've cleaned up and then reunited to cuddle—his word not mine—the fear hasn't dissipated.

Not by one damn degree.

If anything, it claws in with deeper tenacity. Scratches hard, making my gut hurt and my heart bleed. Ruthlessly reminding me of how stupid I've just been. How impossibly reckless, spinning up a fantasy of raising Bastien's baby like I'm the brave heroine who's got to press on with my fallen soldier's love child.

But that isn't the case, is it? Because love doesn't go like this. Not in any tragic war love story and certainly not in real life. Not in just two days, with a man who should be in a centuries-old grave with one woman's name on the lips of his dismembered head.

Magique.

I pull in a long breath and wait for the strength that's got to imbue any second. This is a lot more logic than I'm used to in one string of thought. I should be proud as hell of myself for it. The emotional walls I'm re-stacking. The safety of cold appraisal on the other side. Most of all, the mindset to take the right actions now. Well, one above the rest. To push out from the warmth of our post-coital bed and get my ass down the hall to use the Greene's land-based line. From there, to call Drue.

To ask my friend to make a special trip to the drug store for me. The counter where she'll have to ask the pharmacist for a morning-after packet on behalf of her head-in-the-clouds friend.

"Mon rayonnement?"

The same friend who tumbles back to earth now, courtesy of the naked warrior who dots the question with a gentle kiss to her forehead. Who's making it impossible to think about pushing free of these blankets as he drags one around her with a possessive sweep of his thigh. Who's staring at her with such renewed adoration, she almost forgets where she is.

But not who she is.

Because *rayonnement* will never be the same word again.

"Hey," I manage to mutter. "Sorry. I was just thinking about—"

"Not being here?"

It's impossible to miss his tell-me-I'm-wrong-please undertone, which comes with a squeeze at my shoulder. The kind of touch that's needy but trying not to be.

"Of course not," I chide. But before he can press for more, I rush for a subject change. "I could go for a billion soup dumplings right now. How about you?" I'm hoping for the exact expression he returns. His bafflement gives me an excuse for an excited lurch. "They're the best heaven that'll ever hit your tongue, I promise."

"Then you are already a liar, sweet woman." His drawl is as sultry as his gaze. "Because my tongue has known the succulence of your skin."

And maybe I don't have to call Drue *right* this second . . .

The thought is swallowed by an obnoxious growl from my stomach. "Won't take me long to get the order in," I vow while reaching for my pants.

After getting them on, I reach for his shirt instead of mine. The cheap cotton show shirt has dried faster than my painted denim jacket. I ignore the other benefit of the choice, watching Bastien's male satisfaction at seeing me in something he's already worn. But secretly, I revel in the remembrance of his stare while hurrying down the short hallway. Being quick about this ordeal is the only way I'm going to get through it.

Thankfully, somebody's already on duty at the North Greene's desk. Even better, it's not the same sweet girl from last night, so I can get away with a tall tale about forgetting my phone charger. Best of all, the Liam Neeson look-a-like borrows his namesake's sixth sense and vanishes into a back office as I press Drue's digits onto the pink and green buttons of an eighties-era phone.

As the line begins to ring, I pray my friend will listen to *her* instincts in place of her suspicions. Though she'll see the Manhattan-based digits, the majority of her mind will want to write me off as a pollster or marketer.

Listen to the Force, Drue Skywalker. It's me, honey. It's me.

She picks up.

Thank you, Saint Yoda.

But has she?

I don't hear anything but breathing. And the back-up beeps from an early morning delivery truck.

But then, in a cautious mutter, "Agent...Degas?"

I can't help a small giggle. "Present and accounted for, Agent Lautrec."

"Oh, thank God," Drue spurts. "I honestly didn't know whether..." She huffs, and I hear the frantic clack of her window blinds. "Actually, I'm still not sure if he isn't..." She exhales, underlining the sound with relief. "Okay, he seems to have finally gone home."

"Who?" I charge. "Ohhh, *wait*. Don't tell me you finally got Cy the Security Guy to notice your sweet-sweet girl parts?"

"You're kidding, right?" she retorts entirely too quickly. "Because I'm fairly sure *Cy* stands for *Cyborg* by now. But that's digressing, and we seriously can't afford that."

"Are you telling me something I don't want to hear, missy?" My teasing tone hardly masks my rising tension. The truth my own instinct is confirming, deep in the pit of my gut. "About our friend Dick Gorgeous?"

"Who, I must say, is just as pretty in his stake-out civvies as his just-the-facts-ma'am suit."

"Oh, no." I twist the phone cord around a finger and jiggle my leg until I've burned off triple-digit calories. "So . . . he knows you're *you*?"

D pops her lips with definition. "It would definitely seem that way."

I groan softly. "Does that mean he's got someone casing my place too? And what about Max and Allie's apartment?"

"They're good so far," she supplies. "And you too, girlie."

"Which you're so sure of . . . why?"

"I went and looked."

"Excuse the hell out of me? And what'd you do on the way out of your building? Toss a flash bomb at Mr. Sexy In His Civvies?"

My stunned glower invades my words. A diabolical chuckle peppers hers.

"Remember that horror movie I worked on a few months back? With that kid director who's going to be the next Kurosawa?"

"Oh, shit." I trade out the glower for a shudder. "The one with the zombie babies who morph into cats at night?"

"*Baby Kitty*," she fills in. "Well, they let me sneak out with one of the props. I've been keeping it up in my closet for a special occasion. I got it out and put it into a sling that I made out of an old bedsheet. I got into one of my boho dresses and some huge shades. Our dickster friend was none the wiser."

I give up a soft snort. "I seriously can't decide whether to be really impressed or really scared."

"Come on, girl. You know I always have a plan and even a plan B."

"Oh yeah, I do. But right now, it's just good to hear it out loud."

"Why?"

"Because... funny that you mention being handy with plan Bs..."

I'm done with the not-so-subtle hint, but her silence stretches on. Thankfully, not for too long.

"Ermmm... little Tigger, are you trying to say you boinged on something other than your bouncy flouncy tail last night?"

I duck my head. "More like ... something else boinged on me."

"And you need a morning-after kit for it now?" she punches in a perplexed huff. "What about the other night? Weren't there naughty shenanigans after the Duke of Deliciousness first touched down?"

"Shenanigans, yes. But boinging, no."

"But there was boinging last night. And things got out of hand."

"More like out of this world. Which does *not* excuse the irresponsible choices."

"Hey. Update, baby. You're a human being, not a cartoon tiger. I understand. And, in light of how *le duke* keeps lighting *you* up, I'll toss in some precautionary foil packets. Do you have a preference? Warming? Lubed? Glow in the dark? Double ribbed, *for her pleasure*?"

Her announcer voice emphasis on the old marketing line

has me giggling. Leave it to Drue to ease my qualms without even knowing she is. "Basic is fine," I answer quickly. "Because if there's any more pleasure added to this equation, you may be cleaning my guts off the walls around here."

"Ew. And *damn*," she drawls. "That good? Seriously?"

"Let's just say you should be calling the man king instead of duke."

"And crank up that boy's arrogant knob that much more? I do *not* think so."

"You're kidding me, right? Little D Train, I have never *ever* known a female who craves alpha-boy arrogance more than you."

"Which has gotten me where, exactly—other than facing my thirties with an apartment for one and a nickname based on a cartoon donkey, that's where."

"*Hey*. It's not that shitty, okay?"

"And there's my bouncy flouncy girl, right on schedule."

I shoot out a teasing *grrr* before soldiering on. "Look at the bright side. At least you're not calling your best friend at the butt-crack of dawn and asking her to make the drug store walk of shame for you."

"Don't forget the delivering-across-town part. Especially because I may need to take a boat. Hey! If I look distressed enough, you think a group of hottie sailors will appear in their nifty Zodiac and give me a ride?"

Can't help repeating my snort. "You realize most of those dudes take showers of arrogance every day, yes?"

"Then it *is* perfect weather for a little outing, yeah?" There's rustling from her end, making me believe she's stabbing her legs into blue jeans. "I'll be there in a bit. Meet me in the little den off the lobby. It has a door that leads to the alley behind the inn. You need me to get any other essentials while I'm at it?"

"I'm scared to consider what you think of as essential, but yes. And if it's not too much trouble, a couple dozen soup dumplings from that twenty-four-hour place around the corner from you?"

"Oh, damn. I must say, for a girl who's just had her mind blown by His Majesty of Sexual Prowess, you're on point with the order-in game."

"And *you're* on point with the best-friend game." I work as hard as I can to hug her with every syllable. "Honestly, D. What would I do without you?"

"*Pffft.*" She sees my pretend hug and raises it by a vocal shrug. "*You're* doing *me* the favor. We got word this morning that the shoot is likely to be delayed even longer since the storm has stalled. After it scoots, we have to wait for everything in the park to dry up. Dripping leaves really fuck with the mics."

"So that means Bastien and I can stay put here for a bit?" I twine the cord around my finger hard enough to turn the tip white. "I mean, I hate to even ask . . . and if it's not okay, I underst—"

"No. It's cool," she interjects. "Even gave me an excuse to text Cy because he's been popping over there to check in on the equipment in the room we're using for storage. I didn't tell him the entire truth, of course, but he knows you're there. He thinks you're hiding out from your crazy ex and that Bastien's your brother."

"Oh God." I groan-laugh. "Yeah, that'd probably make things easier, right?"

I wish it was equally easy to ignore the dread that lingers in my gut after D gives a chuckling goodbye. The apprehension that continues well after I find the den and settle in to wait on my friend. Staring out at the rain, even through the stained glass of the inn's back door, doesn't bring as much peace as I expected it would.

Because no matter how I project the days ahead, I'm screwed.

If Logan really decides we're the new bone in his persistent doggy maw, I have to figure out the logistics of where to hide Bastien next. But if the detective moves on to more interesting horizons, we'll be able to freely make our way back to Max and Allie's place—and the portal that will take Bastien back to where he clearly belongs. The time where he doesn't have to worry about being mauled for simply walking through doors and tossed off busses for being a decent human being. Where he can get a head start on escaping the Jacobins and relocate to some quaint German village with Magique.

A village I can practically see.

The church steeple. The rustic Bavarian buildings. The sparkling river running beneath stone bridges . . .

And can smell.

The dahlias along the river. Freshly baked brötchen *and* brezels. *The new grass in the nearby meadow.*

And can hear.

Carts rumbling on the cobblestones. Geese on the river. Children in that glorious meadow.

Our *children . . .*

I jolt to my feet. Violently shake my head. "No. You've had too much stress and too little sleep. Just *no*, Raegan."

But as I fight to resettle my thoughts and form new plans, I wonder why a world without Bastien De Leon already feels like an awful, foreign place. And how I'll ever look at this city, or this century, as home, ever again.

CHAPTER TWELVE

BASTIEN

When the Almighty was molding Maximillian and me, then arrived at the moment to mix patience into the clay, somebody bumped his arm. My brother ended up with the lion's share of the virtue, while the sprinkling that got into me is usually reserved for long nights on patrol or longer days at court.

I am fairly certain neither of those conditions apply now.

Which means I feel no compunction about casting another long glare at the digital timepiece on the table beside the bed and deciding that Raegan Tavish has used up her reasonable allotment of *won't take me long*.

By the time the clock flashes another minute gone by, I have re-donned my breeches. My well of patience is approaching parched.

I march across the room, carefully pull open the door to the hallway, and peer down the corridor.

No sign of her in the mixture of watery light and shadow that leads back to the main entrance of the inn. I also do not hear her, though the place is not at a loss for noise. Every hard surface outside, which is essentially *every* surface outside, turns into a percussive instrument played with ruthless glee by the steady rain.

For a moment, I give in to something besides impatience.

A strange sadness on behalf of the denizens of this metropolis. Many—most?—of them will never know that rain can be an enchanting whisper as well as a raucous din. Across meadows and forests and rivers, storms are the most fascinating symphony of all.

And that is more than enough of *that.*

Where is she?

I am not rankled for myself. This is an unpredictable town, filled with cutthroats, ride grubs, and other seedy ne'er-do-wells. And Raegan, even in all her wit and wisdom, still looks at many of them as if taking their stink for a nosegay.

What if she is doing just that, this very moment?

In spite of the mortifying thought, I proceed with calm steps. Before rounding the corner into the main receiving room, I pause for a cautious moment.

But still no sight of her.

I grit my teeth. And admit, if only to myself, that perhaps I *am* nervous for myself too.

But thank fuck, only for half a moment.

"...had too much stress and too little sleep. Just *no,* Raegan."

Relief tramples me so soundly that I do not detect the stress in her voice at first. When that finally registers, I do not hesitate about striding across the lobby and into the small room beyond.

"Just no to what, *Rayonnement?*"

She startles as if my words are ignited gunpowder packs. "Bastien. What the hell are you doing?"

I roll my shoulders back. "Worrying about you." Relaxing my scowl is not as easy. "Or so I *was.* Evidently, the effort was a waste."

Her features vacillate between soft humility and more of that inexplicable tension. The latter takes over her response.

"I told you I'd be back soon. Drue's on her way with the dumplings and some other provisions we might need."

"Provisions?" I crowd my brows tighter into each other. "For what?"

"For settling in here, at least for a couple more days. D spotted Logan on hardcore surveillance duty at her place."

"*Mierde.*"

"Close enough to what I said. But a silver lining in all these clouds? We don't have to pull up stakes from here until Wednesday or Thursday. That clears some space to consider next moves if necessary. And right now, I think we have to plan on that being *really* necessary."

I am tempted to repeat my profanity, but how would that help her in any way?

"Can Drue help out in that regard as well? And what about contacting my brother? You said he is happy with your friend and successful too? Unless there is a reason for him to be ashamed of me now, I think he will be happy to see me and—"

Her laugh is so high and shrill, I almost think an alarmed bird has gotten inside the building. "Oh, he'll be happy, all right. But right now, he and Allie aren't a viable option for assistance. Even if we did reach out to them in Italy, they wouldn't be able to return until—"

"Next month at best, certainly." I nod, hoping she takes assurance from the commiseration, but wonder why it escalates into her full smirk. I am absolutely not complaining about her adorable expression but push aside my perplexity to push on. "So what additional resources do we have to explore?

And how can I help with the efforts?"

I expect to say farewell to her fleeting smile, but to my pleasure it hitches up by another degree. "You really *are* ready to help, aren't you?" Her gaze turns the color of lush ferns as she runs a hand up and across my shoulder. "Even if I said we had to go out and face a whole battalion of the NYPD with nothing but our bare hands—"

"Oh, *yes* please."

This time, I am ready for her reaction. The light laugh is like church bells. If it were truly so, I would have been more eager to attend services in my youth.

All too quickly, the sound ebbs into some impish quirks at her lips. "Oh hell," she mutters. "I'm in such trouble."

"*Pourquoi, Rayonnement?*" I splay my hands to her hips. "Why?"

"Because now you're making my head swim *without* all the poetry."

I frown anew. "Swimming heads are not usually good."

A playful swat to my chest. "Depends on how you look at it, Desperado."

"I prefer to keep looking at you," I insist. "Though I do see a very tired woman."

"Worth it. Take my word on that, okay?"

I am not so willing to surrender my concern to humor. "Allow me to wait here for Drue. You can go back to the room and rest for—"

"No!" Imaginary fireworks seem to blind her. She blinks at them rapidly before rushing on. "I . . . I mean thank you but no. Who knows where Logan has eyes in the city, and you're rocking the wild Pompeii vibes even more right now. *Not* that I want you to clean up anytime soon,"

Her new quip comes just as she slides her touch across my nipple. A hiss escapes me from the moment she scrapes the tip with her thumbnail. The preening grin on her lips has me tucking closer against her.

"Well," I finally husk. "If this is what my dirt earns me, I shall wallow in a bog forever."

"Hmm. While I definitely approve, I'm not sure our hosts here will go for it. So after we grab some sustenance, maybe I can introduce you to a fun practice of our time called a shag shower."

I am uncertain what has me hardening the quickest. The odd suggestiveness of her term or the silky tone in which she invokes it. "Just *how* soon will Drue be here?"

More church bell laughter from her, which blooms warmth to the middle of my chest. For a moment, I forget every one of the battle scars across it, as well as the rest of my body. Bathed in Raegan's lush gaze, the dark marks cease to be reminders of the violence that has ruled a good portion of my existence. When she studies me, I feel like a warrior who has survived. Even more, a hero who has conquered. At this moment, I might even believe it. I have vanquished time itself.

But not without her.

Before the certainty can solidify in my spirit, there is a loud rattle at the room's stained-glass door. A moment later, Drusilla Kidman appears in the portal, though I only recognize her because of her long aqua braid. Everything else about her aspect is astonishingly different from the woman I met yesterday, down to the strange semblance of an infant peeking from the sling across her chest.

"Greetings from the soggy tundra. Your life-bringer is here."

"Truth. One billion percent." Raegan's tone is thick with gratitude. "I can smell the dumplings already. The gossip mags too. My God, D. How am I ever going to repay you?"

The woman grins so cockily, I am jarred again—but pleasantly. The freedoms enjoyed by females of this time are quite satisfying to observe. Hopefully, I shall soon be adding *shag showers* to my roster, as well.

"Hmmm." Drue drawls while exchanging an affectionate hug with my *rayonnement*. "How about a weekend of true crime bingeing in my girl cave? You can supply the endless carbs and sugar."

Raegan chuckles. "I had to ask."

"You so totally did." But Drue's quip seems threaded with new solemnity as she delivers one more parcel to Raegan. The small item, concealed in a plain white paper bag, has Raegan visibly stiffening. Why? "If you need anything else, you know where to shout, right?"

"Yes ma'am," Raegan murmurs with a strange overtone of affection. At once, I am even more suspicious—but chastise myself for it. *I* have upended *her* world, not the other way around.

But I cannot shake my nagging paranoia. The instincts from a brain that I cannot stop now, with threads spun into dark plots and hunches grown into full qualms. Perhaps that makes me no better than Logan, but Raegan does naught to calm me as she takes all the bags into our room's little kitchen and starts unloading their contents.

"Looks like D found us both a few more shirts. She's officially pumped a few more dollars into every New York stereotype there is, but we'll have some clean stuff to wear. No bottoms, though—but since she also found condoms, I think we can figure out a few ways to amuse ourselves after I hand wash those. Yay for drip-dry time, *oui*?"

"Raegan." I wait until she stops for longer than half a second, hoping to dam her babbling brook with the firm log of my tone.

"Ohhh. She found Peanut Butter Boulders! With choco-twigs! Buddy, you haven't lived until you've had the sugar rush from this stuff. Best cereal *ever*."

"Raegan."

More logs. But her brook is now a rambling river.

"There's extra cheesy pasta swirls too. Fortunately, these are cook-in-the-cup, so we can nuke them in the microwave. And hot cocoa for afterward! With rainbow marshmallows!"

"*Raegan*."

At last, she jerks to a halt—but not without adding an obvious huff. "Sweet panic at the disco, Desperado. I'm just as hungry as you are, okay? Just wanted to get some of this put away first."

I step over from my watchful location against the wall, spreading my hand to the counter while leaning fully into her personal space. "Including the small package Drue slipped to you, not intending for me to acknowledge?"

Her whole form goes still. "Sometimes women just have shit they need to handle." She angles her head, nailing me with the force of her pursed lips and flared gaze. "You know ... *female concerns*. Now come on, let's eat."

I push off, letting her think she has triumphed by appealing to my stomach over my sensitivities. But now is a moment in which she could learn from her two-hundred-years-removed duplicate. As soon as I requested—well, decreed—to Magique that she would be my woman exclusively, she informed—well, decreed in return—that I would have to be privy to her *female concerns*. Ohhh *oui, all* of them.

But for now, I will let the woman be at ease. A self-woven web is often the easiest to be trapped in.

Very quickly, I learn of some additional advantages to the decision.

Not the least of those is the pleasure, complete and altogether carnal, of watching Raegan Tavish enjoy her food. Not just any food. As she soon demonstrates, soup dumplings, also called *bao*, are apparently among the most heavenly of foods.

The plump dough pouches contain a savory broth that is rich with chunks of pork and vegetables. But better than eating them myself is the experience of learning how, my eyes unblinking as she bites off the nubby peak and then sucks away at the juicy filling.

"*Mon dieu.*" The exclamation erupts from me in a choke while she prepares to slurp at her third dough ball.

Her eyes dance at me over the edges of the sticks in which she expertly holds it.

"He's not going to help fill your belly, Desperado. And I'm definitely not going to finish all these by myself. It's okay to use your fingers if the chopsticks feel weird."

I narrow my gaze for a telling look. "And you do enjoy it when I use my fingers."

She giggles around her new bite. "Indeed, I do."

"As well as . . . my other body parts."

The impish lights in her eyes continue to sparkle, but her reaction does not get close to the looser mien upon which I was counting. I have no opening to pursue the subject of her secret delivery from Drue—and nor does she plan on affording one.

Damn it.

Before I can shift to another approach, Raegan pushes to her feet and turns toward the sink. Not all the way. I can study her profile, even as she bends over to rinse off her plate.

"More for you," she says with a forced breeze. "Guess I'm not as hungry as I thought."

I tamp down a smirk. Why was I worried about a new opening? The woman herself has all but served it up with perfect garnishes.

"Is that why you look so tempted to empty your stomach into that basin?"

She whips her head up. "Would you seriously stop? I am perfectly fine."

"And I am the king of fucking England."

She pivots around. Her hands brace to the edge of the sink, poised as if to help her lunge forward any second. "Why have you suddenly decided I'm the enemy here?"

I arch one brow. "Because I am concerned about your health, *ma chérie?*"

"Because you're watching every move I make." Her knuckles get even whiter against the counter. "Honestly, what's with the Bond-level antics now?"

I listen to intuition, holding my reply until another break ticks by. "And *honestly* . . . what was in the small parcel that Drue snuck to you?"

"Not a bomb or a gun, if that's what you're getting at." She sniffs when I give her no rise for the quip. "And as I already told you—"

"*Oui.* I know. *Female things.*" I push away the food container, clearing room to spread my elbows on the small dining table. "Regrettably, that is not an answer to my satisfaction, *Rayonnement*. You see, I am the man privileged enough to have enjoyed your *female things* most recently. And the man who would also be honored to delight in them again. But if, in my passion, I have caused you pain or injury—"

"*Unnnhhhh.*" Her outburst is small but significant. Her head falls between her shoulders. "Okay, I should've known you'd go there. And I'm sorry for calling you out about it." When she looks back up, her features have softened again. "I really *am* fine. You have my word. Takes more than some epic love bites and mind-bending orgasms to break me, buddy."

"I am relieved to hear that." I rise as well. "But it also takes more than a sweet smile to deter me from my ultimate purpose. You have been tense and conflicted since the moment Drue gave you that white paper package. Was it truly for feminine needs, or is there something troubling that you are keeping to yourself? Are there new developments about Logan and his activities?"

"No!" Her urgency rises in proportion to mine. "I mean that, okay? As soon as I get the latest on that front, you'll get it too."

I smooth the air with my hands, assuring her I believe that. But at the same time, I prod, "So what is really going on here? And why is it causing your spirit such contention?" From the moment I observe how hard I have struck her target, I move back around the table to re-approach her. "Your intimate tissues . . . are they tender or sensitive? Or is it time for your courses? It is naught to be discouraged or embarrassed about. I can certainly be . . . more creative about things."

But the desirous dip in my tone does not comfort her.

"*Gah!*" she blurts, wrenching to the side as I approach. She crisscrosses her arms until gripping her opposite shoulders and visibly shivering. "Please, Bastien. *Please*. Can't you just drop it? You … this … Being so *nice* isn't helping shit at all, okay?"

"Ah." It is the verbal version of how I brutally halt myself. "Well, then. My humble apologies for annoying you with my *nice,* Mademoiselle Tavish. But perhaps if I had some explanation to be *less* nice—"

"Seriously?" She whips back around. "Oh, that's such a mature recipe to follow. Hold on, I've got to make sure I post all this. Hashtag *wokeandwonderfulguy.* How does that one work for you?"

"What works for me is helping *you.* If hashing is required for that, then give me a sharp knife and point me to the sideboard. But love of Christ, let me into the kitchen first. To me, *that* is a mature recipe."

She opens her mouth as if a ready rebuttal is already there, but not a sound spills out. She remains there, her back against the wall, visibly raw but tough—just like a sideboard full of uncut vegetables. I am just as stoic now. Out of ideas about wrestling her for the big blade. I cannot help without knowing where to dig it in first.

Our impasse continues, silent and inelegant. I have nearly resigned myself to walking away without expiation when she inhales and then exhales with ponderous intent. Her arms fall to her sides. She flattens them to the wall.

"I'm … sorry," she mutters. "And I promise that's sincere. I'm just facing a dilemma that's new for me. There are lots of weird feelings because of it. But if anyone has a right to know about it, that'd be you."

"Me? Why?" I let my own hands drop, though it is impossible to keep them idle. With measured purpose, I flex my fingers in and out. "To know about what?"

At once, my flexings are not so steady and slow. It is not comfortable to witness the creep of tighter tension along her slim shoulders.

"Drue went to get me...a morning-after pill. That's what's in the white bag."

I honor her sincerity with my own. Admittedly, my confusion is not difficult to summon. "Assume I am from the eighteenth century and know naught of what you speak of. A pill? You mean for medicinal purposes? The morning after what?"

She straightens her stance. Visibly pulls in another breath. "After having...relations...with a man and not taking precautions about it."

My hands go limp. I start to regret my persistence. More than I want to.

"And this pill is a precaution...after the fact?"

"In basic terms, yes."

"So it terminates anything that has begun to live inside you?"

"*No.*" She is flustered again, her face in conflict. And damn it, I have never been happier to observe the emotions. "I mean, not usually."

"Not *usually*? What about the *un*usual times, then?"

"Don't you think that this—*us*, whatever the hell this is— checks enough of the boxes for *unusual* already?" She lifts her arms and splays her fingers. "Eventually, we'll get you back to the wardrobe. Do you really want to be climbing back inside that thing, wondering if you've left a child behind? Or technically...ahead. *Shit.* Where's the user's manual when a girl needs one?"

Only now do I realize that I have stomped sweaty footprints onto the floor between the kitchen and front window. I halt them with a pair of loud squeaks and make more noise when pivoting back around. My posture is already rigid. I impale the woman with a strict thrust of my glower. "Do you think, for even a moment, that I would crawl back into that cabinet if there is an inkling you are with child?"

As soon as I finish, I nod with satisfaction. That should be fucking enough of *that*. End of discussion.

But it is the end of nothing.

Raegan's chest pumps with agitated air. Her nostrils flare.

"Let's go again with that whole guy-who-knows-nothing-about-this-century theory," she snaps. "Because in this case, it's a good one. Because in *this* day and age, even if we *can* skirt the rules of your gypsy friend's spell, this is a lose-lose proposition."

Thankfully, I am already stopped in my tracks. Still, I sway as if she has flung open a window and let the rain pummel me.

"My gypsy fr—" More figurative rain now, drenching my mind in icy sheets of. "Are you referring to . . . Kavia?" I narrow my stare. "How do you know that about her, *Rayonnement*?"

That detail that *nobody* in our family ever speaks of . . . inside or out of Château De Leon . . .

As more wild conjectures daunt my mind, the woman slams hands to the graceful curves of her hips. "You remember the part about us figuring out how Max got here? And then stayed without becoming two-hundred-year-old ashes?"

"*Oui.*" I mean to state it but barely croak it. The conjectures have turned fiercer than I think. "*Mon dieu.*"

Fiercer . . . to the point of agony. Clear, sharp, shards of it all.

I have cheated the universe. Fucked over history. Eviscerated fate itself.

By the laws of time, I should be naught but a pile of bone and dust in the De Leon family crypt now. To avoid that, providence has certainly demanded a specific tariff.

A price attached to a gypsy spell.

Kavia's gypsy spell.

The toll that she never had time to impart. The instructions I still have not heard.

I scrub a hand down my face as the realization sinks in. As my memory fills with the last few moments that I saw Kavia and Carl, cut short because the revolutionaries were closing in on our hiding space.

Good. Very good, my boy! Now there is only one more thing to remember...

"I never heard it." My admission is barely a rasp on the thick air. "The conditions of the spell," I explain. "Kavia never had the chance to tell me. There was a mob. They were after my life—"

"You don't say."

Her comment brings some needed levity, as well as a moment to catch my breath. Revision: to snap up whatever air my lungs will allow in. They are as constrained as the rest of me, braced in agonized battle against the memories that keep tumbling on me. But I accept the paltry oxygen as a blessing. It helps me to blurt out the rest.

"They wanted to kill me. But instead, they slayed Magique."

RAEGAN

"Wh-What?"

I'm shocked I'm able to get that much out. As my mind absorbs the truth of his confession, it surrenders its hold on other parts of reality. The room is rotating. My head spins in the other direction.

They slayed Magique.

What the hell do I do with that?

Bastien loves her. And he's supposed to get back to the mystical-magical wardrobe, hop back in, and return to her. Then he'll still be alive, and I'll be back to normal. That was the reason for making Drue go out in the storm, right? The reason I talked myself out of the ridiculous baby-mama fantasy. Normal is good.

Okay, so it's ... fine.

But *fine* works too. It's workable. Predictable. A stable safety net, giving me freedom to get back to work and create for my clients. The work I love, despite the insecurity that's been a tiny roadblock lately. But just a small one. It'll pass ...

So why haven't you taken the pill yet?

Why are you letting the minutes race by, closing the window on when that medicine is going to be effective?

Why are you so determined to watch that bridge burn?

I step back, needing a second to regroup here. Maybe more than one. More like a thousand.

After I scoop up at least sixty, letting a minute pass, Bastien speaks again.

"It is true. She was in my arms when she went to the angels—with her own brother's dagger buried in her chest. A dagger he meant to plunge into *me*."

And there go all the rest of my seconds.

Along with all my air.

The breaths that his words snatch from the space beneath my scar.

I curl a hand into that space, as if that's enough to calm the agonized pulses against the jagged line of marred skin. The ragged heartbeats that I still have but Magique does not.

Magique. The woman he truly loves. I am so sure of it, even now. *Especially* now. The grief in his words as he speaks. The agony that creases the corners of his eyes and compresses his mouth. And consumes his broken heart . . .

I know it because mine cracks too. Not in the way of sympathy or empathy. In the way of *feeling* this stuff, like I did last month when things fell apart with Justin.

Only a billion times worse.

It's searing and shattering. I feel like I'm bursting, in none of the good ways. I can't breathe and sure as hell can't see. I grab the back of a chair, intending to plummet into it, but I stumble until falling against Bastien again. Nearly *onto* him.

Yearning to crawl *inside* of him.

But I can't do that either. Never again, no matter how right it feels to think about it.

So what now?

I don't know.

I don't know.

I'm so desperate about it, the words tumble from me aloud.

"*Je ne sais pas. Je ne sais pas.*"

And the room is careening harder.

My senses are screaming louder.

I shove at Bastien's chest. As I stumble back, I tear at my

head with both hands. It's not enough. The action confirms that my skull is still intact, but my mind isn't.

What's happening? What the hell *is happ—*

"Raegan?" Bastien isn't helping either. His gentle tone and brushed bronze gaze are like silk sheets after I've only slept two hours. I long to melt back into him. But...no. *No!* "*Ma magnifique.* It is all right. I do not know either. Perhaps we can fathom it through together?"

The question is a luxurious comforter on top of the sheets. But I shake my head, forcing myself to resist. *Needing* to. "*Je ne sais pas.*" Especially when nothing but that spills out. "*Je suis désolée, Bastien!*" And then that.

I have to get out of here. And then I have to run.

But where?

I can't risk being seen anywhere in the city. But I *know* I can't stay in this room any longer, with this man and his world invading more and more of my thoughts. My senses. My emotions.

And dear God...my *memories?*

I rush across the room. When I'm at the door, I yank at the knob. When I'm on the other side, alone in the hallway, I still don't feel any better. My thoughts are racing. My body fights my mental urges for calm. I'm thankful for D's reassurance that nobody else is staying at the Greene. At least I don't have to stress about faking nice to someone on their way back to their room.

A jolt of energy pulls me around as the pretend lightbulb flashes in my brain.

The other rooms...

They're all unoccupied.

Five of them, if I remember correctly from Drue's

rundown yesterday—holy shit, was it only yesterday?—and all fully paid for another nine days. If I'm calculating correctly, two out of the five must be upstairs. That means I can try my luck at the other three.

The first two, located off the same narrow hallway as the room that Bastien and I were given, yield no joy. Secured snug and tight, without a chance of hairpinning the locks loose.

My determination pays off on the third door.

I walk right into the room, which is clearly a catch-all holding space for extras and crew. The disassembled bed parts are stored flat against one wall. Instead, two portable banquet tables are set up and surrounded by more chairs than they should really accommodate. A few used coffee cups and soda cans have been left behind, along with some jackets and aluminum water bottles.

But my eyes latch on to the best discard of all. In this moment, my ultimate treasure.

A cheap doodle pad and a cup of dull pencils.

It's not the bells and whistles of my electronic design program, but maybe that's a secret blessing too. Now is *not* for normal. The cosmos have made their point, loud and clear.

Maybe now is also a time for embracing that—but in the same stroke, forgetting it too.

From the moment I sit down, pushing back a page of hangman rounds to begin the image that takes life in my mind, I'm also celebrating it.

CHAPTER THIRTEEN

BASTIEN

It is agonizing to let her go, but I push through the pain and set her free. This time, due to no small miracle, I keep my impatience in check, as well.

Or perhaps there is no miracle at all. Maybe it is a simple lesson called *understanding*.

My poor *Rayonnement*. All the elements that struck her at once in here . . . would that I did not commiserate with every one of them, but I did. With cruel clarity. The sort a person can only have from recent experience. I know what it is like to be so stunned, only a dazed fugue is possible for relating to the world. Of forming sentences one painful word at a time. When even that fails, of withdrawing into safer places inside one's spirit. But even then, not finding the familiar fallback— and deciding to run.

And being given the freedom for that flight.

She gave me that gift yesterday, so I compel myself to return the favor today. She has left behind her phone device, so I know she will not go far. Or perhaps that is a desperate wish, since I doubt my tracking abilities will be of use in a forest of concrete and glass. Or my talents for hunting, fighting, and falconry.

I do congratulate myself for determining that the little

box labeled *TV Remote* has something to do with the shiny monstrosity crafted by the artist named *Sony*. This modern wonder serves to gobble up the next three hours of my existence, as I discover that foam packing pods are useful in city rooftop gardens, the Knicks shall be playing the Nets tonight and are favored to win, and someone on *The View* is making a great deal of other people upset and they have gathered on a net to express it together.

But out of all that, I am most fascinated with a selection that features dazzling minstrel performances called *Big Apple Spectaculars*. I am puzzled about the title, since no apples of any size are in the scenes, but the pageantry of the presentations has me overlooking the omission in favor of an awestruck stare—especially since several of the musical stories are said to be set in Paris.

But if the set pieces are to be believed, the city has grown into more than anything I dreamed. Paris, not Versailles, is now heralded as a global icon, with a soaring opera house, a grand golden tower, a mysterious phantom, and courtesans more elaborate than Louis's palais beauties. Those courtesans do a dance called the cancan, and I wonder if my pupils separate from my eyes while watching it.

Thankfully, I recall Raegan's lesson from yesterday, about the signal lights on the streets. *Green for go* led me to activate the Sony, and I am relieved when *red for stop* yields the same results before I am ogling those frilly derrieres like the full-blooded caveman I am beneath my gentleman's breeches.

If I am going to indulge that side of myself, it will *not* be with Monsieur Sony and friends. As marvelous as it all is, nothing on that palette is real. Here and now, I need as much reality as possible.

As I step out into the hall, I only hope that reality is ready again for me.

Everything out here sounds exactly like it did before. Naught but the plunking rain and whistling wind fill my ears. There is no significant movement from the small vestibule at the other end of the corridor. The shadows are a little longer, since the day is shifting from afternoon to evening, but the storm eliminates all other modes of determining that.

Still, I am glad for the gloom. Raegan was not a joyous puddle stomper in the torrents yesterday, which gives me hope that she has avoided a repeat stomp today. All my instincts hail the validity of the thought before I notice the leak of golden light from a doorframe at the end of the hall.

As I watch, the light flickers. Movement in the room. From something or some*one*?

I am willing to gamble on the latter.

As I approach, a smile grows on my lips. The door has a small steel lever attached, which is flipped around to hold the portal slightly ajar. My lips lift higher once I push into the room and inhale the sweetness of herb-infused violets.

The scent of my heart's home.

Oui, even the one from two hundred years ago.

But I already know to keep that to myself. Raegan's frenetic aura dictates the boundary, even from the little seating area across the room. She does not look up, too focused on whatever she sketches on the paper sheets in her lap. Between her swift strokes, she jostles one knee and then the next. Clearly, her mind is seeking answers just as mine was yesterday. I am simply grateful she ran down a hall to sort things out instead of tearing across the city again.

Yet as I also learned yesterday, *sorting things out* is not as simple as those syllables.

Another temporary blockage of the light, which comes as she rises with her sizable sheaf of papers. Fortunately, they look to be bound at the top in some manner. She tucks the pad against her left elbow as the pencil in her right gets pressed back into service as she begins a circuit of tense pacing. I do not want to admit that the stress makes her even more beautiful, but that is like denying my very humanity. It is almost like watching a dance number from one of *Big Apple Spectacular*'s hip-hop musicals.

Sketch-sketch-one-two-three-four.

Sketch-sketch-five-six-seven-eight.

"Raegan?"

She does not answer my hail. I am not thrown. In many ways, I understand. Before I spotted the consulate, a fly on my arm would have spooked me—and several times did. The disjointed terror was what kept me running. Anything to keep up the hope that I would eventually escape.

Sketch-sketch. It is her own version of running.

"Raegan."

"What?" *Stumble-stumble.* "Huh?"

"Ssshhh." I can extend a hand, soothing her from afar, when she whips around with a startled gawk. "It is only me." I long to toss aside the haphazard tables and chairs just to be near her again. I have to settle for dropping into one of the faded chairs next to window since she quickly reclaims her place in the other.

"I'm sorry," she rasps, pressing several fingers to her forehead. They are littered with pencil smudges, which helps her create a cute gray bridge between her tawny brows. "I needed to put my head back on straight. In the process, I guess

I found some inspiration. Once the fever hits, I give in and get lost, especially when it hasn't happened for a while."

I lean over, sneaking a glance at the first drawing of the sizable stack she has formed the round table between the chairs. "Well, inspiration has been good to you. Magnificent gowns, dreamt by a *femme magnifique* herself."

And more modest, at least in sketch form, than what the designers for the cancan girls imagined. *Oui,* I see the generous cleavage, but breasts are...meant to be there. Natural and exquisite parts of feminine couture. Even a man of turbulent passions, such as myself, can and should contain his baser side at the sight of a bare nipple. Better yet, at two.

Raegan's laugh is light to the point of dismissive. "You're being kind," she scoffs. "I mean, obviously I've been influenced by a certain historical hunk in my world lately, with the split skirts and statement wigs, but these are just for messing around. Something nice for the concept files if a client wants something vintage-y and unique."

"*Concept* files?" I drop my bantering side, glauming a hard frown. "Why would your clients not want you to execute on these in full? Obviously you have a skilled eye for dramatic impact. And I know naught of intricate fashion construction, but the details in these suggest that also possess that."

The splotch bridge breaks apart as she tosses back an amused spurt. "Much easier said than done in the twenty-first century, mister. Thanks to your people in particular, fashion is a high-prestige industry that takes connections, clout, and a shit ton of pixie dust." She leans her cheek against a hand, causing her curls to tumble over her neck and shoulder. "I've got lots of number one and even a little of two, but the fashion fairies have been mighty stingy with the magic dust. So, for now, I've to get on with the styling gig."

I set aside her sketches but do not waver my gaze from her gorgeous face. "Which entails doing what?"

"Working with celebrities and other notables as an advisor, of sorts. Making sure the current and upcoming trends work for their figure and brand, in the context of whatever big occasion will help them break the internet."

I only grasp every third word of that part. Thankfully, it is enough to inform my reply. "So others employ you to tell them what *more* others are creating, rather than benefiting directly from your unique talent."

Her lips compress. "In about twenty pissy words, yes."

I hike my brows. "Is *pissy* now a word for *accurate*, as well?"

Thankfully, she abandons her brusqueness. I have not come searching for another imbroglio with her, but my vexation is too real to hide. *Very* thankfully, she seems to see that too. Moreover, she also seems . . . stirred by it.

"Do you really think these are that good?"

She scoops up the stack and ruffles through them. I am delighted about the new consideration in her gaze, as if she too is beholding her handiwork in a new light. My chest puffs a little higher. *I* put that look on her face and am damn proud of the fact.

"It's been a while since I hit a jag like this," she confesses quietly. "After a while, when you start telling yourself you're irrelevant so many times, you just start believing it. It gets easier to ignore the inspiration because you doubt that too. You just doubt . . . all of yourself."

She slides the stack back to the table but does not yet surrender her reverent touch. Looking there, at her slender fingers with their functional oval nails decorated in green and gold swirls, I am awash in a wave of new awareness. An unignorable need to lean for her. To wrap those fingers with my own.

"And now, you have stopped doubting."

Raegan lifts her head. The motion is like the moisture in her eyes. Misty but meaningful.

"Yeah. I really have."

I draw in a breath. It hurts. I have never savored such perfect pain in my life. "What made it stop?"

Her grip tightens in mine. "You."

RAEGAN

And here I go again.

Letting the truth tumble out of me before contemplating what it'll actually mean. About the effect it's going to have on everyone around me.

This case, in which *everyone* equates to just *this* one, is no different.

Because he's the *only* one who shouldn't be hearing confessions like this from me. Not when there are other things I had prepared to tell him. More vital things.

Well, one thing in particular.

Using my hands to sketch always frees my mind for strategic thoughts. To show for it this time, I have a theory about getting him back to Magique—a living, breathing version of her—but also ensuring the two of them will escape the Jacobins' crosshairs. It all hit me sometime between my second and third sketches, but now it's like my creativity damn got busted open.

My flair is definitely back. My confidence.

Best of all, I don't worry about Bastien seeing it all too. He actually seems to enjoy the wild and crazy view. The swirling, bouncing me. The imagination parade that used to drive Justin, and so many like him, so nuts. But like a moth to a hundred flames, I kept craving creative geniuses. Kept thinking they'd be the ones who got me the best.

But they all ran. And they all were fine that I blamed myself for it. They were scared of my light. Intimidated by it.

I do *not* intimidate Bastien De Leon.

I know it with thorough brilliance. With such awesome completion, I don't even have to ask him. But the man leans in as if I've done just that, already knowing how to halt all my misgivings.

He kisses me.

At the same time, he sweeps over me with his broad warrior's body. Before I can discern whether to gasp or groan, he drops on his knees in front of my chair. I decide on both. Good plan, since his hands plummet onto *my* knees—right before he pushes hard and spreads them wide.

Not. Intimidated.

And now, with the new plunge of his tongue, not taking any prisoners either.

He's just as voracious when continuing his kisses down the front of my throat, scraping my skin with his teeth until the neckline of his big T-shirt won't stretch any lower. By now, my moan is a frustrated growl. Half an inch more, and the man's magical lips could be in contact with my aching nipples. It's beyond time to make that happen . . .

But the moment I stretch back my hands to go for an over-the-head T-shirt strip, Bastien captures both my wrists between one of his. With another sweep, he pins them over my head, caught atop the chair cushion.

"No," he orders at last, the growl low and lethal in his throat. "No, *Rayonnement.* Sometimes it is better . . . without so much skin."

He debates his side with incredible effectiveness. The warmth of his mouth over my left nipple, aided in its spread by the abrasion of the cotton fabric, has me already crying out. The next second, I'm bucking against him. And God, it feels *good.* The wetness. The friction. The pulses that careen through me, not stopping until they curl my toes.

Yes. Oh yesss.

"Oh, my freaking *hell.*"

"Or heaven?" he teases, still tracing maddening circles around my thimble-hard nub.

"Speak for yourself," I grouse. "This is officially hell until you fill me up. *Please,* Bastien. Please, just do it this time. I stashed a rubber in my pocket. I don't remember which one, but it's there. *Please.*"

"Of course, *ma chérie.* Soon, I promise."

"Soon?" I retort. "Not good enough. Damn it!"

Here's the part where I inwardly shoot myself for celebrating the man's steel nerves. And matching self-control. His cock's already a ramrod beneath his fly, but he's as determined as a porn star to draw this all out. To keep caressing my breasts from atop the T-shirt. To free his other hand from my wrists so he can stroke in under the shirt's hem, tracing soft figure-eights along my ribcage. And at last, to tug my yoga pants all the way off . . . In the process, he somehow locates the condom.

"Is this what you are after, *ma magnifique?*"

I manage a grin. "Getting much warmer, Desperado." And then roll my hips. "But that's only half the prize. It's to help you with navigating the ... treasure map."

He angles back over me. His hooded stare is also a collection of bronze lights. "But I already have my treasure. And I thoroughly intend on reveling in the bounty."

"Oh, my word." I flourish it with a high sigh. Even arch my head back and bite my lip. I'm acting like a total porn princess, though I should be stifling a mortified snicker about his corny declaration.

But from him, it's not corny. It's silky and sexy and heartfelt ...

And hot.

Oh, my Technicolor tiger stripes, *so hot.*

Searing a path up the inside of my right thigh and then my left, his fingertip like a firestarter rod cranked on high.

Enflaming the quivering flesh between that leg and my core, his thumb a ruthless branding iron.

And then igniting me ... right *there.*

The start of the inferno that refuses to be doused. The first decadent shivers, preparing me for the perfect unraveling at my center. The throbs that begin so deep and then spread up and out, pushing against his knowing fingers ... and rushing to my parted lips.

"Bastien!" There's so much more I need to say but so many words that my mind won't supply. Not when my body is rapidly succumbing to his carnal control ... his ravishing mastery. "Monsieur le Duke. *Please ...*"

And that's what I have go with—but why not, since it's taking us in the right direction? At least I hope so. Oh damn it, how I pray so. We could be cleared to leave tomorrow, even tonight. Once we're on our way back to Max and Allie's, he'll never be mine again—though technically, he was never truly mine to begin with.

But oh, how I can pretend. At least for now.

Maybe that's wrong. At best, a gray area. Yeah, just like the pill I've conveniently *forgotten* to take so far, still in its white paper bag back in our room. If he's never been completely mine, why am I clinging to the one-in-a-million chance that part of him has taken root inside me? Is this fair to either of us?

Yet how—honestly, *how*—is it fair for the man to keep taunting me with his touch like this?

Taunting.

I can think of no better word as he rolls my trembling clit beneath his circling thumb. As he takes me perilously close to the edge of lust only to back off again. Making me moan and shiver and beg again. Mercilessly answering with that languorous timbre in his throat, thinning my patience to an agonizing nub.

"Hmmm," he murmurs with a wicked smile. "Such a tantalizing treasure, indeed."

I gasp again. Lurch my hips again. "It's much better if your cock gets involved. I promise."

"And *I* promise you shall have it, *belle chérie*. So very soon."

"Aghhh!" I spew. "Not soon enough! *Bâtard!*"

He's driving me so crazy, I don't have a free brain cell to stress over my new *laps de Français*. Fortunately, neither does he. His rumble escalates to a snarl. He's clearly contemplating even more parts of his primal side. *Good.* If this is our last time for naked fun, I long for it to be *fun*. Like our first. Dirty and determined. Raw and real. Only this time, with some actual fucking. Oh, yes. A good dose of that, please.

"*Mierde.* Who has suddenly gotten herself a saucy little mouth? Is discipline in order for you this afternoon, little *magie*?"

And oh my *word*, another few of these inner thigh smacks would be perfectly nice too.

"Will discipline get your penis inside my pussy faster, *Monsieur Bâtard*?"

Another pair of perfect spanks. Harder and louder than before.

And I think I'm in heaven.

While whips and chains have never been my full saucer of milk, I've indulged some kinky fantasies by way of a few favorite porn sites. But never have I been brave enough to actually ask for stuff from a lover. Never has one been able to see right through me and deliver it. Not until now. The only *now* I want to think or care about. The only man I want to spend it with.

"You shall get fucked when I say it is time," he grits out. "But for now, my sweet Magiq—"

He freezes before my eyes. Remorse drenches his face and clouds his gaze. He gulps hard, clearly trying to summon the proper regrets in the proper ways.

I abhor every second of it. Further, as I communicate with a frantic shake of my head, I don't agree with it. Not at all.

"No. Look at me. Just *no,* Bastien. Stop thinking it. Stop *feeling* it. It wasn't on purpose. I understand. I look like her . . ."

He grunts viciously. "That is no goddamned excuse."

"It is *every* excuse. You love her—"

"*Loved* her."

"And you can't be expected to just turn your feelings off!"

No matter how completely you've helped switch mine back on. So many of them. In so many wonderful ways...

But he doesn't get to hear all that. He can't ever know it. If I go there, it'll also be to express the preciousness of the gift he's given me. The gift of *me*. Yet I won't stop there. I'll have to also let him know how my soul feels changed. How indelibly he's stamped me. Undoubtedly, that insignia is shaped like a fleur-de-lys. The symbol of his land...of *him*. An emblem of unity, strength, power, and light, patterned on one of the world's most beautiful flowers. *Fleur de lys...*

De Lys...

De Lys...

The echo continues across my mind, layered like church bells across the city on New Year's Eve. Except in my mind, they aren't American bells at all. They're somewhere else...

Just like *I'm* suddenly somewhere else.

But am I? Because Bastien is still here with me...

Except that *here* isn't exactly *here*.

And I'm not exactly me anymore. Not completely. But somehow, that's all right.

It's...better than all right. It's strange but astounding. Unreal but extraordinary.

De Lys. Magique De Lys.

I feel her.

Everything she knows right now, staring up at this incredible man. How he grins when she sings because she's crappy at it. How he tells her every story from his patrols, and she knows all the places in which he embellishes for drama, but she lets him. How he has taught her to read stories for herself, written in words across pages, and opened up new worlds for her because of it.

I feel her.

And I want so badly to tell him that but don't dare. There are other things she needs to tell him. Things that can't be put off, especially if he decides I'm really crazy this time and bolts out again.

Dear God, no.

This time, I can't guarantee finding him before Logan or his friends do. And while Bastien is still more on the right side of the law, *Agents Lautrec and Degas* definitely aren't. He needs to be right here with me, not Logan's bargaining chip in some holding cell.

I feel her.

And God help me, I yearn to feel so much more.

"Feel." That part, I *can* let out. Not too far astray from where our subject is already. "Please, Bastien. Stop fighting it. Can you try... for me? For *her*?"

No more of his skewed glower. He rivets the look straight into me now. "You want me to think about another woman? Here? Now?"

"What if I do?" It's shockingly effortless to be serious about it. But still scary. Oh, still plenty of that. "You were all-in on obsessing over her a couple of nights ago."

"That was different! This is—"

"Still no different, if you time-jump your mind back. If we both do."

His nostrils flare. I glimpse the grit of his teeth, with those front four a little more prominent than the others, emphasizing his bossy side by delicious degrees. "Why are you doing this? She is gone, and I am struggling to accept—"

"But what if you don't have to?"

What if we get you back to the wardrobe, and you can fix it all? What if you can save her?

More astral concepts that I keep inside. I've already hit the poor man with all he can handle for now. All that he still hasn't embraced—and that I might have to convince him of with the dirtiest tactics. With my naughtiest side.

"Raegan."

"No." I stroke a hand down the center of his chest. When getting to the ridged path below that, I keep going. "My name is Magique now. Come on. Try it. I think you'll like it."

With a terse sweep, he halts my caress. "What are you about? And why? Is this some strange new sorcery?"

"No." I purse my lips. "Okay, maybe. I don't know myself. But you believed Kavia's spell enough to go for all of it."

"Because there was an enraged mob after my balls!" he protests. "And a lot of everything else."

"Well, I don't blame them. I like being after your balls too." I take advantage of the moments in which his surprise loosens his grip, and I can slip free to continue my downward stroke. "And now, I want to know what it's like to have *them* craving *me*. To know what it's like to be the woman you desire the most in the world."

The lucky woman who's captured your whole heart.

And there's the part I should have left out of *my* heart. Because its absence from the air doesn't stop his dukeness of discernment from spotting it on every inch of my face.

At once, there's a defined change across his. *Not* one I'm fond of. The man can keep his tender pity, damn it. I don't want it. I've actually told him what I *do* want, so why isn't he listening?

"One day, one unbelievably blessed man is going to

claim yours too. And he shall know the true gift he has in his possession. And he will cherish that prize with every ounce of his heart, soul, and body."

Okay, so he did pocket the pity—only to replace it with everything worse. Words like that.

"So let's pretend, just for a few minutes, that *you're* that blessed guy." My offer is joined by my smile when he doesn't try to stop my caress anymore. "You get to role play him, and then I get to be Magique."

But he hitches again. Damnably hesitant again. Even an extra undulation of my pelvis doesn't affect him. "I am not one for *playing*, little one."

His expression is true to his tone. Not a single bantering quirk around his lips. Not a wink from his unblinking eyes. The small glitterings in his irises have been buffed and blended to a take-no-shit sheen. A glaze that now seems to bleed into the air around us, tinting everything in an old movie sepia.

What . . . the hell?

The golden glow spreads, transforming everything else in the room. *Holy shit.* I'm no longer in a cheap boardinghouse chair but reclining on an old-world chaise covered in tufted velvet. The craft services tables are gone, replaced by a giant canopied bed that belongs in a musketeer movie.

In Bastien's world.

Which is now . . . *my* world?

No. I mean, no. *What is all this?*

But as the words careen in my mind, they never take form on my lips. The only thing that emerges there is a phrase as stunning to me as it is to him.

"Tu préfère te battre?"

Yes, I really just did that. Literally asked the man if he

wants to fight instead of fuck. And yes, it felt totally awesome. All the flippancy of it. All the *French* of it. Like it's come out of me before. Like Bastien has been here, in this room with me, responding exactly like he does now. With that sultry smile and even that pronounced laugh...

"Must I select this very moment?"

And holy crap... with those very words.

"If your testicles want to make it out of this room in the same sac, I'd highly advise it."

No more French from out of nowhere, though once more the words are all kinds of wrong and right at the same time. It's as if I'm in a Broadway play that's already a hit. I already know how well the lines are going to land, and they're special because of it, but they're still *lines*. Words that weren't created by me. That surely *aren't* me...

Right?

Why doesn't my psyche automatically answer that? Worse, why is Bastien already making me doubt the instinct, his stare turning into something I can't decipher?

"Little lily."

More bewilderment, trying to absorb how he utters the endearment. Like it's a poem in and of itself. No. Like it's prayer from the depths of his soul...

Before he pushes back in and softly kisses me.

"*Oh, Magique.*"

Once more, everything feels so right. A memory that's been perfectly imprinted on my senses.

But as he kisses me again, I fight to recall what a memory even is. As he fits his body tighter against mine, I give up the battle. And as he angles my hips up, wrapping my legs around him, I simply succumb to it all.

To desire. To connection.

To him.

"Bastien. My duke. My love. *Je te veux en moi.*"

There's more to say, so much more that feels so right now, but he robs the words from my throat while stealing the breath from my lips. How do his kisses keep getting better? Brighter. Bolder. Nastier. Wetter. Everything I want. Everything I've waited so long to have . . .

Over two hundred years . . .

I should be the one jolting back now. Hard and fast. But that would mean leaving him, and no way am I doing that. Not again. Not ever again.

Until death . . . and beyond . . .

More of the words that I remember but don't. That are new to me . . . but not.

Because . . . this is me. Whispering it to him, right now—if even just from my soul.

But I need to do better. To let *her* speak it to him. To let him know . . . that she's here. That she knows. And sees. And still needs. And still loves . . .

At last, *at last*, he breaks his lips free. He's dragging them through the salty drops that have crept down my cheek. The bittersweetness that's leaking from my senses. From *her*, now so awake and happy and sad and adoring him. Crying to him.

"Bastien. *Bastien.*"

"I know. I know, my sweet love."

But he doesn't know. Not really. How can he? All the words I hear. All the things I see. All the *changes* I feel. What's going on? Who am I now?

"Raegan!"

It takes a moment to fully identify the sound. It's not

from my head. It's from Drue, who repeats the shout from somewhere far away. *No.* Not so far at all. From just down the hallway . . .

The hallway of *this* place, just beyond the closed door on the other side of the banquet tables . . .

The North Greene. A boardinghouse thingie of the twenty-first century, not a roadside inn somewhere in eighteenth-century France.

Yes. I'm here. I'm me, altogether now.

So why does that make me so sad? Even forlorn? So much so, I can't even choke out a reply to my friend's new hail.

"Raegan Karlinne Tavish! For the love of fuck, where are you?"

She strides down the hall with enough force to sound like two people. Maybe three.

"They've got to be here somewhere. Her phone and *a lot* of uneaten dumplings are still in the room. But if one of Logan's minions picked them up, I'd have been her first phone call."

"Unless they're still getting booked?"

The reply, so clear because it's issued from this side of the hallway, elucidates the pitter-patter-for-two that I just heard.

At once, I rush to my feet.

"Allie?"

"Aha! Wonderful supposition, *mon miracle*, but they are certainly *not* getting books. Unless these rooms have books in their amenities?"

The third voice in the hall has my poor Desperado jostled worse than me. He pops up like a GI Joe figure that's been plucked by an eager kid. Apt comparison because he's gawking with as much glee as that kid.

But his joy is only half that of his brother's.

"*Mon dieu*," Max blurts from the second he leads the way into the room. His hair, a few shades lighter than his brother's, is damp and disheveled. His eyes, also lighter than Bastien's, are glowing as brilliant as gold. "Bast! It *is* really you!"

I smirk, filled with a flood of girlish pride that flows as Bastien dips half of an unassuming bow. An equally adorable grin yanks up one corner of his mouth. "It is *very* good to see you again, brother."

"Good?" Max counters. "It is a fucking *miracle*!"

"Well, that's almost taking the words right out of my mouth." I drawl it in the moments before hauling Allie into a hug. "How did you get back here so fast? Did you guys spend all of fifteen minutes in Italy?"

"Hmmm, maybe sixteen." Her concession comes with an it's-all-good glance, as if she already hears my inward fret about her forced interruption to an essential work trip. "We weren't even unpacked. We were going to do that after enjoying a drink at the hotel. Fortunately, their lobby bar had several English language news feeds turned on—and we caught a very familiar face on one of them."

Drue takes that occasion to saunter deeper into the room. "You hear that, Duke of Daring? You made the international feeds!"

I wallop her with an exasperated huff. "And that's a reason for celebrating *why*?"

"Because it got us back here," Max announces, lurching to thread his way between the tables. "Back *here*, to where *you* actually are." He doesn't hesitate about yanking Bastien into a hug that takes *bromance* to seriously fresh levels. "My brother. My beautiful *brother*. It is you—with your whole head on your shoulders, at that!"

Bastien's smirk isn't so pronounced now. "Where else is it supposed to be?"

CHAPTER FOURTEEN

BASTIEN

I intended the question in jest. Mostly.

Maximillian has hauled me away, beneath the awning that covers the boardinghouse's back patio, to issue his answer. All too swiftly, I have learned why.

His answer is nowhere near a laughing matter.

"A revolution."

I shake my head while reiterating my brother's terminology—and extending some silent gratitude for the cold air that gusts up the alley. Fortunately, the rain has abated for now. But if Maximillian has more stunning truths to impart, I might be wishing for another downpour as well.

"For eleven years?"

A grim nod from Max. "What you experienced—and me, shortly after—was barely the beginning of it all."

Of it all.

Another collection of words, atop his others, that should not represent so much more. Revolts and revisions. Arrests and accusations. And a horrible Reign of Terror . . .

"And Robespierre led the chaos?"

"Among *many* others," he supplies. "Sieyès, Danton, Lafayette . . . but the most famous was probably Bonaparte."

"*Bonaparte?*" I lurch to my feet. "That small, twitchy

man? Now I *know* you surely play, brother."

He is too damn somber for comfort. "Well, the twitchy gentleman was eventually crowned emperor."

I pace a few steps, about all I can manage in the confines beneath the alley's large puddles. "Perhaps it *was* fortuitous that Kavia got us out."

"Both of us."

He stresses the syllables as if they are incantations of their own. Meaningful ones. Before turning back around, I am already aware of the places from which they emerge. His huge heart. His boundless spirit. Max is a unique human being, genuine and intense about the way he loves—applicable, as well, to the way he grieves. I cannot fathom what it was like for him to do so in such a strange new world, thinking I was murdered along with Mother and Father.

But clearly, he has found his way here. And done so with so much joy, shining from his whole being, as he grins anew at me. "St. Peter's balls, Bast. I still cannot believe you are here."

I lean back against a dry part of the wall. "I do not think *I* do yet."

But now, beholding the ongoing awe in his gaze, I am beginning to. No matter how staggering it might be.

My God.

I am supposed to be dead.

But I definitely am not.

I already know the *how* of it, especially after confirming it all by exchanging a few cursory sentences with Max. A few key phrases were all I needed to hear.

Escaping from a mob.

Kavia and Carl.

Wardrobe on fire.

Surreal. *Un*real. And yet the truth...that now feels like so long ago.

I am a different man now.

And, just a few minutes after being reunited with him, I know Maximillian is too.

"But now...we must focus on keeping you here."

I snap my head up, shaking free from my newfound fascination with the tops of my feet. It takes another second for Max's declaration to set in—and to formulate a reply as dazed as my first one.

"Keeping me?" I cant my head. "Why the hell would you want to do that?"

He scowls as if my brain has toppled out of my skull. "Because the alternative is not acceptable." He emphasizes with a stomp, turning a smaller puddle into silver drops against the alley lights. "You do remember what happens in the original version of this story, right? In 1789, you *die*, brother."

I attempt a smirk. "As you have made me well aware, Maximilian."

He clenches his jaw. "Then why—"

"Because if I do not go back, or even try to, *she* dies."

That relaxes his jaw but puckers his brow. "She who?"

"Magique De Lys." I have to order my shoulders down from my ears before going on. "Just before Carl and Kavia found me and put me in the cabinet, she was murdered before my eyes."

"*Désolé.*"

While I know he means it, the sentiment does not get completed in his eyes. His gaze rakes across the empty air, as if he is searching the invisible molecules for specific information. "Magique de Lys," he repeats "Was she not the

Versailles salon servant with whom you were having a fun bit of bread and butter?"

"You mean the *woman* whom I asked to be my *wife*?"

At once, his gape grows. "Oh."

That rings with more sincerity. I dip a nod of appreciation. Max had no way of knowing what Magique had come to mean to me. How much she still means, considering it has been impossible to forget her. These bizarre circumstances have given me no choice.

A predicament that Maximillian deserves to know in full.

"I was with her . . . minutes before Kavia put me into the wardrobe. But she was killed before my eyes. Taken by the blade of a Jacobin lunatic."

He swears. I yearn to join him but must focus on holding back the additional part of the revelation. That the zealot was Magique's own brother.

"I thought my own story had some insane parts."

I flatten my spine along the wall. The reinforcement is needed now.

"And that is hardly not the end of mine."

Another gritted swear word. "There is *more*?"

I steel myself again before going on. "Raegan Tavish . . ."

Despite how calmly I approach the pronunciation, the syllables are like sparks on my lips and tongue. More markedly, they ignite things in Maximillian too. Things that have my posture stiffer than the wall behind it.

"Is part of the team who saved *my* life," he growls. "So just to be clear here, brother. If you have led her to believe—"

I pummel the wall with both fists. Just one pound. Fortunately, it is enough. "*I* have led *her* nowhere."

The corners of his eyes tighten. "Meaning what?"

Another long inhalation. An exhalation that feels like hell. "She is a mirror image of Magique."

I am unsure what to expect now. But Maximillian's continued calm is not on that list.

"You are mistaken," he decrees. "You must be."

He is not the only De Leon with knowledge of quiet control.

"If Kavia reappeared and hurled you through time again, would you forget Alessandra's face?"

His nostrils flare. He flicks a glance toward me—a silent and grudging *touché*. "But just her face?" he prods. "There is nothing *below* her neck to tell you—"

"I have learned enough." While I know he will not press for every intimate detail behind that, I acknowledge he will not settle for four plain words. "The scar on her chest... it is the exact same location where Magique was stabbed."

He believes me. I see it now. I just wish the confidence felt better, especially as he paces toward the other end of the awning.

Once there, he does not turn. One of his long arms extends over his close-coifed head, bracing to a support pole for the canopy. He looks up into the mist that clings to the air. The blue-silver light from the artificial lights traces an interesting line along his strong, determined profile.

"So you think they are connected somehow? Magique and Raegan?"

"Unsure." I drop my stare back to the tops of my feet, hoping my tone conveys that sincerity. "But ever since I got here, there have been instances..."

He jogs a look over his shoulder. "Of what?"

"Moments," I supply. "None more than a few seconds

long, but all that have given me pause to think . . ."

"Of *what*?"

His pressure is not necessary. It is a relief to free these admissions, especially to him.

"She has . . . lapses," I say. "I cannot describe it any other way than that. She . . . goes away from me. Even from this time and place. She is lost, as if possessed—except the force inside her is not malevolent. Sometimes she will even start speaking there—and that is when I am most jarred. But not in an awful way . . ."

"In what way, then?" Max demands.

I pause, if only to allow myself a few seconds for the affirmation again. *He is your brother. He cannot disown you. Just say it!*

"There have been times when I swear . . . I am speaking to Magique."

Encouraging news—he does not bolt out of here. Or openly scoff.

But troubling news—his dark contemplation does not change. I am hard-pressed to notice if the man even blinks, even after he turns around and walks back over. Though his body is clearly still capable of movement, I wonder about everything going on behind his face. In the far reaches of his bright brain.

"So now what are you intimating?" he charges. "That . . . what? They are the same *person*, centuries apart? *That's* the reason Raegan's going on about you trying this stunt in reverse?"

I set my feet apart, bracing them for the thrust of my full standing weight again. "I know it sounds crazy. But is it any more outrageous than how we got here to begin with?"

"All the more reason to leave the fuckery alone!" he retorts. "Bast. *Brother*. What is so awful about the idea of staying here? Would I suggest something that I cannot vouch for myself?"

"Says the *salaud* who recommended I take Bluebell out for a ride for my tenth birthday?"

"What?" he snaps. "The horse was always fine to *me*."

"Just like the twenty-first century has been?"

He huffs. "You have simply had a skewed introduction."

"Ah. Of course," I bite back.

His expression remains even. "You have seen, and experienced, some of the more challenging aspects of the city. So I understand your initial reticence."

"*Initial?*" I laugh but it is slathered with bitterness. "And you plan on changing my mind about that, I take it?"

His own spine stiffens. His countenance turns so dark, I wonder if he shall start breathing fire on me. "I merely hope to show you that not everyone in this place is rude and bloodthirsty." Not the most dragon-like thing he could utter, but damn it, he believes it. "Christ, Bast. Fighting and warfare have been woven into your veins even before you knew what the words meant. So perhaps that is what you always look for in those around you." He relaxes then, enough to clap a hearty hand to my shoulder. "Maybe you can find new ways of living that don't involve killing and dismembering people."

I let a brow jump up. "New ways of living. You mean right here, of course."

"Selfishly speaking, yes," he answers at once. "But also . . . concernedly speaking."

I squirm but scramble for a note of levity. "Concernedly? Well, well, *mon frere*. Has your Alessandra been as good for shoring your left hook as your interesting vocabulary?"

One edge of his mouth twitches. "She is good for me in many ways—even though there was a time that she did not believe it for herself."

At once, I discern his discomfort. The memory is clearly not easy for him to relay. I express my gratitude for his exposure with a sincere reply. "But you changed her mind? How?"

"'Twas not my doing at all—but her own bold proposition, the very night the wardrobe arrived from France. It was her Christmas present for me. A wonderful surprise, indeed—that she upended with all of her doubts about whether destiny had known what it was doing when delivering me here in the first place."

I pucker my lips and emit a low groan, empathizing with his wounded expression. "So the evening concluded with the woman over your knee, counting out her spankings?"

"Only after I called her bluff by getting into the cabinet right away."

I drop the pucker. It joins the rest of my amazed gape. "And what happened?"

"I went time traveling."

"*Mierde.*"

"By five minutes." He is more relaxed about the recall now, seeming to warm to the moment in his memory. "And only to the other room in our apartment, where my heart was truly longing to be the whole time." He returns to reptilian inspiration for the look he casts now, his gaze as knowing as an old crocodile's. "So you see, I have learned from personal experience. The wardrobe is not like a hired livery driver. It will not take you where you are not destined to go. I am not even certain it has a *reverse* mode."

His pause is deliberate and watchful. I return the scrutiny with as much determination. Does he think his assertion will dissuade me that easily?

"But you were not *focusing* on the past," I claim. "The cabinet gets its direction from our energy and desires, *oui*? Your heart already knew where it wanted to be. You merely needed to prove that to Alessandra."

"And you are still certain that *your* heart is not here?" Max rebuts. "Just *wait*, Bast, and stop to consider that. If Kavia told you—"

"The same thing she told *you*," I snap. Damn it, he knows that. We have already reviewed the many details of our experiences, noting the uncanny similarities of them—especially this part. "Which is exactly what I did."

"So why did the wardrobe not cast you back instead of forward?" he charges. "Why did it not fling you back to a place where you could get to Magique and then flee France with her? If it was indeed possible, why were you propelled here instead of there? Would 1788 not have been an easier push than the twenty-first century?"

I fume. Not vociferously, but enough for him to feel my pique. *Cheeky fucking churl.*

"Perhaps I should just summon Kavia up to our little chat, hmm?" I drawl. "I am certain she would love to expound on the subject, as long as we toss a few soup dumplings at Carl and keep him amused."

My cynicism does not dissuade the man. Secretly, I would be disappointed if it did. "I just think there is more magic at work here than we think," Max asserts. "Obviously Kavia found a way to harness the divine—but she is *not* the cosmic author. The Almighty, in all its different and magnificent forms, is still in charge. In this case, perhaps it also exercised some mercy. If Magique was snuffed from this realm before her sacred time, perhaps parts of her have been secured and brought back as Raegan. Maybe those are the parts your own soul was drawn to and now has found once again."

I sway where I stand. The *bâtard* seems to savor that, grinning like the few occasions when he bested me on the combat training field. But I cannot summon a shred of malice—because yet again, all his words sound so right. *Feel* so right.

Good God.

What if he truly is right?

That moment when Marq's dagger sank into Magique's chest...that terrible sweep of violence, with every moment that felt so *wrong*...

What if it was?

What if that fratricide was a gross gash in the canvas of divine destiny? And what if the cosmos recognized that her soul was too precious to expire with her? What if a troupe of angels themselves flew across time and retrieved everything they could before her body gave up breath and form? What if they searched through centuries for the right person who could share her perfect magic—and they flew to *this* year to find it?

To find *her*...

My mind feels like it is juggling cows, but I manage to keep them all in the air while reviewing the ramifications of Max's suggestion.

That perhaps I *am* meant to remain here. Ordained to all this oddness. Fated for this wilderness of the future. But for what? Not just to save my sorry skin. *Not good enough.* Not by half.

But a reunion with my beloved…

If I can truly stretch my mind around the concept…

She would be worth staying for. Worth trying for. Even fighting for, if it comes to that.

I nod with definition, attempting to say as much to Maximillian with the motion. Aloud, I offer more. "All right, then. How do we figure all that out?" I note the change across his face, a reiteration of his earlier earnestness. "How do we… focus on keeping me here?"

A long pause. Perhaps his face changes again, but I don't know because of his deeply dipped head. When he raises it again, at once casting his stare down the alley, the situation is no better.

This is either very good or very bad.

I wish my heart wasn't hammering so hard with the need to find out.

"It is a specific set of conditions that must be met," he finally says. "Within one rotation of the moon."

The pressure in my chest subsides. A little.

"Fair enough," I reply. "Unless it is a trip to hell and back, or locating Atlantis, or some insane quest such as—"

"No." Max lowers onto a decorative bench. He braces elbows to his knees and steeples his fingers. "It is based on the power of the force that got you here."

I slant a quizzical look. "Fire, then? A crucible of flames?" At a village fair a few months back, Magique and I stopped to watch a troupe of traveling performers. They appeared to swallow fire and even walked across burning coals. Is that the kind of test I am to face?

"Not that." He presses his fingers harder. Everything but his palms are touching. "The power of what's inside your heart. Of touching another's with it, until they declare their love for you before witnesses."

A long pause.

And another.

Because my brother's urbanity is going to crack any moment. And then he will confess that jibes are just another form of fraternal fun and we can return to the subject at hand.

After a minute, his game gets grueling.

To the point I realize it is not a game at all.

Fuck.

I husk the word beneath my breath. When I am done, I rake a taut hand through my hair while stabbing a stare *up* the alley. In the distance, a few sunbeams pierce through the last vestiges of the soggy day. For a few moments, they turn the wet pavement into colorful fire. If only they were all *actually* fire. A burning maze that would dazzle Kavia, even two hundred and thirty something years in the past, into changing her mind about the insane *condition*.

But I only stand here, as blinded as before. As blind*sided* as before. Having to concentrate on bringing enough air to my lungs for a miserable mutter to my brother.

"Are you *certain* I cannot just discover Atlantis instead?"

RAEGAN

I lean against the little kitchenette table back in our room, hoping one of my two best friends will help erase the awkward pause after the story I've just laid on them. Okay, not the basic plot part of the tale. The figurative crickets in the air have more to do with my crazy conclusion . . . which I'm desperately hoping one of them will talk me out of in some way, shape, or helpful form.

But I still get nothing but their silent blink-blinks.

I should already know better. Like the fact that neither of them are going to bullshit through an awkward moment just to make things less hinky for me.

I should also know that if *the look* is happening, it'll be now. That momentary trade of their glances, silently confirming that they need to be talking about some *outside help* for the friend who's been locked down for a few too many hours with a guy who just touched down from time-traveling orbit.

So maybe—hopefully—that *is* the only issue here. Maybe I'm just under-slumbered, oversexed, and too damn desperate to make the impossible happen.

I try to say as much by leaning back in my chair, refusing to qualify the cold dumplings on my plate as a dismal metaphor.

"You know what?" I finally mutter. "Seriously, just forget I said anyth—"

"Ohhh, no." Allie's the first to speak up, almost gleeful about the insistence. "No way do you get to be the one running from your De Leon when *you* led the mission to smuggle mine onto a trans-Atlantic flight last year."

"You mean after she made room for him on the castle tour hop." D's even more eager about hopping on the memory lane tour bus. "And finagling secrets out of the new De Leons about the legends of the old ones."

I lob a fortune cookie at her. "I seem to remember having help with that one, Mademoiselle Kidman. And now that I think about it, exactly *who* had the original idea about stowaway Max?"

My question seems to enter the ether as Drue extracts the fortune from her shattered cookie pieces. "Ahhh. *Changing the subject is only painting the truth in a worse color.*"

Allie taps her fingertips against her opposite palm as if applauding a new course during high tea at the Pembroke. "Very nice!"

"And a wasted effort." I grab for the slip of paper, only to watch D swipe it through the leftover puddle from the dumplings I managed to get down earlier. "There's no subject to change here, okay? Obviously Bastien was transported here by accident. Obviously it was an eleventh-hour effort to save his neck—which worked, but not because of me. His heart led the way because *Max* is part of his heart too. So it's just coincidence—"

"That you look completely like the woman who was going to be his duchess?" D inserts.

"With a scar in your chest, where that same woman was daggered?" Allie concurs.

Drue tosses her head like a starlet giving sassy game face for the press corps. "As long as we're on a roll, how about the flashbacks into a language you barely know, referencing occasions you've never lived?"

"Not to mention the tall, dark, and decadent detective who's taken a keener-than-keen interest in our little Eeyore?" Allie adds, earning herself an instant blush-glower from D's side of the exchange.

"Let's chalk that delusion up to your jet lag, yeah?" The woman's aqua ponytail nearly becomes a lethal weapon as she switches her attention back to me. "I stand by my original theory. It won't be long before Logan has to obey his superiors and move on to leads that yield better results. A day more. Two at best."

"If that's true, and I'm not saying it *is*"—Allie absently swipes at crumbs from the cheesy fish that were part of D's earlier care package—"we should use the time wisely. We have to burn both your FBI agent outfits, such as they are, and entertain ourselves by thinking of a new hair color for Tiggerfina here."

"Aha." Drue brightens with unnatural drama. "Saved from the hotel room hair dye job by the dominatrix wig." And then pulls out her hair tie and blithely toss-tosses her lush blue waves. "But also because this shit's a bitch to switch."

I smash a few fish and wobble my left leg. "Maybe all I need is a simple haircut."

Allie frowns. "Not with that distinct color, darling."

"Biggest asset. First thing on the APB broadcast," Drue adds.

"Thanks for nothing, thumbtack butt."

Deftly, she catches the fish-shaped cracker I've hurled. As Allie throws her hands up to celebrate the clean pass, I give in to a heartfelt smirk—right before my sincere confession.

"It's so good to have you guys here." I reach for their hands. "I mean that. Thank you both. For absolutely everything."

Drue smirks with definitive purpose. "You're just saying that because I took the bullet of going to the pharmacy counter."

At once, I groan. It barely edges out Allie's fresh gasp.

"What bullet? In what way? The *pharmacy*? Rae, are you okay?"

I fling another cheesy fish. "Well, *there's* the topic transition we didn't need."

After fishing in her bra for the cracker, Drue flicks it

back at me. "And there's the response that tells me everything."

"Everything about *what*?" Allie's all but bouncing in her seat. "Damn it, what loop am I out of?"

I jerk my head back and forth. "Not important."

"Which means it *is*," she insists. "You're never this cagey about trifles and trinkets."

I roll my eyes. "Because my professional reputation depends on trifles and trinkets?"

"Good try but no good." She darts her scrutiny between D and me. "Come on. You both going to tell me to chalk *this* one up to jet lag too?"

Silence stretches.

Drue stares at me.

I scrutinize three more smushed cheesy fishes.

But she finally speaks. "You didn't take it, did you?"

Allie huffs. "Take *what*?"

All of a sudden, I'm restless. Surging to my feet barely helps, especially because I twist my fingers together like some fretting frau from long ago. All right, maybe only two hundred years ago. But that's far enough away for a full-on conscience crisis. An inner debate that hasn't set me free since this morning.

"Well, you have seventy-two hours, right? So there's still time to decide."

"Seventy-two ho—" Allie interrupts her snit on a blunt snag of breath. "*Oh*. You mean *that* kind of a decision?"

I leave the kitchen area, pacing out across the bedroom. "You know, fifteen minutes ago, we were deciding *other* things. Girls' night in, remember? Passionflix? HBO? Nail polish? Maybe even hair dye?"

Allie rises too. "Fifteen minutes ago, I wasn't aware that

you and Bastien had tumbled quite that far over the edge."

I stop. Pivot. And then snap, "Well we did, okay? But I'm working it out for myself, and—"

"Hey." She holds up both hands. "No judgments, chica, especially not from me. Things happen when one is dealing with a naked De Leon."

Drue tosses a cracker high and again catches it in her mouth. "I don't know whether to order you both for details or puke up everything in my stomach."

I stop and let a laugh burst free. "And I don't know which one of you should get a harder hug."

"Probably her." Allie thumbs toward D. "Because I'm not letting this subject go so fast." She endures my frustrated groan while sitting on the edge of the bed. "Don't get a rash, Tavish. You're a grown woman and have every right to your ultimate decision. You also don't have any obligation to share that with us. But if you really haven't chugged that pill yet, it does say a few significant things."

I settle onto the couch with folded arms. "*Only* a few?"

She presses her hands together in her lap. Her nails are a stunning shade of *Roma Red*. Of course. "Well, one in particular."

"And thank God someone *else* said it." Drue sidles over and leans on the threshold between the two spaces. "Well, not yet, but . . ." She jabs up a thumb in Allie's direction. "Take the shottie, *Hemline* hottie. Right here for you, missy."

Allie throws her a grateful look. The expression solemnifies as she swivels it back to me. "This possibility . . ." she says, "of what might already be going on in your body, because of Bastien . . . I think it's your way of still being connected to him. A tangible way, that you can understand—

instead of all the other ways, which are freaking you out."

I look down. Like that's going to confirm . . . what? That I spilled a stupid amount of dumpling gravy on my soon-to-be-burned yoga pants?

Or maybe . . . that she's hit my emotional bull's-eye more accurately than I thought and now has glaring confirmation of it?

"I'm not freaked out."

"No?" Allie returns. "Because you know, I was the megaphone for freaked when all I had to deal with was a two-hundred-plus-year-old lover. If he'd also told me I was a ringer for his dead fiancée, who then started uploading scenes from their life into my mind, I'd start—"

I hiss in aggravation, pushing again to my feet. "That's not—*she's* not—that's just—"

"Sounding very much like the truth," D comments. "At least from where I'm sitting."

I scowl. "You're *not* sitting."

"And you're not accomplishing anything by running," Allie asserts. "And before you start, you know exactly what I mean." She moves fast, reaching and grabbing my hand before I can step back. "Dearest wench whom we love so much. Would you just come and sit down? You too, Drusilla."

While we're all readjusting against the headboard, Drue snickers. "Is this the part where I get to turn the room into a winter fantasy bower?"

Allie groans.

I giggle, and it feels so damn good. "Don't stress, Allie-rific. She's got a *long* way to go before this place approaches a *bower*."

"We're not talking about her right now." She drapes a

comforting arm around my shoulder. "So what makes you so sure that you're not the miracle reincarnation of Magique De Lys?"

At once, I sit forward. "And what makes you so sure that I *am?*"

"Seriously?" Drue tilts her head back, regarding me from the top of her cute pop star nose. "The man is clearly knocked on his ass for you."

"The man doesn't *know* me. It's been *two* days."

Allie spreads a wide smile. "It was about the same blink of time before you two saw the same thing in Maximilian."

Drue nods. "And there are a lot more flukes going on *this* time."

"Okay, Jesus toast is a fluke," I volley. "That doesn't mean it's got to be tossed in a manger." I scoot up and then turn around, regarding them with crisscrossed legs and my chin on my knuckles. "I have a life, you guys. And full memories of my *own*. Birthdays and snow days. Old schoolmates and new heartaches. Vacations with my parents to Vermont and the Vineyard. One time, they even bit the bullet and took me to Orlando. And yes"—I press at the middle of my sternum—"I even remember every second of how I got *this*. So if all that's legit, then what's another woman doing in my psyche? And why?"

Allie unleashes a long breath. "If any of us knew that, we probably wouldn't be having this conversation."

"Because maybe it's a pointless one?" I nervously rub at my kneecaps. "Bastien... He's as charismatic as his brother. It's in a lot of different ways, but it's still there." *God help me, is it ever.* "Maybe, in some way, I'm experiencing his psychic overflow. *His* recollections, pushing out through the air and hitting me. There's probably even a word for that, right? Like telekinesis, only with memories?"

For a long moment, they're both silent.

Finally, Drue snorts. "And you think *our* theories are whack?"

Allie joins in with a soft laugh. I don't join their little party. Damn it, how I wish I could.

"Honestly, I don't know what to think," I admit, newly miserable. "Which is why I've probably been trying not to."

Including the decision about what to do with the little wrapped box in the drawer.

Letting go of Bastien, in any way . . . it's like thinking of hugging the Statue of Liberty. Impossible. I know that won't always be the case. When the time comes to set him free, I'll do what's right. It'll feel that way too.

But right now, even with him in the next room, there's a physical ache inside. My fortitude feels like nothing but thin girders and rivets, bravely supporting my shell. I keep wishing Bastien and Max would be done with their reunion so they can get back in here and I can light up my torch again. Just for a little while longer . . .

"You know what?" Allie offers it in her latte-foam voice, soft but significant. I'm grateful for the chance to stop thinking of French scowls for a moment. "I have an idea about figuring this out. Or at least getting us closer."

I cock my head. "You remembered a secret tunnel entrance to your building?"

"Good one, but no." She motions with a finger between her forehead and mine. "Though remembering *is* a key verb to it."

"Meaning what?" Drue asks.

ANGEL PAYNE

"There's a big party—a gala, actually—taking place at Grand Central Station. They're celebrating the depot's hundred and fiftieth anniversary with a period costume thing benefiting the city's budding fashion designers."

"Is that already here?" I ask with a flared gaze. "It fell off my list mostly because of how many clients I bid on and lost for it. Once the Met pushed off their event by a month because of the refurbishments at the museum, the Grand Depot's thing became the hottest spring event. Everyone opted for name-brand stylists, if not the leading historical costume designers."

"Honestly, I wiped it off my radar too," Allie replies. "Max and I declined the original invite because of the Italy plans, but Hemline is one of the big sponsors for the thing. I know they'll be zazzed if we show up as surprise guests." She adds an impish wiggle to her quick wink. "I don't even think they'll mind us bringing along a few friends, either. I can call our showrunner to hook us up with last-minute ensembles."

"Errr..." I tilt my head the other way. "Just how last-minute?"

Allie checks her watch with twisted lips. "About three hundred of them, give or take a few seconds. I'm not quite the mathing maven."

"Three hun—" D sits up straighter but still looks like there's now a dozen tacks in her ass. "That thing is *tonight*?"

"And the method to your obvious madness about this is *what*, Ms. Allie Fine?" I add.

"Well..." The woman beams her pearlies in the engaging smile that's earned her millions of fans via Hemline Network's fashion-forward programming. "What better way for you to find out if you've lived in the past than to *live* in the past for a few hours? They're transforming Vanderbilt Hall into an

229

exact replica of life as it was when the railroads first began."

"Okay . . ."

I say it slowly, hating to convey the full scope of my skepticism. Allie's being so sweet, offering us VIP access to an event that's going to rival the city's *other* themed gala for celebrity wattage, and there's nothing on my mind except a massive *but* to her proposal.

As always, Drue to the rescue. "Okay, shitty math maven, even you know that only lands us somewhere toward the middle of the 1800s, not the late 1700s, yeah?"

"Surprisingly, yes. But Rae will back me up on this. After the Revolution and the Regency, fashion silhouettes circled back around in some ways. If I can get some gowns and embellishments delivered within the hour, we can make fast alterations and still be on the arrival carpet in time."

"The . . . *what*?" I'm not shy about speaking up this time. "Honey, you know I'm more than grateful for all this sugar, but we're hunkered down on this side of town for a reason. Liam Logan . . . I wouldn't be surprised if the man's middle name is *Tenacity*. On that note, if he also didn't know every single cop patrolling every single foot of tonight's big welcome mat—"

"Which actually makes that idea a pretty good one," Drue cuts in. She swings half a smirk Allie's way. "That's your second point, isn't it? The ol' hiding-in-plain-sight option?"

"Yes and no," Allie hedges. "Is it *hiding* when one happens to duck behind their demure makeup and gloved fingers at the same moment half the world—and the cops—are gawking at Miley's wig or Lizzo's bustle?" She waggles her brows. "Because we *know* Liz is going to *bring it* with the epic bustle."

"Another winning strategy," I concede. "But only good for *us*. Even Lizzo's bustle won't divert knowing eyes from identifying Bastien."

Once more, my friend dances her brows like she's simply teasing a segment of her new fashion competition show. "Do you know how many alternative entrances there are to Grand Central? Don't guess, because my man already has the answer. I'm positive he'll take great delight in planning the perfect route for *your* man."

I scowl. "He's *not* my m—"

"And surely you also know how different a man can look after a haircut and a shave," she interjects. "So if worse comes to worst—"

"Can we also not talk about *worse*? Pretty freaking please?"

D flicks up her fingertips with energetic emphasis. "I'm already calling the win on this one. Gold stars to Ms. Fine for the logistical win."

Allie swoops up from the bed and returns to the kitchenette table for her phone. "Not sure you can call it *preplanning* with only two hundred and ninety minutes to spare, but what the hell." After a second, her confident composure gets a fresh glow. "Well, hey there, Hot Stuff. Yeah, I know you're right down the hall, but you *know* I like it when you growl like that. Besides, I need you and Bast back in here right away. We have . . . an interesting little proposition for you two." She's silent for about three seconds before a sultry giggle breaks free. "Oh, *Max*. Of course you shouldn't be scared!"

As soon as she says it, I flash a new glance to Drue. "Why am *I* a little scared?"

And why doesn't her silence, filled by her way-too-knowing smile, do a thing for easing that angst?

CHAPTER FIFTEEN

BASTIEN

"Man, can you *believe* this shit?"

The man who issues the exclamation, a character bizarre enough to defy just one describing word, adds a grand sweep of an arm toward Vanderbilt Hall's ornately carved ceiling. His other arm is occupied with clamping around Maximillian's shoulder—not that the sloshed sot cares a whit about my brother's answer.

I step around to issue an answer on Max's behalf—and mine. It is my most intimidating stare, the look that shrivels every man at Versailles save Louis.

Until now.

A more foreboding conclusion, to be sure—if the days of Versailles were more than just past pictures in my head. The caricature of humanity before me now simply rears back his own head before snorting out a chuckle.

"Yo, buddy. Stop being so *mad as hops* and get yourself some from the *tavern* instead."

He chortles again, inflated with pride about his ability to read and absorb some of the slang from the Chatty Cheat Sheets that were distributed to the gala guests upon arrival. Maximillian and I have discreetly discarded ours, having already recognized half the expressions from our youthful adventures in Paris and London. But after a while, debauchery is as tiresome as gluttony and vanity. A man knows when to leave all that uselessness behind. I am grateful one of the men next to me is also aware of that fact.

As for the other . . .

"Seriously. You'll thank me. They're making something called the Regent's Revenge, and it has left me shoook, babyyy!" The character takes a stumbling step, stopping only when he collides into Max's chest. "Yo. Sorry, dude. I mean, I should be saying it's got me *half-rats*, right? Maybe even *full* rats?"

"Of course." My brother grits out a smile while tactfully prying free from the man. "That is all . . . delightful, my friend."

As we step away and weave through the thickening crush in this grand space, I mutter, "Do you even know who that is?"

"Not one fucking clue."

My scowl deepens. "And that is . . . acceptable to you? Amenable?"

"The two are not one in the same, brother."

"Which means what?"

He stops when we find a waist-high table near the wall, shockingly unoccupied. "That I accept many things that are *not* amenable so that I can have what is amazing."

I do not demand details after that. After seeing my brother in the same room with Alessandra Fine, I already know the answer. "Your life with your woman."

Though the light in here is a mellow tone because of the large chandeliers overhead, his irises glint like a long-lost goldmine.

"It is a very good life," he professes. "Like nothing I ever imagined, that is most certain—and yet it sometimes feels as if

I never were away."

"You are sincere," I say, exposing my awe about it. "You do not think of our time . . . your very history . . . and marvel at the masses of differences? Well, at the masses *themselves* . . ."

He chuffs with quiet mirth. "Not every place on earth is like Manhattan. You have truly had a twenty-first century trial by fire. But on the subject of fire . . . of course I think about what life was like, before the inferno in the wardrobe." As he tilts his head back, a small smile spreads along his lips. "But mostly, my thoughts are of what I assumed as utterly lost. Our home and friends. Our duties and purpose. Hell, even Chevalier."

I grunt. "That mangy hound of yours? Seriously?"

He drops his head, stabbing me with narrowed regard, but goes on like I have merely commented on the flower arrangement on the table. "Mostly, I mourn for Mother, Father . . . and you."

I watch my hand lift and then my thumbnail gouge a little crescent into a rose petal. And try not to think of ripping into his memories in the same way. "Chev was a good dog," I mumble. "Mostly."

He elbows me with the brutality only a brother can get away with. But his smirk is still smooth, his easy demeanor having nothing to do with the drink in his hand. It is likely the same smooth-as-silk whiskey I am nursing. I am *so* glad it is not a Regent's Revenge.

"This is good," he says after a sip of the dark-gold liquid. "*Very* good."

"On that, I *will* agree with you."

Another extended pause, in which I observe the conspicuous angles of his royal heritage along every inch of his profile as he looks around the room. "Whiskey is not the only thing they have improved in the last two centuries. Wine and weather prediction. Crémant and music concerts..."

"Does every part of this point get companion spirits? No wonder you have been enjoying yourself."

"All right, then. Put down your drink and join me right here and right now. Look around you, brother. Truly *look* at it all. Not just at the lights overhead, or the intelligence that created the moving period pictures on the walls, or even the advanced machinery that enabled our women to alter these suits within an hour..."

"Ah. Yes."

I straighten and spread a proud hand down my embossed satin waistcoat, as well as my fancily tied stock—now called a cravat, according to my fashion-shrewd brother. My dove-gray breeches have been renamed trousers. They now cover my entire leg. Though this is called *historical* attire, it already makes more sense than what I am used to.

Yes. I do like the suits. A great deal.

That must have tumbled out of me at some point, because Maximillian smiles wider. "Wait until you wear one that has not been sitting in costume storage for God knows how long." He jogs his head and waves across the hall—this time, to someone he actually knows—before wheeling around to me. "And until you sit in a tub with three-speed jets at eight angles. And sample gourmet sushi. And ride in an Airbus A350!"

His zeal has climbed so high, I do not have the heart to declare how soundly he has lost me.

Especially when he really *loses* me.

When the forest-thick throng seems to thin between us and the dancing area.

When, through that sparser fashion foliage, my stare fixates...

On a fallen star.

It is poetry in a moment when there should be none—especially in the private chambers of my soul. Because surely, Raegan will see them, as she always seems to do, across my whole face.

And when she sees them, she will fight them.

She will find a way to trivialize them, exactly as she played down all the steps of Alessandra's fascinating, *terrifying* plan.

In the hours since, I dared not expose my own hopes—and, of course, fears—about how this would all proceed. My twenty-first-century acclimation skills have been more like a mongoose in a snake pit instead of a butterfly in a garden. In this crowd of strangers, was I doomed to repeat all those vicious mistakes? Am I going to in the steps I must cover to get to the dance floor? To Raegan's side?

Raegan.

My *rayonnement.*

Is it really her? I am unsure whether to believe this vision before me. How she has suddenly *appeared* here, looking like this... How did I not see or notice her before? How has every male in the whole room not?

For she is *not* just a star.

She is a galaxy.

The brilliance of comet trails in her intricately piled curls. The twinkle of moondust in the barrettes that hold them up. The boldness of sunfire in her welcoming smile. And then the stars, so many of them, embroidered from gold threads into the froth of her diaphanous dress...

I rush faster toward the dance floor. Even faster. If I do

not get to her—

But thank Christ, I do.

After I reiterate the gratitude aloud—my aversion to church does not preclude my respect for its holy son—Raegan tosses an unsteady laugh.

"Errr... pardon?" she asks, equally nervous—and utterly beautiful.

"I thought you might float away before I got here." I seize one of her hands, just to assure that does not happen. "In the way that perfect fantasies often do."

She darts her free hand up to the throat that stutters on air. "And you really want to keep claiming you're a fighter instead of a poet?"

I take another small step toward her. The cloud of her skirts engulfs my leg. "I am a fighter to many, *ma chérie*—but a poet for only one." Gently, I draw her trembling fingers to my lips. Beneath my kiss, they shiver even harder. I pull away. But not very far. "Am I overstepping? We are in public... I should have more of a care for your reputation and sensibilities."

"Oh, don't you dare let me go, Desperado." She twists our grips until she is the one securing *me* tighter. "My sensibilities don't know half of what they're doing under all this stuff."

That is entirely too good a reason to wrap my other hand around her waist. As I already suspect, there is no give of her flesh anymore, with her torso now cinched beneath a corset. But that damned lingerie is also part of the reason I pull her in so tight.

"Are you well, *Rayonnement*? Your color is adequate, though I cannot say for certain past your rouge. Your eyes are bright, your speech coherent. You do not seem ready to belch or vomit."

Oh, but she definitely knows how to spit out a small laugh. "Gee, *thanks.*" And then a more hearty one. "Just so we're even, you don't look ready to hurl either."

And now, when I need the cue the most, she refrains from any and all chuckles. I go still, wondering if I have cleared my figurative slate for another disastrous faux pas. Does she expect me to be actually hurling something now? If so, exactly what? And to where?

Concerns that I stow away, since that is exactly what she seems to do.

Making this moment more perfect than ever before. More fitting.

This decade, represented by all the special decorations and lighting . . . yes, it should be as foreign to me as the modern world outside the building, but there is so much more I recognize now. Definitely enough to let me settle into a theoretical easy chair. The themed prop sets with their horses and buggies. The moving pictures, staged to depict promenading citizens and verdant landscapes. The finely presented food and drink. Even the people themselves, behaving with gentler manners and regal actions.

"Bastien?"

I startle but only for a moment. "Hmmm? Yes, Miss Tavish? You are welcome, of course," I add, directly addressing her previous quip, but she pierces right through my attempt at urbanity.

"What is it? You're a million miles away."

I do not growl or snap or defend. My point is better made another way. By transforming our handclasp so I control it and cinch into her waist again. Not by a great deal. Just enough so her breath catches once more. And mine with it.

"I am right here with you, magnificent woman." I husk it slowly. Deliberately. "And I know that so clearly because there is nowhere in space and time that I wish to be more."

Her lips purse. "We both know that's not—"

I tug at her again—so forcefully that our chests collide. And our hearts share their beats. And our bodies exchange a hot, heavy pulse. Oh yes, even through all our costume layers. Oh yes, even with all these people surrounding us.

Oh yes.

Oh *yes*...

Thank Christ—perhaps not so thoroughly this time— for how the musicians in the corner break from their quieter repertoire and begin a lush waltz. As the couples around us frame properly for the dance, I reluctantly step back to do the same.

Raegan sneaks the tip of her tongue between her gorgeous lips, readying for the same but also not relishing the idea. Quickly, I take consolation from that.

But once the dance officially begins, my bloodstream pumps one unimpeachable thought to my swirling senses. It is not ready to give up its new flames. Not by a single degree.

The rigor of the dance is no help. Yes, the *rigor*.

I move better with battle cries instead of music, especially when struggling not to step on a woman's skirts while my fixating on the steady throb in her neck. On the beats that flow fresh color beneath her topaz pendant and then down... farther. To the place where her decolletage meets the graceful rise of her breasts. To where I want to lower that fabric froth and taste the smooth flesh beneath...

I clear my throat. Pointedly. Attempting *any* dance in this growing... condition let alone a fucking waltz, is like asking one's pants to become their unique torture devices.

I have to focus on something else. Right away.

The witless boor from earlier. The inspiring grandeur of this room. Subways. Busses. Feeling so lost for so many days . . .

Feeling so found every time Raegan Tavish has reentered my atmosphere.

Especially right now.

At last, a thought I hope she can decipher on my face. When she seems to do just that, letting me know with an uptick at one side of her mouth, my desperation dissipates. My steps smooth out. Better words—my clunky poetry, just for her—brim to my own lips.

"*Rayonnement.*"

The other edge clicks up, and I am nearly back to missing a step. Or ten. Before she takes the stumble with me, I rush on.

"The word has always been perfect for you, Raegan . . . but now it is a struggle to say it." I attempt to shake my head. "The word simply does no justice to how you shine tonight. Not just . . . all this." I indicate toward her sparkling gown with my head. "But . . . *this.*" And then funnel my focus on her face alone. I must appear more potshotten than any other male in the room, but I am past caring. I only need more of her enchanting face. More of its freckled sweetness and bright, attentive light. Such brilliant *life* . . .

"You ever stop to think that you're looking at a lot of reflection, buddy?" she murmurs with adorable ease. "Because you clean up pretty well yourself, Bastien De Leon."

I cock my head back, carefully regarding her. "Which does not fully explain your quizzically themed curiosity."

"Curiosity?"

"Do I have that word incorrect, as well?"

"Maybe not," she confesses. "Well, not completely." An impish expression frolics across her face. "I just didn't think I'd like you so much with the totally clean face."

I join her in a soft laugh. "My face is *usually* clean, mademoiselle." And because I cannot resist, I poise my eyebrows with salacious intent. "Unless the...mess...is worth it."

"Hey!" She pouts. "Good thing we're occupied with dancing, Monsieur De Leon. I don't have time to pull out my fan and—"

"What?" I rejoin, warming to her resplendent repartee. The quick and sexy wit that first attracted me to her identical version, not so long ago. And yet, forever ago. Back at that wondrous day at Versailles, at the beginning of our journey.

Of *this* journey?

How I want to believe it is true. How I do not dare to.

"So what, exactly, *would* you do to me, *ma magnifique*? Or...with me?"

My gaze borrows the weight of the innuendo, dipping to peruse her lips—especially when my words cause those sweet pillows to part a little. My feet keep miraculous time as my mind takes imaginary hold of my own mouth, envisioning it could drop to claim her there. Pushing in to taste her. Conquering her with commanding sweeps of my tongue...

A strangled sound spills from her throat. I edge up a slow smirk. It feels good to be the one in charge again. Knowing that I am affecting her in so many ways again. And exactly how.

The only thing that would make it even better...

"*Bastien.*"

Starts with her pleading my name like that.

"Oui, ma chérie?"

My senses fill with an equal petition. Needing more of these ties to her spirit. Craving more of this fervor from her deepest nature ... this bond with her deepest soul. Most of all, seeing that she yearns for it too ...

"Je veux faire ... tout."

No. Not just the yearning. So much more than that.

So far beyond what I hoped ...

But entirely beyond what she has planned.

You want to do ... how much of everything? With how much of me? With how much of you? In how many ways?

Her fear, so apparent and instant, has me shackling all questions. Instead, I concentrate on gently guiding her to the side of the dance floor.

When we are clear of the throng in that area, I tug her fully back into my arms. If it is indecorous, even in this crowd, I do not care. This is no longer about flirty physicality. It is about exposed vulnerability. Hers *and* mine. Raegan's, because of the presence that keeps intruding on her self-control. Mine, because I can no longer hide what I keep hoping here. What my heart deeply longs for.

That somehow, in some amazing way, heaven has gifted me with *two* souls to cherish in *one* incredible form ...

Damn it.

It is the thought so good to be true, I violate too many boundaries by letting it take full bloom in my brain—and across my face. Raegan does not miss a nuance of it.

And at once shoves away to be free from it.

"Raegan!"

And now lifts her skirts, stumbling to be free from *me*.

"Rayonnement!"

We are approaching the far side of the cavernous room, closer to the stand with the barkeep who is not as busy as his friends. He eyes us with interest. To his view, we are a pair of squabbling lovers. But we are also potential patrons. If Raegan keeps fleeing me, the tapster might get what he wants.

As soon as I get close enough to reach for her again, I do—this time, without a word of warning. I manage a decent grab around her elbow. She hurls back a not-so-proper glower. Her irises are green fire. Her breaths emerge as furious hisses.

"How do you *even* dare?"

Bizarrely, my pulse does not jump to the same temperature. Oh, she still has my heart racing and my cock pulsing, but her virulence is already my much-needed spigot, turning on instincts that have been honed from years of subduing outlaws.

"I might ask how *you* dare, sweet one." I crank my grip tighter. "'Tis not a wise move to turn your back on a trained operative of His Majesty's royal army, let alone a—"

She wrenches her arm. I hold on fast—until the clever thing writhes in such a way that the shawl around her elbows, light as the dust from its infused stars, is now the only thing left in my hand.

"If you pull the fucking *duke* card right now, I'll scream at the top of my lungs until every uniform in this place is salivating to arrest you."

Her language is not as sparkling as those stars.

And God help me, I am doubly hard about it.

"That is *Monsieur le Duke De Leon* to you, girl."

She spurts a sharp laugh. "Ahhh, of course it is. Well, profuse apologies, your grace. *Mon dieu.* My complete bad!"

In another time and place, the airs and the attitude

would have resulted in her backside over my knee and her flesh under my palm. But in this exact moment, she is spared by my sudden wonderment.

And, if I am observing accurately, hers as well.

She has spoken that before.

Not fully. And maybe not exactly. But enough that I am swept away from this place, my eyes no longer beholding the grandeur of the huge hall around us. I am in a low-vaulted room on the top floor of an Orléans inn, naked in bed with her. And she is apologizing—but this time, there is not so much sass in it.

Sass that, in just a few days, I have come to ... anticipate. And savor. And adore. And celebrate.

Sass that I long for again ... even now, in this bittersweet memory ...

But is it? *A memory?*

But if not, then *what* ...

"Monsieur ... le Duke ..."

Her voice, as soft as the wrap in my hand but filled with the same confusion in my mind, has me blinking hard. I am back at the New York party. Fully dressed and clean-shaven. The ale slinger is still intently eyeing me—but his inspection is a trifle when squared off with Raegan's.

Raegan—who stares as if I have still been transported far away.

"Monsieur ... le Duke," she blurts again. "Le Duke De Leon. Because ... because ..."

"Rayonnement?"

I do not cloak my concern about it. No. My alarm. Where are the gorgeous glints in her eyes? The fresh color in her cheeks? What has suddenly unlatched her from me like this?

"Because what, Raegan?"

Dieu, I would be happy to accept the lash of her fury again, instead of this bizarre distance. The strange haze that continues to cover her face, as if she has figuratively reclaimed her sheer shawl from me, only to wrap it around her head.

"Because of the scroll," she finally states. "The decree... that Louis signed for you." She gasps, and I am too damn sure it is not because of the shock taking over my own countenance. "The scroll that you left on the night table... before Marquette came in and... and..."

"Raegan?" It is a raw demand from the depths of my throat, coinciding with the horrified gasp from the pit of hers. "*Raegan?*"

She releases another harsh breath, verging on a sob. "Oh, Bastien," she rasps. "Oh... no..."

Before she is done, I have enough time to toss aside her shawl and brace myself—to stop her plummet from an all-consuming faint.

Her head lolls against the crook of my arm. All the strength in my body funnels toward her. All the air in my lungs is stolen and frozen.

Which means the stunned *what the hell* on the air is not hers. Nor mine.

Through nothing short of a miracle, I manage to swing my head around. "Drue," I dimly croak. "Thank Christ."

"Holy shit." She yanks the peacock-blue fichu from her bosom, at once using its satin surface to dab at Raegan's forehead. The crinolines of her blue-bows-everywhere gown are a mass of urgent rustles. "What happened?"

"Eh?"

"Holy shit. Okay, scratch that and oxygen in your lungs. I

need you to pick her up because I can't in all . . . *this*."

I dip a quick nod before securing Raegan and most of her dress into my hold. At least five times, my frustration echoes what Drue has just expressed. I yearn to rip out the ridiculous crinolines and toss them into the shadows. But the last thing we need right now is undue attention—exactly what Drue is attempting to steer us clear from.

"Come on," she directs, rushing beneath a sign that says *Main Concourse*. We round another corner before entering a small room with doors that slide shut after we enter. I am too absorbed with watching Raegan to wonder why the little room seems to be rattling and then slowly descending.

Less than a minute later, we leave the room and again turn to the left. Drue leads the way toward a flight of stairs heralded by another sign.

THE CAMPBELL APARTMENT

"This is out of the way," Drue explains before I can ask exactly who Campbell is or why he wants the whole world to know where his apartment is. "And, from the scoopage I overheard around the party, it's also been clammed for the night because of the hoo ra-ra over the gala."

Only half a dozen of her words make sense, but I latch on to the main points like they're my new air. Hopefully, we are headed away from prying eyes and suspicious curiosities, most notably belonging to anyone who knows Detective Liam Logan.

At the top of the stairs, we confront a locked door. Drue unlatches the jeweled pin from her bodice and uses the long point to release the lock, mumbling something fervent about not having to find her way around "digital fuckery."

I am equally thankful the digits and their fuckery have stayed away, especially as we enter a room of sweeping grandeur. If I had moments to waste on being fully impressed with the space, I would indulge them. The wall sconces are made of sleek stained glass. The high hand-painted ceiling leads my gaze down the long room. At the end, on the other side of a bar topped with polished stone, there are plush chairs and couches. Across from the bar, there is a grand storage cabinet fronted by five carved doors.

I rush Raegan to one of the black leather chairs in front of that huge chest. My muscles strain as I take care not to jostle her. She moans now, fluttering her eyes as if struggling to focus.

"*Rayonnement?*" I lean in after grunting in gratitude to Drue for bringing over a damp cloth. I dab it along Raegan's face, but she flaps and shoves at me. "Sweet girl," I urge. "Please—"

But she *thwacks* at me again, which has me darting a scowl toward Drue.

"She's not totally conscious yet," the woman says. "What the hell happened?"

I shake my head. Trying to give her the answer would take hours we do not have. "Do you think we should summon a physician?" I demand instead. "I care not if Logan finds out. If she is unwell in some way—"

"Okay, slow up. Right now, that might be the password before the log-in."

"You want to bring in a *log*? All the way up *here*?"

Drue opens her mouth. Closes it. Clamps the front of her head as if talking herself out of saying something but speaks anyway. "I'm just saying first things first, all right? Let me go find your brother and Allie. All hell's going to bust loose, with or without logs, if those two look around the party and don't find us. Plus, if we really do need a doctor, maybe Allie can pull some strings and find one who's willing to slide in on the DL."

That ensures she has my fast and fervent nod. "Most excellent plan, then. Go."

The woman turns, requiring no more treatises or encouragement. Once more I acknowledge how valuable an asset Drue Kidman would be on a clandestine mission or on a battlefield. If she had been but born two hundred and fifty years ago . . . and as a man . . .

It is all the thought I have of that subject. Or any others. No considerations are of matter, in any form, other than the freshly moaning woman at my side. But while her burst is full of new strength, her countenance is not. She is still writhing in a dream world, crying out at her own apparitions . . .

Though all of her invisible ghosts now bear a name I cannot ignore.

Mine.

CHAPTER SIXTEEN

RAEGAN

"Bastien!" I cry, and then again, though the sound is so far away. So raspy and weak. "Bastien . . ."

Why isn't he answering?

What is going on here?

Am I dead? About to be dead?

Mom and Dad, in the name of peace, love, and magic crystals, always held to the view of letting me try any "natural substance" anytime I wanted. None of those wild trips from my youth compared to this. *All of this.* The threads of my sanity, slowly unspooling over the last two days and nights, tugged much harder with these episodes I keep trying to explain away . . .

But not now.

There's no excuse for this. Not the tidal wave of crazy that pours in now.

The waves of recall, making my head spin with their detail. Big things, like the size of the night sky—*where did all these stars come from?*—to the enormity of Versailles' stench in the summertime. But there is no time to process a grimace because I am dancing with Bastien again. A waltz—*where did all these spins come from?*—during which we are flirting in too many ways. With each other. With danger. With the idea of a union that can never be because Louis has now made him a duke.

A duke.

Never will I ever be accepted as the wife of a duke.

What?

I force myself to blurt it aloud, no matter how much it feels like a gong against the inside of my skull. *I'm worth ten dukes, damn it! Twenty!*

Too late, I realize I've let all that spew out too. The gong is now a hammer. A huge one. But as I grimace and fight it, equally mighty arms hold me close and tight.

It's all okay. I'm safe. Supported. Better than that, I'm alive.

I...think.

Because Bastien is still here. Closer than ever before. Caressing my forehead with his lips, which recite a nonstop litany of French. His voice is earnest and rough. Too rough. Filled with too much...of what?

I can't figure that out right now. Where would I even start? Weirder still, why is he thanking saints I've never heard of—and even some of his dead ancestors? At least that's what I think he's saying.

No. That *is* what he's saying. I understand it. Every single word of it. But I shouldn't.

I shouldn't.

"Bastien."

I'm not sure if it's a plea for him to stop or continue. But when he halts, I hate the silence. A world without his gruff baritone and adorable archaisms...it's terrible. Terrifying.

"Bastien?"

"Here," he assures, but it's not enough. I have to see him.

But that means compelling my eyes to open. It's painful, but I thank myself for it at once. "See? I am right here, *ma magnifique.*"

"Yeah," I whisper. "Oh *yes*. Hi there, gorgeous."

Every syllable carries my heart-deep worship. He's never been more beautiful, with his eyes a pair of blazes past the tumbled disarray of his hair. New stubble has returned to his jaw, shadowing the formidable angles in unbelievably alluring ways. As soon as I run a hand along the spiked plains, the rest of my body wakes up too. All too quickly. All too awesomely.

"You had me utterly dicked in the nob, woman."

I don't ask him what it means. I already know. His eyes are stark and unblinking from one obvious force. Fear.

"I'm sorry," I whisper.

"Do not do it again."

I lift my other hand to his face. As his breath audibly snags, so does mine.

And it's happening again . . . already.

The embrace of our intentions . . . already.

The stitching of our souls . . . already.

"Then give me a good reason not to."

Still no breath out of him. I see the oxygen being used in another way. The blazes in his gaze are stoked high enough to set the city on fire and me with it. Oh God, I hope so. *This* is where I need to be. Where *we* need to stay. The place that's not so scary. The place with so much fire and thirst and lust, it burns away all the confusion and trepidation.

But I can't do it alone. I need his combustion too. He's starting to get it but still isn't sure, so I take him tighter in my hands and pull hard.

Our lips touch but don't kiss. I won't give him that yet. I

refuse. He needs my words first.

"Bastien." A caress of breath. A fast press at the corner of his mouth. "*Please*. Give me . . . the reason." And then a lick along his lower lip until I can bite into his opposite corner. "Maybe . . . a lot of them."

His exhalation is heavy but ragged. His hand, feeling beneath my crinolines for my thigh, is steadier. Thank all of his obscure saints.

"*Ma magnifique*," he husks. "*Dieu aide moi*, I cannot refuse you . . . even now." He leans over me with ease, and I thank those saints again for the accessibility of the wide leather chair into which he has placed me.

Where exactly *has* he placed me? But why do I even care?

"Ah!" he exclaims once his fingers find their way to my naked center. "*Especially* now."

No. I really don't care where we are.

Not as his shoulders flex as he strokes me down there.

Not as his jawline tautens until it could feel like a private gift box in my grip.

Especially not as he dips and then twists his touch, entering me with a swoop of long, aggressive fingers. Two of them, and then three. Pumping until I'm sighing. And then gasping.

"Oh, my. Oh, *Bastien*."

"Is this what you meant by *reasons*, little Raegan?" he croons into my ear. "Perhaps . . . three of them?"

I answer his roguish chuckle with another high-pitched sound. Not a gasp this time, but not a sigh. Something in between, seeming to arouse him like a caress of its own.

I savor every second of the moment. I revel in causing his blood to race and his libido to rise right along with mine. I preen, just a little, that he gets this way by simply touching me.

"Three's a good number," I tease out in a murmur. "But one can work too . . . if it's the one and only of your cock."

His throat convulses. The sound within . . . it's dark and lusty and immediately addicting. It entrances me so much that I raise myself a few inches, sealing my lips over the vibrating knob in his neck. When he makes the sound again, such a primal and perfect drone, I suck harder.

"Méchante *fille*," he growls. "Such a nasty girl, demanding my body like this. Making it so easy for me to find your sweet little *minou*. As if it already misses me fucking it . . ."

"Well," I cut in with a sultry drawl, "there *is* such a thing as historical accuracy. Especially if it comes with delightful perks."

"Oh, no one is coming *yet*, my sweet."

It's more command than flirtation, and every syllable has me shivering. He's going all-in for the *King and I* vibe, and I couldn't be more delighted. But the next moment is even better. As he picks up the tempo, languidly pushing back and forth into my channel, my clit ignites. My thighs clench. My hips buck at him, needing more. *Oh, so much more.*

"But . . . soon? Please, Bastien . . . tell me soon."

"Perhaps," he grates out. "But perhaps I shall make you wait for it. And beg me more for it."

"Just as long as it's with your dick." I rearrange my hold, securing his nape with one hand and his huge shoulder with the other. "*Please*, Desperado."

I lock down his gaze with the pleading desperation in mine. In the pit of my gut, I sense we've run out of time on the twenty-first century bus ride. If this is the last stop on our line, I want to be closest to the gas tank. Ready for explosion on impact.

"I even came prepared," I offer. "I mean, just in case, right? Under the elastic at the top of my left stocking…" While I could never bring myself to take the special pill back at the North Greene, there's still no need to spit in karma's eye. "You'll find—"

My own giggle, nervous and high, is my interruption as Bastien secures the condom packet. His motion is almost too slick for comfort. Funnily enough, his wavering smirk has me relaxing again. Good damn thing because wasting a second of this man's sensuality on my stress feels like twelve kinds of a crime. Maybe more.

"You know, I might need a little help with this," he murmurs. "Do you know of any naughty little seductresses willing to apply for the position?"

I snatch the small square package out of his fingertips. "Only if they want me to separate their pupils from their corneas."

He snorts, but the mirth fades once I twist at one button, and then the second, at the front of his breeches. As soon as the flap falls free, so does his cock. And it's wonderful. Swollen heat, pulsing in my hand. Needy drops at the slit, ensuring that the rubber will slide on without problem. Another good thing. The sooner this flawless penis is inside me, the better.

"Oh, Mother Porn and all her filthy minions. I should've known better."

The voice, drenched with so much irritation that it's comforting, yanks me from the task at hand. Well, *in* hand. I've only gotten the rubber halfway up Bastien's length when he and I startle together.

Also in tandem, we stare to where Drue's voice emanates—across a huge room that's disconcertingly familiar.

"Oh, my hell." I sit up straighter as recognition sets in. By a lot. The delay in my cognizance isn't just from the reality escape that my brain just took. It's because the last time I was here, the room was packed. We were celebrating Allie's first signed contract with Hemline. "The Campbell," I utter. "Oh, holy shit. We're at Grand Central. Wait. *Wait.* We're here because . . . *The gala.*" I jolt a new gawk up at Bastien. "Where we were dancing . . ."

Before my mind decided to mess with me . . .

In scary ways . . .

"Oh my *God.*"

But now, I'm not the only one dealing with baffled bewilderment. Allie's first three words are the same as my last three. As they burst from her, the woman rushes over.

She's dressed in a gown that's similar to Drue's in the bodice but styled like mine from the waist down. The lavender color, nearly her trademark by now, is adorned with small purple rosettes and a poofy satin underskirt. It all billows even more as she drops to her knees beside us.

"Baby girl. Oh, my word, are you all r—" Once her gaze sweeps down, she chokes. "Oh, you certainly *are!*"

I'm positive I'm a hundred shades of red, all from the neck up, despite how the equal number of gown layers are a sufficient shield for my modesty. Bastien isn't so lucky. There he is, half-gloved and fully erect, gloriously on display for our three new guests. Fortunately, two of them are friends who've received enough dick pics in their lives to handle the unexpected view. And the third is a person who's probably seen Bastien's crotch more than me.

"And now we *know* he is a De Leon," Max declares. His punctuating shoulder roll is a combination of Buffalo Bill and Steve McQueen.

"On that note, it's time to turn off the bounce house, kids." The creative verbiage only enhances Drue's strictness. When she has even Max backing down, my own tension takes over again. "We've got to focus on ways of sneaking little Rae-Rae right out of here-here."

"And then right to a physician," Bastien inserts, only to be speared by a sterner look from D.

"It's on the priority list. Just not the immediate one."

"No. Not acceptable." Bastien stiffens. "Do you understand that she lost consciousness in my arms? Do you understand—"

"Desperado." I bolt to my feet now too. Though all the blood in my body recirculates in crazy directions, I push past it to bypass him and beeline for Drue. "I think we need to listen to her." I stop and sway but tack on a silent look in the nick of time. D doesn't say anything. "What is it?" I demand. "Is Logan—"

"No." She pulls in a tight breath. "I mean . . . not yet, at least."

"Not *yet*?"

"She's trying to say we don't know," Allie offers. "About a half hour ago, the Hemline brass summoned Max and me for a photo op with the other network personalities. We had to walk through the area where MTA security is coordinating with the police for tonight." She reaches for one my hand. "They were on the radio, talking to Liam Logan. About you."

"Shit." I mutter it at the same time that Bastien spits it in French. "So, there's no time to waste." I throw my gaze to Drue. "Do you think we can double back to the Greene?"

"You mean can *you* go back." Allie squeezes my fingers,

taking on an expression I haven't seen since the night I threw up in her foyer bathroom for hours. "Yours is the only name on the alert, sweetie. They're not talking about Bastien or Drue."

D now looks as miserable about that as her. "When we walked into the consulate, a lot of my face was hidden by that dorky wig and beret. And officially, Bastien doesn't yet exist in this century. That means they probably got a positive face match on you alone."

"Double shit." I plant my left foot to add traction for the inevitable leg jiggle. "Okay, so I'll just try to sneak out through the bar's Vanderbilt Avenue entrance—"

"And I shall be at your side," says the proud soldier who's reinserted himself next to me. I let him see the grateful smile in my eyes before I go on.

"We'll get a cab from there to the Greene," I say. "I'll change into fresh clothes and then cut my hair—"

"What?"

"You have a better idea on how I can throw off Dick Logan?" I rebut to Bastien's outburst.

"Dick Gorgeous is *such* a better way of saying that," D says.

"Huh?" Allie flings. "What *else* have I missed?"

"Fun story for later," D rejoins. "With better lighting and tastier cocktails."

"All sounding like *idées parfaites*," Max cuts in. "But, as Drusilla aptly expressed, for later. *Much* later."

Allie, D, and I honor his wisdom by wasting no more time—except to bunch together in a tight triangular embrace.

"Don't you worry about a thing, Sister Tigger," Drue decrees. "We've got your back, okay?"

"We'll redirect Dick Gorgeous and his friends to

someplace fun. Maybe Brooklyn. Or Siberia."

As I giggle, a few nervous tears slip through. "Well, *there* are a couple of great ideas."

"We'll find a way to get in touch," Allie assures. "But not until it's safe."

"Which it will *not* be if we do not depart in all haste."

The charge is wrapped in so much of Bastien's bossy bearing, I don't even think it's strange to look up and see him in his full regiment regalia for a couple of seconds. But I blink and the vision is gone, thank God. If he had stayed in his time for even a few hours longer, that uniform would have been the ultimate signature on his execution orders.

But while the hallucination is gone, it hasn't given me back my spine. Every vertebrae is a chunk of ice, enough to make me tremble in place. Bastien, attempting to tug me toward the Campbell's entrance stairwell, already peers at me in concern.

"*Rayonnement?* What is it?"

I shiver again. Even harder. "I don't know. I . . . can't move all of a sudden. I don't know why. I—"

"Ssshhh," he admonishes. "It is going to be all right, my sweet." He scoops up my other hand. "I am right here with you. Just stay with me this time. You promised you would. Remember?"

"I did," I rasp, but that's all I can get out. My heart is an ice-covered mallet against my ribs. Everything between my neck and knees is locked as if already frozen.

The most inaccurate comparison of the night. Perhaps of my whole life.

Because when I look back up to Bastien, praying his strength is enough to melt my biological iceberg, I instead gawk up and over his shoulder.

At the huge curio cabinet along the wall behind him.

The ornate thing has held many treasures and oddities in the nearly hundred years since John Campbell installed it, but right now it looks to be consumed by . . . *fire.*

The same surreal flames that flashed in the wardrobe in Max and Allie's apartment—right before Bastien stepped out of it.

The same heat that casts frightening shadows across my friends' faces as they acknowledge the bizarre sight.

The good news? I'm really not going crazy this time. Everyone else can see this too.

The bad news? I'm *not* the only one experiencing this.

It's real.

And it's frightening.

This cabinet is *a lot* bigger than the one Allie had shipped over from France.

So what does that mean? Is this thing *another* time travel machine? If so, who's in it? Or *what*? Have the Jacobins found a way to follow Maximillian and Bastien here? Is there an entire battalion of them braced inside? If so, what are we going to do about it? Fight back with barware and expensive bottles of booze?

Already, the answer flares in my mind.

Yes. If we damn well have to.

The light show doesn't go on for too long. As it fizzles and dims, Max stomps forward. Bastien joins him. The looks they shoot back at Allie, Drue, and me aren't to be brooked. This definitely isn't the time for reckless one-liners.

"Halt! Whomever you are, inside the closet, you are commanded to show yourself. Keep it slow with your hands where I can see them!"

Though as reckless zingers go, Bastien *does* know how to fling them.

Until one of the cabinet doors swings open.

And then one more.

Two people appear. Only... *two.*

As the pair cautiously emerges into the light, I watch the soldier-commando-alpha drain right out of my Desperado's spine. Maximilian's too.

The man and woman look like they've stepped from a production of *Les Miz*, with slightly better costumes. The woman's bodice is demurely pinned, with a faded crimson fichu that matches the kerchief around her head. The man's long vest is the same regal color, with gold buttons that match the closures at the bottom of his breeches. They look older, causing astonished bells to chime in all my instincts—*did the guys' parents find a way to escape too?*—but that's before I notice the sun damage to their skin and the work calluses on their hands.

They're not nobility. But they're also not strangers. Not to the two men between us and them—the secret prince of France and his newly ennobled brother—who now rush the pair of arrivals like *they* are the heralded royalty in the room.

But once they are before the man and woman, the brothers do not bow or kneel. Bastien and Max wrap the pair in impassioned hugs, as if determined to wipe away their dazed stares with the force of the embraces.

But I'm damn glad they do. I look over to Allie, seeing that she is too.

The guys' gestures are what make us both certain of what we're watching. A reunion that's a little less shocking now.

But only a little.

All right, maybe not even that.

As Max growls out one name and Bastien the next—both coated in layers of total shock and joy.

"Carl."

"Kavia."

BASTIEN

"By the saints! It *worked*!"

While Kavia's happy gasp is a warm bloom on my shoulder, her grip on my neck is nearly the opposite. I groan from the brutal clench but manage to end with a laugh.

"I think it certainly did," I say. "And left you no worse for the two-hundred-year wear either."

The woman, as equally precious as precarious to see here, bats at my sternum. "*You* are an impossible spade, sir."

If she only knew the half of it now. How I could truly let fly with the flattery if I so chose, courtesy of the wild and random streets of this place. New York, for all its hard and strange edges, has also taught me about lighter wonders. Juice boosts, falafel, day spas, night basketball, hot yoga, cold sodas . . . and so many hundreds more. *Thousands*, perhaps.

The things I am still craving to see and do with Raegan by my side, if the woman would only give up the wild idea that I am not meant to be here anymore. That urgency inside her, to return me quicker than an ill-fitting sweater to the Macy's service desk—before I have had a chance to see Macy's *at all*— which has not been helped by this new development in our night.

Development?

And just whom do I think to fool with that awesome underplay?

The development stage was back at our decision to come to the gala at all. *This* is far beyond that.

Carl and Kavia, standing here before us ... well, it is ...

"And you both are incredible miracles, madame."

And here is my brother, coming through with the perfect word at the perfect moment. *As usual.* Normally, it would be so simple to add the qualifier. But I wonder if *usual* will ever be a word I use for *any* part of life again.

At the moment, I focus on easier subjects. Such as *miracle* absolutely being better than *development.* I only wish it were a sentiment that either Carl or Kavia felt too—but clearly do not. The somber intent starts with our former house man but swiftly dominates his wife's face as well. They link hands, also not a gesture I expect before turning to face us again.

"We wish we had hazarded this trip for miraculous reasons, my boy," Carl murmurs as if he has added the duties of the Château De Leon's undertaker too.

"Hazarded." The echo comes not from Max or myself. Drue is the one moving forward now, rapt interest in her gaze and voice. "How *did* you two get here without using the time warp wardrobe?"

It is a question pounding at my own mind, but I wonder if Carl and Kavia will accept it from an aqua-haired female with such forward manners. I should have known never to worry. As Kavia lifts a ready smile at Raegan's friend, she also brandishes a small strip of wood.

"By using this," Kavia announces.

"And a great many prayers," Carl injects.

The glorified splinter is not long or thick enough to qualify as a witch's wand, but my intuition already hints at what it is. More vitally, where it came from. I obey that instinct to offer a theory out loud.

"A part of the original wardrobe itself."

Kavia nods. "But not taken on purpose. It broke off when we moved the thing back into the château. I wrapped it up, wondering if there would ever come the bizarre chance of needing it while away from home . . ."

Carl fills in her pause with a heft grunt. "And Christ help us, that occasion came."

Kavia winces. "Faster than we imagined."

I exchange a knowing glance with Maximillian before murmuring, "The Revolution." And then look down, knowing better than to return my regard to the people who were like a second set of parents to us. My emotions are already spiking too high. My temper, too heated. "When the new Assembly seized the château, they made you leave."

Carl, normally glad to let his wife be their main mouthpiece, braces his stance and provides the next commentary.

"Seized it, they did," he relays. "But they were emphatic about wanting us to stay and help operate the place." His high forehead undulates courtesy of his arching brows. "Their offer was surprisingly decent, for a pack of wild mutts with bloodshed on the brain."

"But you left anyway?" Maximillian prods. "Why? Because of what?"

"Not because of *what*." Kavia's gentle declaration is also a departure from the norm. She is normally like a kitchen-bound version of the town crier, undaunted about word she utters. "'Twas because of *who*," she continues, just as caring.

"And that *who* was *you*, Bastien."

"Me?" Though I stand taller, my head rears back. "But if you already had the fragment from the wardrobe, that means you had already sent me off, behind the inn at Orléans. So if I was no longer there—"

"Ohhh no?" Carl nearly chortles out the interception— yet another odd occurrence. Carl does *not* enjoy chortling. More so, with such gusto.

"Bastien." Kavia reaches for me. "We truly have not traveled this far just to see if we could. We came to find you— so we could bring you back with us."

I whip my hand away. "Pardon the hell out of me?" And at once am questioning the spew. Just two days ago, after traversing the wild montage of New York City, I would have been jubilant about this. I would be madly snatching the woman's hand and leading the way back into the big cabinet.

But now...

What do *I want?*

I know not. *I know not.*

This place and this time... I still do not belong here. My very bones confirm that. But walking away? Just vanishing and going back...

To... what? And to whom?

Kavia doubles down on her own insistence. "Bast. My boy. It is about... Magique."

Six quiet syllables on her thin lips.

Six chaotic clangs through all my senses.

I grab my head, digging fingers at my scalp, but the din goes on. It is tamed only when my brother steps up, a protesting glower on his face.

"Magique is dead, Kavia. *Oui,* he told me all about it. The woman was murdered before his eyes, and then—"

Kavia tosses her head from side to side. "No. *No.* We are trying to tell you ... as absurd as it seems ..."

"Stop!" Maximillian stomps to the right, inserting himself between her and me. "I will not allow you to torment him like th—"

Kavia cuts his air short with a vehement shove. I doubt anyone but her could get away with such an affront to my brother. "You think *that* is why we did this? Risked ourselves together like this? To deliver empty *torment* to you boys?"

When Max's opinion is still glaringly clear in his coiled posture, Carl moves forward. "Let her speak, Maximillian. Believe me, if we *both* had not seen it with our own eyes ..."

"Seen what, damn it?" I finally break in. "We are all standing here on borrowed time. You must gather your thoughts and your words, Kavia. Just tell me. What about Magique?"

At last, Max capitulates with a terse nod. But now that Kavia has the full floor, her jaw has nearly dropped to it. At the end of my patience, I am about to prompt her again—when her mouth finally forms around a word.

"Here," she stutters out. "H-H-Here. She is ... *here!*"

I wheel around—and realize that from her angle, Raegan has been invisible until now. But still, her shock sends me into a similar daze. Only at this moment do I recognize what has felt like impossibility for so long. That Raegan is not invisible to me. More so, that she is not the unusual but passable proxy for Magique. She is ... *Rayonnement.* A unique radiance in my existence. In my spirit.

In my heart.

"Hello there." Raegan arcs an awkward wave and then

drops into a small curtsy. As I battle the urge to sweep her up and kiss her soundly for the beautiful respect to my alternate parents, Carl joins his own gawk to Kavia's. "So sorry, I know this is mega weird. But... my name is Raegan Tavish. I was apartment sitting for Max and Allie—errr, Maximillian and Alessandra—when somehow, Bastien burst in via the wonder wardrobe and—"

"Oh, no." I pivot from Kavia in order to wrap my arms around my adorably bumbling woman. "Not just *somehow*, Raegan. My God... if even I see it by now, how are *you* so blind to it?"

She huffs, conveying her affronted puzzlement. "Listen, buddy. Somebody's got to see the forest through the trees, okay?"

"To the point that you do not see the purpose through the providence?" I counter.

"Huh?"

She scowls. I do my best to erase the fine lines of it with my fingertips.

"It was not just *somehow*, Raegan. None of it. It was *somewhere*, in a very specific *sometime*. My collision into you, into this *here and now*, was a reminder that I had to keep putting steps in front of each other. You reminded me why I received that dukedom... 'Twas not just for how I wielded my sword. It was for the courage I had to keep fighting, even if all the odds seemed absolutely impossible. To keep believing I had been spared for a reason, even if Magique was not."

There is more to tell her—*mon dieu*, so much more—but Kavia surges at us, now appearing and acting like the real woman who inhabits her body.

"No. *No*. My boy, this is the very reason we are here!

This—by all the saints that were ever lifted to heaven—*this* is why we are here!"

She ends it by rushing in and clasping Raegan in her own exuberant grip. My *rayonnement* darts her wide stare between the two of us.

"I ... ermmm ... not quite sure I understand ..."

"The purpose through the providence." Kavia punches harder on every syllable than I did. "The *somewhere,* the *sometime*—and the *someone.*"

She nudges in between us. In a numb haze, I let her. My obeisance is more than being the De Leon brother who knew the wrong side of her paddle too many times. It is also not about the shock of actually having her here.

It is the acknowledgement of the words she has just reiterated. The truth she is now staring into Raegan's soul. The verity I have seen so many times in Raegan's eyes and been too staggered to admit. To truly see.

"You know it too, Miss Raegan Tavish ... *oui*?" whispers my determined sorceress of a former kitchen maid. But right now, Kavia wields no charmed wood shards or alluring incantations. She summons no extra power but that of the truth. "You have already seen it. Smelled it. Touched it. You have already been touched by ... *her.*"

And there it is.

Too outlandish to consider.

Too terrifying to dream of.

So I do not dare.

"Kavia." I lower my arm between Raegan and her. I keep going, pushing vehemently enough to make her stumble back. "You will stop." I swing my gaze up to hers. "*Please*. She is gone, and I have to accept that. I *have* accepted it."

"No. *No*, my boy. Do you not know it? Do you not *see* it?"

"Of course I see it, damn it. But that is not the same as wishing such a thing into existence. Rebirth is for Bible passages and folk tales. It is *not* for—"

"But what if it is?"

My mouth is already open, drawing more air to settle Kavia into her existential place, but stop short when realizing the retort is not hers.

As usual, Raegan Karlinne Tavish has toppled my mind like a brimming apple cart. The fruit tumbles through my mind at wild velocity. Just like her bold, bustling city. Just like her vibrant, passionate spirit. All the ways she challenges me . . .

But none so much as now.

"I said, Bastien De Leon, *what if it* is *possible?*"

She rolls a sweet but strong hand along my outstretched arm. With gentle guidance pulls it around her waist. Along the way, her hair tickles my knuckles. After all the jostling tonight, her shiny strawberry curls have started to tumble free, exactly the way I like them.

Just a tiny part of everything I have grown to love about her.

"*Rayonnement?*" I hook my other arm around her. "What are you saying?"

I draw her yet closer, needing her here now. Unable to see her anywhere else. More than just my connection to this place and time. She is my bridge back to . . . me. The life I thought so lost to me. The soul I had all but torched in that loss.

"The whole of it, Raegan." It is a demand I do not intend but cannot ignore. Something already tells me that her answer is too important for a simple whisper. "You have never distilled the truth from me, woman. Do not begin such disrespect now."

If she is going to insist that I depart with Kavia and Carl, then she *will* honor me by saying exactly that.

But dear God, how I pray it is everything but that.

Oh yes, this is me—*praying.*

And now this is her— smiling.

"Well, I'm not dictating it in code, Desperado."

She adds to all of the sudden lightness with a small giggle. *Laughter? Why?* What am I telling myself not to hope for—but dare to do just that anyway?

"Hey. I really *am* asking this, buddy. I mean, what if… all of this … really *is* the freaking miracle? What if, in a weird way, I was right about the ultimate plan but wrong about the spark for it?"

I scowl. It is not a proper reply for her mirth, but her honesty deserves the wholeness of my own. "Which means what?"

"Which means … what if you really were just here for a stop-over but not a full arrival? What if you were always meant to return to your own time—but not to rescue Magique? What if you were meant to travel here so you could bring her back with you?"

At once, there are wings springing from my heart. But then I realize they have always been there. All this time, I have been carefully cutting them back, refusing to let them take complete flight. They are poised now, so ready to carry me into the heavens…

But not yet.

"*Rayonnement*…" The endearment is equally as tenuous. Waiting… for what, I am not fully sure. But it feels like something good. So right. So huge. So full. "Are you really saying…"

"That I love you, Bastien." She wraps her hands along my face again. Pushing her warmth and life and adoration and *love* into me again. "I think I've loved you for a very, very long time. Yes, in another life. In *our* life, the one that we were planning that night, until everything went so awful and wrong."

"*Mon dieu,*" I breathe out. "I love you too."

I can no longer hold back. I lean in and take her lips beneath mine, sealing myself to her with a bond recognized by the ages...symbolizing a promise that has survived the centuries.

Until death...but beyond...

The words resound in my heart and soul—and now, I know, from Raegan's, as well. She returns my kiss with all their strength and magic...and *oui*, all their time-defying power. It makes me tremble, and I part her lips to delve in deeper, but we are interrupted by thunderous rhythms in the walls around us. A sound I know all too well.

The pounding force from determined footfalls. The lockstep sprints from focused, coordinated soldiers.

For a second, but only one, I am amazed how some sounds survive the trounces of time. Passion, joy, sorrow...violence.

But at this exact moment, I do not choose violence.

I focus on the power that betters it.

The purpose through the providence. The love that got me back to her side, at the exact moment that I should have been there. The love that pulled me through so many minutes, days, years, decades...*centuries*. The destiny that she believed in, even while she lay dying in my arms so long ago.

Until the end of time, my love...

I am praying again. This time, it is to give every kind of

ANGEL PAYNE

gratitude I can put words to—though there is so much inside that defies syllables or syntax. So much I want to say and ask but cannot.

Only one line seems to crawl its way from the clamor of my mind and take discernible form upon my mouth. "So... what do we do now?"

"Hmmm." Raegan tilts her head, eyeing me with intent that is all Magique. The sly slant of her lips, joined with the open honesty of her gaze, that pummels me ten times harder than when we first locked gazes at Versailles.

This time, it carries the best of both worlds. The magnificence of both women. The doubled treasure I have been given, in one stunning beauty.

The love I will cherish for the rest of my days—no matter what time and place they are in.

"I think we should go home, Monsieur le Duke," she murmurs at last. "I mean, if Kavia and Carl are right, it seems we have some catching up to do..." Her quizzical glance is met by Kavia's confirming nod.

I tug her even tighter. Dip my head so that our eyes fully meet again. "You are absolutely certain?" I prompt, wondering if I have ever meant any words more.

"Oh, believe me, I think she's *certain*." Drue is the one to laugh that out, with Alessandra chuckling by her side.

"We'll tell your mom and dad everything," Alessandra states. "I think they're the only parents on the planet who'll actually get it."

"I love you two wenches."

Raegan pulls from me long enough to rush into a three-way hug with her friends. When they pull apart, I am skittish about getting back a woman with hesitant steps and teary

271

eyes, but my *rayonnement* steps back over to take my hand with more surety than before. Her emerald gaze is clear and bright and adoring.

"I'll write them, and you, some long letters," she promises to them. "They'll be in the wardrobe. In the meantime . . ." She pushes all the way back against me, snuggling her cheek atop the heart that now beats because of her. *For* her. "Tell everyone that I've run off with the hottest duke of all time."

EPILOGUE

RAEGAN

1798 — Montjoie, Germany

Morning mist clings to the tops of the lush Eifel hills as I make my way along the narrow cobblestone road, fighting the urge to break out in a song or three from a favorite princess-y type Broadway show. I mean, in this setting, any of them will do.

Instead, I hum a simple folk tune while turning right to cross a stone bridge over the happily babbling Rur. Along the way, I pass a couple of fellow shopkeepers. Neither of them startles at the pair of bulging baskets dangling from my curled elbows. They already know I've not been to market for fruit and bread.

My treasures are better: new lengths of fabric from the Troistorff and Red House cloth layers, who have turned wool and cotton and thread into lengths of beautiful inspiration for me today.

Already, my senses are zinging. If I embellish the sage velvet with gold thread, it'd make a stunning new coat for Bastien—just in time for the town's harvest ball. At once, I'm sizzling in other places too. The years have been very good to my hottie desperado . . .

Correction. They've been very good, period.

As if fate thinks I need more convincing, it times the next moment to perfection.

As I round another corner, the sunlight finally breaches into town and illuminates the little shop at the end of an avenue straight from a storybook. The sign, a birthday gift from Bast so many years ago, thrills me as intensely as the day he mounted it over the front door.

RAYGIQUE: MODISTE MAGNIFIQUE

Business hasn't stopped since that day, though I've had to start double-checking myself on what provincial German townswomen will accept as the newest fashion sensation from the big cities. I'm not sure Frau Kraus has yet recovered from my Aphrodite-inspired sketches as suggestions for her daughter's wedding ensemble.

Massive note to self: the Regency isn't here yet.

But it won't be a chore to wait.

Sometimes, I even wish time would hold still a little more.

"Mama! It's her! Mama's home!"

Times like right now.

Though I tenderly place my baskets aside, the attention isn't half of my care for the five-year-old dynamo who fills my arms. "Oof!" I groan and mean it. "Christophe Maximillian Tavish, have you sized up since I last saw you?"

His giggle tickles my neck while his meadowy smell delights my nose. "Silly mama. You only left an hour ago."

"Whaaat?" I tease, squeezing him close again. "Well, they were sixty of the longest minutes of my life."

I duck my head, ready for another wonderful whiff of early autumn mixed with rambunctious boy, but he's already squirming for freedom. *Aha.* I should've known there was a purpose to Chris's willing cuddles.

"Yo, buddy," I prompt. "What is it?"

The little furrows in his forehead, so similar to his father's, intensify to full grooves. And now he's practically a carbon copy of Bast—a recognition prompting my wider smile. And his tighter scowl.

"Christophe? Come on, now. You can tell me. You *need* to, young man."

The hell *yes,* he does. Because there are still too many moments like this. Seconds in which a schism like *this* is shooting along my spine, afire with worry and wonderings. Too many of them.

Have we escaped far enough away?

Taken enough precautions, even with the new identities?

Watched all the shadows and corners that we can?

Another year and a few months, and the Revolution will officially be over. Though Napoleon has already returned Château De Leon to one of Bastien's cousins, we don't dare return until then—if we choose to return at all. Right here, in the damp dirt with this sweet boy, I already swear I'm in heaven.

Except for this anxious rope I used to call a spinal cord.

"Are we really the Tavishes?"

And now the petrified punctures I used to call skin pores.

"Ermmm . . . why on earth would you ask that, buddy?"

As Chris steps back, he rubs at his eyes. Only now do I notice the emotional red rings in them. *Holy shit.*

"Izzy was teasing me. She says our last name isn't truly Tavish. That we are pretending for everyone." He drops his head to one side. "If that is so, are we . . . *lying* to people? And don't you say lying is bad?"

I open my mouth. Clamp it again. Shove heavy air out through my nose.

"Where's your father?"

Thankfully, he points inside. I nod, thankful that Bast hasn't left to start his newest job. The Hoftstaders' privy is going to be quite a project, and he mentioned wanting to get an early start. For that reason, Kavia was here before *I* left—not that she had to come far. She and Carl live above their small ale house around the corner.

When I walk through the shop and into our living quarters, the woman hasn't moved from her place at our dining table. But a couple of elements *have* changed, so I don't feel completely batshit. She's made progress on the embroidery along the hem of Lady Horseley's gown—*thank you, helper angel*—and the little lilt in her lips has ticked up by quite a few notches.

I borrow from my son, slowly tilting my head. Do I dare ask her if the look is a good or bad thing?

The serene gypsy at the table takes away my dilemma with her humorous chuff. "They're upstairs." A jog of her chin toward the ceiling. *"All the way."*

I straighten my head with a jolt. "In the attic?"

Waiting for that answer isn't an option. Our attic is like the West Wing from *Beauty and the Beast*. Full of all the off-limits stuff. The kids *know* not to trespass its boundary. Bast and I have intimated at everything short of a child-eating goblin king inside the low crawl space.

Now, as I climb the ladder up through the hatch hole, I wonder if I should've had Kavia cast a goblin snarl across my face. Maybe that's what I'm going to need to teach this young one a proper—

The concept vanishes as fast as my fury.

As soon as I push up completely into the attic and discover that *I'm* the intruder now.

My arrival has very nearly destroyed the careful array atop one of my old fichus. It's spread across the floor, now doing duty as a tea party table linen. Two chipped saucers, centered by two old china cups, are on opposite sides of a plate full of breakfast biscuits.

Well . . . not completely full.

Telltale crumbs are dotted across my oldest child's pretty lips. Across from her, Bastien is licking away his own tasty morsels, looking entirely too breathtaking about it. His strong jaw is stubbled to the point of stunning, and his gaze is better than the bright sun outside.

But none of those factors are what kills the air in my throat and the strength from my limbs.

I stop cold, still on the ladder, when realizing that Ysabeau Eleanor Tavish is playing tea party dress-up in the gown from the night that changed my existence. The ivory and gold confection makes her look like a precious doll in a wash of endless sea foam, despite all the pink of her practical day dress. Clearly, she's pretending that's not even there. She keeps hoisting up the sheer shawl, wrapping it around her shoulders like the belle of the ball she longs to be.

How I yearn for the chance to tell her exactly that. But other words tumble out instead.

"Holy shit."

Words I have no choice about, once my stare falls to the sizable parchment resting next to Bastien's knee.

Our marriage license.

The really official one, obtained through lots of money

making it into the right clergymen's hands, making it possible for Bast and I to travel quickly together. *Really* quickly. As in fleeing France as rapidly as humanly possible, despite my lack of identification and his supposed death. Ironically, the madness that we fled from was also the institutional chaos that made it possible to slip free.

But Izzy doesn't want to hear that right now. My daughter peers hard at me, her mind obviously spinning with a thousand stories to satisfy her curiosity. Not a one of them could possibly come close, but how is she supposed to know that?

I look back to Bastien, certain he's thinking the same thing. But he's also had time to sort more conclusions—and that's the part that has me wobbling on the ladder like a spooked cat.

"*Rayonnement.*" He leans and steadies me. His hand is a welcome clamp of granite around the ball of my shoulder. His soft baritone is even better. I soak up its fortitude, already knowing what he's about to level next. "Come. Sit here with us. Ysabeau has been asking some very good questions of me. Perhaps you can help me answer them."

My daughter sits up straighter. Though one shoulder of my gown slips and turns the thing into a diagonal slouch across her torso, she disregards it—to raise a stare at me that's serene and serious.

"I am nearly ten years old, Mother. I can handle the truth now." She settles her shoulders with determination. "I have a *right* to know now."

My gut twists—but not as harshly as I expected. It even calms and smooths as I flick my regard to Bastien. In the fortitude across his high forehead, down to the firm cords of his neck, I observe everything I need to know. All the reasons for me to stretch my hand out, pressing it into his own. To feel the warmth and courage of the man who traversed so far to find me—and then braved that journey again so that I could have this life with him. This world that is my complete, everlasting joy.

"Desperado," I rasp, hoping he hears that my love for him has never been more sure or strong. "She's right . . . isn't she?"

Bastien re-secures our handclasp. I remember so many other times he has done it, always to affirm that he's right here next to me. Reminding me of our connection. Our destiny. The life and love we will never take for granted.

But part of that fate is our full story.

There's a fluctuation across Bastien's demeanor, as if he's plucked that conclusion right out of my head. But that's no longer weird for me.

"It is time to stop hiding, my love."

I smile and softly kiss him, but our daughter is already grunting with impatience. I pull away with a giggle, already readjusting and reaching for Ysabeau's small hand too.

"Well, Monsieur le Duke . . . time has always been on our side."

ACKNOWLEDGMENTS

It was such a wonderful labor of love to revisit the world of the dashing De Leons! I really want to thank everyone who loved the first book enough to ask for this second story, especially the team at Waterhouse Press: Meredith Wild, Jonathan Mac, Jennifer Becker, Robyn Lee, Keli Jo Chen, Haley Boudreaux, Jesse Kench, Kurt Vachon, Yvonne Ellis, and Amber Maxwell. You all keep me going with your encouragement and support. So grateful.

Scott Saunders: I am so lucky to know you and to have the gifts of your wisdom and talent! You really *are* an editor extraordinaire, but I am also thankful to call you friend. My profound gratitude for your hard work and input on this story. We just found out what's harder than writing a time travel story: writing a *second* time travel story! So thankful for you!

Profound and special thanks for my writer and reader sister friends: Carey Sabala, Shayla Black, Stacey Kennedy, JL Drake, Kika Medina, Corinne Akers, and Victoria Blue. You all held my proverbial (and sometimes literal!) hand through this one. Thank you!

Continued gratitude and love for the Payne Passion nation. I love you amazing gods and goddesses! Special thanks to Martha Frantz for keeping things sane and organized!

The best for last this time. My wonderful Thomas . . . this journey is nothing without you. Thank you for being my rock, my friend, my heart, my love.

And my amazing Fortune . . . how blessed, proud, moved, and dazzled I am to be your mom. Your wings are only starting to spread . . . and look how beautiful they are. I am so proud of the life you are building, and the love with which you are doing so. You amaze me each and every day. Love you, kiddo . . . to the ends of this world and all those beyond it.

MORE MISADVENTURES

Misadventures in the Cage
Misadventures of a Biker
Misadventures with a Sexpert
Misadventures with a Master
Misadventures with a Lawyer

**VISIT MISADVENTURES.COM
FOR MORE INFORMATION!**

ABOUT THE AUTHOR

USA Today bestselling romance author Angel Payne loves to focus on high-heat romance starring memorable alpha men and the women who love them. She has numerous book series to her credit, including the action-packed Bolt Saga and Honor Bound series, Secrets of Stone series (with Victoria Blue), the intertwined Cimarron and Temptation Court series, the Suited for Sin series, and the Lords of Sin historicals, as well as several standalone titles.

Angel is a native Southern Californian, leading to her love of being in the outdoors, where she often reads and writes. She still lives in Southern California with her soul-mate husband and beautiful daughter, to whom she is a proud cosplay/culture con mom. Her passions also include whisky tasting, shoe shopping, and travel.

Visit her at AngelPayne.com